Green

Mango

Chow

David Kalloo

1

Copyright of David Kalloo 2020

British Library Cataloguing-in-Publication Data
A catalogue record for this book is available on request from the British library.

ISBN 9798664144734

© David Kalloo
Published April 2020

Cover Design by: cashewmedia

Dedicated to my mother and my family. My
thanks for the passion they infused in me.

Special thanks to:
Nasser Khan,
Dianne A. Alphonse-Kalloo,
Renuka Koniger,
Karen Thomas and
Claire Shepherd
for your time and valued feedback.

CHAPTER
1NE

The Drapers had the biggest mango tree on Farfan Street in Arima, with the biggest mangoes of its kind you would ever hope to see. The mangoes would ripen to a rosy yellow, red and purple hue. Its distinctive aroma, led to the name mango rose and colloquially, it was known as hog mango. The tree glowed with the abundance of this fruit and was busy with birds of all species that came to feast on the succulent ripe mango pulp - Keskiedee, Sici Yea, Semp, Blue Jays, Black birds and Parakeets were just a few of the varieties that flocked to the tree during the mango season. The tree stood alongside the front of the Draper's house, tall and magnificent, partially obscuring the brightly painted blue pillared structure.

Ma Draper had spent many hours during the construction making sure that Mr Draper followed the architect's plans. Had he his way, Mr Draper would have installed different windows to the back of the house and only use the fancy ones at the front. Ma Draper was obstinate and insisted that everything should be according to the architect's specifications. Mr Draper was a dutiful husband and Ma Draper's best friend. He respected her wish. The house was completed plan perfect and much to Ma Draper's approval.

Since the death of her husband, Ma Draper spent her days sitting on the veranda, humming a hymn and every so often, she would vocalise a refrain. "Yes, Jezess loves you...hmmmm...hmmmm...yes, Jezess loves you..." She would stop only to acknowledge a greeting from passers-by who would shout. "Mornin' Ma Draper."
To the schoolchildren, her reply was always the same.

"Mornin', mornin' dear, God bless eh child. How yuh mammy?" Her tone was always in a whisper as she raised her hand from the veranda to signal her response.

Ma Draper was not a tall woman. She was merely five feet five and her square shoulders and trim body showed off her strength. She walked purposely, with a brisk gait and short strides. Her once thick black mane was now almost all grey. After the death of Mr Draper, she had taken to wearing a head cloth, whether at home or when she was going out. She removed the headcloth when she retired to bed. She dressed elegantly, mostly wearing printed floral dresses and skirts that were tailored for her by a local dress maker at the end of the street. Ma Draper had smooth, toned skin with a silky sheen that seemed to self-moisturise without effort.

Mr Draper would always comment on her skin saying. "Agnes gyul your skin smooth like glass oui!" Rubbing his rough hands along her arms. She would tease and him push his hand away screaming at him. "So, you want to damage it now with dem concrete hands of yours?"

There was a lot laughter in the Drapers' home. Since the new house was built, they both sat in the veranda or on the steps, sharing jovial moments together. They both enjoyed just sitting, talking and laughing. Ma Draper would smile remembering the days when Mr Draper would get the hairbrush and brush her thick hair, making two neat plaits. Her hair although greying, was still thick, soft and well groomed. She was never consciously preening. However, she was always well dressed, even at home. She would often wear a coconut shell or dolphin shaped earrings dangling from her earlobes. She had especially loved wearing them because Mr Draper had made them from dried coconut shell which he polished and varnished to a high gloss finish. The dolphin-shaped ones were fashioned from the seed pods of the sandbox tree. Mr Draper had collected them on one of his fishing trips to the countryside.

The mango season kept Ma Draper occupied. Most of her time was spent tidying the front yard where the mangoes fallen, littering the ground. Many of them were half-eaten by birds and dislodged from their stems because of strong winds or, simply by the birds tugging at them for their luscious pulp. Tediously, she sifted through the bruised and half-eaten mangoes, setting aside the unblemished ones. She would carefully place these on a tray and put them on the concrete pillar at the front gate. Here, passers-by could help themselves to the ripe rosy fruits. Despite this daily routine, people hardly ever bothered to help themselves to mangoes. This somehow never deterred her from refreshing the tray daily.

Although the mangoes were beautiful looking and had a honey aroma, most people did not eat mango rose. The rosiness of the fruit and its luscious aroma were not reflected in its taste. The flesh of the mango was very bland. The mango was mostly collected by pig farmers who used it as a supplement food for their pigs. It was through this that the colloquial name 'hog mango' was derived. Ma Draper never cared too much for the ripe fruits herself. She always preferred the semi-ripen one, which she used for making mango chow. Ma Draper used a long bamboo pole with a wire hook, fashioned from a wire clothes hanger, attached to one end, to select and pick mangoes for making her green mango chow.

First, she peeled the rosy skin off the mangoes; she then cut the fruit into half inch strips, placing it into a large enamelled bowl. Once this phase was complete, she would put a generous helping of Shadon Beni, which she crushed between her fingers, black pepper, chopped garlic and finely chopped scotch bonnets over the mango strips – the recipe was the same each time she made the chow, she never measured. Ma Draper would take a deep sniff at the mixture and sigh, 'ahhhh' tossing the contents until the seasoning was evenly distributed, forming a coating on the mango strips. She covered the bowl with a plastic lid and left it to marinate in the sun for at least half-an-hour before inspecting it. She gave it a final toss leaving it for another fifteen minutes.

It did not take long before neighbours started smelling the aroma of the chow. Mr Dhanraj whose shop was not far from the Drapers' house, was often the first to get a whiff of the chow. He would shout, "Aye Draper yuh make chow?"

"Eh heh." She dutifully echoed.

Dhanraj would hastily gather a bowl, skipping over to Ma Draper for a share of the mango chow.

"Macumere yuh must make dis ting an' gimme; I go sell it in de shop for yuh."

"Yuh always saying dat boy, but de old gyul eh what she used to be yuh know." Ma Draper groaned as Dhanraj filled his bowl with the aromatic mango mixture, pausing only to fill his mouth with strips of mango.

"Macumere dis pepper hot too bad, oh goosh!"

Ma Draper laughed, "I t'ought allyuh Indians did like pepper?"

"Yeah we do! Buh since I get creolised ah cyah take de pepper too much."

She erupted into laughter and said, "Careful wid it den, it nice in yuh mouth now, but it go be fiery in yuh backside later. Look it have ah man in yuh shop, go before he t'ief something an' run."

Dhanraj turned on his heels and made off to the shop. "Ah comin family, hold on." He yelled to his customer.

Ma Draper shouted after Dhanraj, "Don't forget de green mango for Yvonne!"

Sitting back on her rocking chair, she replaced the lid on the bowl and started to sing another hymn to herself, softly. Suddenly, there was a loud bang on the iron roof, the noise startled her slightly. "Dem blasted bird and dem go give meh ah frigging h'art attack yes!"

The mangoes hitting the iron roof would often bring out some subtle profanity from Ma Draper, quiet enough only for her ears, laughing at the ease at which a cuss came to her lips. She remained sitting in her chair with the bowl of mango chow resting on her legs. Ma Draper adjusted her head tie, sticking her index finger under the cloth to scratch an itchy spot on her scalp. "Jezess, de sun hot today eh!" She murmured softly patting the bowl on her legs. She lifted her head to peer into the street, casting her eye as far as she could see. Her head turned trying to catch a glimpse of the large clock on the living room wall. The clock face was busy with a print of birds, alien to Trinidad. The clock was a gift from a visiting relative in England, the birds were native to Europe, Fitzroy once said to her. She took note of the time as eyes followed the second hand sweeping across the face of the clock. Nodding to herself she said with a whisper, "Just now is lunch time, dat chinee shop going to get *really* busy. Ah hope Elsa pass today yes. Ah make plenty chow."

Ma Draper's anticipation was short-lived. Moments after her thought, she peered over the low wall of the veranda. She could see Elsa dragging one foot after the other, slowly marching down the street, franticly waving to Dhanraj. He leapt from behind his huge oak desk and began flirting with Elsa. Dhanraj shouted to Elsa from the doorway of his shop. "Gyul you and I could have some nice dougla children yuh know!" Elsa blushed, blew him a kiss before crossing the road to embrace Ma Draper who had made her way to the front gate. The two women greeted each other with kisses and a warm embrace. "I didn't expect to find you home nah! I say yuh gorn in town today." Elsa said with a concerned frown.

"Nah gyul! Fitzroy say he go pay de insurance, so I eh bodder."

"Well is ah good t'ing ah could lime wid yuh ah lil bit today instead of dat Dhanraj. He rude fuh so yuh know, he good heckle me yesterday." Elsa mused.

"Dat Dhanraj rude for true, but yuh does encourage him too. I see yuh givin' him sweet eye and t'ing." Ma Draper chuckled with a teasing grin.

"Come mum, enough about lover boy Dhanraj, whey de chow?"

Ma Draper laughed and proceeded to lift the lid off the bowl releasing the aromatic flavours of the *shadon beni*, followed by a wave of scotch bonnet, lethal enough to clear a stuffy sinus in a few seconds.

"Mama yo! mudder dat t'ing smelling good!" Elsa lamented as she brushed her fingers across her jeans and dipped into the bowl carefully lifting a strip of the mango to her mouth.

She chewed slowly then swallowed and cried, "Oh gorm! Dat pepper hot for so."

"Is de same t'ing Danny said. He say, since he creolised, he cyar stand de pepper."

"Mudder yuh should sell dis t'ing yuh know, people will buy it without ah fuss."

"Allyuh all right wid all dis commess yes. Who in Trinidad go buy mango chow?"

"Yuh going be surprised." Elsa chimed, "Ah bet yuh if ah Chinee man make chow an' start to sell, all ah we go buy it."

"Is true gyul, we people too lackadaisical."

"But A-A...mum yuh know big word an' t'ing." They both erupted into a spell of laughter, their fingers finding strips of mango chow as they conversed. Stopping only to fan their mouths or wave to someone passing in the street.

"Doh put dat hand in your eye yuh know, dat pepper not easy. Is from de plant yuh fadder bring from Moruga."

Ma Draper surveyed Elsa curiously, lifting her head she smiled. "So how much months you is now?"

"But mum you eh bet yuh fas' nah. Who tell you I pregnant?" There was a sheepish grin on Elsa's face, she tried to hide it but burst into a spell of short laughter. She rubbed her belly, patted her jeans, and sucked her teeth. "Yuh know I wear these damn jeans to hide meh belly but yuh still notice!" Elsa chuckled, selecting another strip of mango from the bowl.

"Come den gyul, gimme de scores nah! Who is de fadder?"

"Is nobody from Arima, he from Tunapuna. He's a really nice man mum."

"Ah hope is ah nice boy an' not one ah dem vagabonds yuh pick up with and swell up yuh belly."

"No mum." Elsa got hold of Ma Draper's hand and gave her an assuring squeeze. "Trust me mum he is a kind and decent man, I am so glad I met him and to have him in my life."

Ma Draper was apprehensive, she stared at Elsa suspiciously, clasped their hands together holding them firmly as she offered a prayer. "Lord bless dis child, an' clear ah righteous road for she to walk. Is all ah ask of you Lord Jezess." Ma Draper prayed and recited the Lord's Prayer, she put her hand on Elsa and they both chorused amen.

Elsa grabbed Ma Draper and threw her arms around her, kissing the old lady on her forehead, tears trickled across her cheek and settled on her chin. Ma Draper brushed the tears away. "Yuh best be getting back to work oui, is almost two 'o' clock. Before yuh leave, go up by the corner and buy meh two Doubles and some Pholourie. Buy from de short, dark lady, her Doubles does taste better."

Ma Draper fished out a beaded cloth purse from her bosom, selected a green note from the purse, and handed it over to Elsa. "Is five dollars, buy two fuh yuhself as well."

Elsa smiled at her generosity, assuring Ma Draper. "Mum I do know what ah five dollars look like you know."

CHAPTER
2WO

Ma Draper did not eat any of the delicacies that Elsa had bought her. She did not move from her rocking chair since Elsa bid her farewell in the afternoon. She rocked the chair forward and back, humming a hymn to the rhythm of the chair, the cool wind rustling through the veranda applauding her melody.

She stopped abruptly, whispering to herself, secretly, as though she was aware of someone listening to her conversation. "Oh, my lord. Look at all dis mango to clean up in de yard again!" As Ma Draper looked upon all the fallen fruits under the tree, she let out a heavy sigh. "I think ah go leave dat for Fitzroy to do when he come home yes."

Fitzroy was the Drapers' only child. He had grown into a handsome young man with his father's looks and, a little taller. Fitzroy sported a low afro hairstyle and groomed a pencil thin moustache. He was infatuated with the idea of working on a ship so he could see the world, without having to pay for travel. Every day, since Mr Draper died Fitzroy would journey to Port of Spain docks seeking work on any ship that would have him. Ma Draper was not amused by Fitzroy's ambition. She had hoped that one day he would join the civil service, like his father or, become a writer because of his love for books. He was an avid reader. Ma Draper would sometimes call out to him in his room and say. "Fitzy take ah rest from all dem books boy, yuh go damage yuh eyes."

For a short period, Fitzroy had written articles for one of the radical newspapers, writing mostly about politics.

His articles had caught the eye of the editor of one of the daily newspapers. He offered Fitzroy a small weekly column but cautioned that he would need to tone down the attack on the government. Fitzroy declined the offer. He replied in a letter explaining to the editor that to accept such an offer would be stagnating his freedom and his moral duty to speak about political failings by the government. The editor never responded to Fitzroy's letter.

Ma Draper could hear the radio in the living room, where the news bulletin was being broadcasted. With her head perched, she poised attentively, listening as if waiting for a specific news item. She settled her head back on the chair and continued the rhythm of the chair. Across the street Dhanraj shop was a hive of activity. The brisk afternoon trade had begun. Apart from early morning trade, the afternoon was normally the busiest time of trading for Dhanraj. Market, shop traders and roadside vendors descended on Dhanraj wholesale store to restock their retail establishments. Dhanraj boasted competitive prices, attracting a steady flow of business from his existing customers and from those who learned of his prices compared to the other major wholesalers in the area. Traders could find cheaper prices, but they had to venture further out of town. Most were happy to purchase from Dhanraj who, in some circumstances; extended a credit facility to his loyal customers.

Almost every small gathering in Trinidad served as a platform for political debate and those who gathered at Dhanraj would engage with their political knowledge. Customers all manner of topics, from international topics, crime, unemployment, CARICOM and local politics. Others, not keen on politics discussed what *whe whe* mark could make them a winner. Dhanraj, catching the tail end of the *whe whe* conversation joined in, "Play 26 or 21." A few heads in the crowd nodded in agreement.

Someone in the small crowd yelled. 'Nah 15 is ah boss mark today!'

Roland, one of Dhanraj employees came out from the storeroom balancing a four-foot long snake on a piece of wood and asked. "What number is snake?"

People scattered on seeing the snake. Dhanraj shouted to Roland. "Boy take dat in de road and kill the kiss-me ass ting nah."

"But Mr Dhanraj de snake eh do nobody nutten."

Roland manoeuvred the snake into the gutter and the reptile slithered into the nearby manhole. A voice in the background said, "It look like a Ma Pepere Zanana."

Roland looked around in the direction of the voice and responded, "Nah is ah Macajuel."

Dhanraj shadowed a slap at Roland, "Ah tell yuh kill de blasted snake yuh let it go."

Looking over to the shop, still humming. Ma Draper gathered the hem of her skirt and squeezed the tips of her fingers and brought the chair to a halt. She stood up with relative ease, making her way down the wooden stairs to the yard, intrigued by the commotion at the shop. A firm mango crashed through the branches hitting the hard earth exposing the yellow pulp inside. Ma Draper was not startled, she shook her head and complained. "Dem blasted mango, dey go kill me one day yes." She laughed to her own amusement, adjusted her head tie and walked slowly to the front gate. She gazed at the sight of the un-blemished mangoes placed on the tray early that morning. They were all still there, absorbing the heat of the intense sunshine and, warm to the touch. Taking a long look at fruits, she mumbled, "Hmm, people, doh know how good dey have it dese days nah! All dis mango going to waste."

Car horns tooted and people shouted at the top of their voices amidst the hustle and bustle of the afternoon. At Dhanraj shop, customers were in a haste, shoving their list forward for Dhanraj's attention, hoping to get served quickly. He ignored them and dealt with everyone in their turn, distributing the lists to the storeroom workers to manage the orders accurately. These young men would disappear with the list in hand, behind a heavy plastic curtain into a dimly lit warehouse. They emerged later with trollies filled with an assortment of merchandise, ready to be carted away by their customers.

Dhanraj would scan each trolley in relation to the list and, would always make a comment. "Bertie wha happen, the grape sweet drink eh selling these days?" He scanned the list and the trolley again, double checking everything was correct before putting a line across the list with a red marker pen.

Dhanraj was a multi-tasker; he counted money with amazing speed and accuracy. He did so, while carrying on several conversations with several different customers, as well as checking the lists and trolleys in front of him. He would then interrupt, "Jagdeo, yuh two dollars short here man! Yuh trying to rob meh or what?"
A voice in the small crowd shouted, "Anybody could rob you Danny?"
"Okay, okay. Ah go owe yuh dat next time." A voice belonging to Jagdeo bellowed from the crowd of customers.
"Yeah, but doh forget yuh owe meh seven dollars from last week." Dhanraj reminded Jagdeo with an assertive response.

"Doh dig nutten; ah go send it with de boy later." Jagdeo promised.

Dhanraj looked over the crowd and saw Ma Draper standing by her front gate. He gazed at her, still shuffling the notes from one hand to the next and lifted his head. "Yes Bernard, all correct and proper here. Roland," Dhanraj called to one of his packers, "Take ah grape sweet drink over for the Draper 'oman for me please."

"But mister Dhanraj I on meh break man." A timid voice called back from the warehouse.

"Oh gosh boy is only ah sweet drink for ah old lady. Take ah extra five minutes then." Dhanraj grumbled, shook his head, engaging with the customer in front of him, he laughed. "Young people eh Samuel, wha yuh go do?"

Roland skipped over with the drink in his hand and a dark red pommerac for Ma Draper. Ma Draper watched him as he dashed across the street towards her. He smiled at her and said. "Mister Dhanraj sen' de sweet drink but de pommerac is from me. The tree laden dese days ah go bring some more tomorrow nah."

"T'ank yuh boy, God bless yuh. Say hello to mammy for me, yuh hear?"

Roland was halfway back when he shouted, "Okay Miss Draper."

She watched as he skipped across the street before disappearing into the shop and out of sight. Cupping the fruit with both hands, she inhaled its exotic aroma and bit into its juicy flesh, cotton white inside.

The evening sun battled with the onslaught of darkness. Bats darted about in crazy zigzag chaos in the fading sunlight. High above them, egrets flew in arrowhead formation as they made their way home to the Caroni swamp to nestle down with the flocks of Scarlet Ibis that sought refuge in the verdant foliage of the mangrove trees. Against the house, the mango tree cast an eerie silhouette as birds fluttered about the thick leaves for an ideal sleeping perch. On the low orange tree, a young hen, her wings fluttering to garner balance as she took up her position for the night.

The radio played the melodious vocals of the Indian singer, Lata Mangeshkar, which could be heard from the front gate. Fitzroy had just come in and shut the gate behind him. He pulled the neck of his T-shirt, blew a mouthful of cool air onto his chest, he sighed and repeated the motion. He stopped and looked up at the mango tree and then at the bowl that was left on the veranda. He shook his head lightly and wiped beads of perspiration from his forehead with his index finger. The neighbour's mongrel barked knowingly from behind the iron fence. Ma Draper's head lifted with a knowing suspicion, "Is dat you Fitzy?"

"Yeah! yeah is me Ma. Doh worry."

"Is how you take whole day so man?" She quizzed.

Fitzroy never bothered to answer. Not that he was purposely ignoring his mother, but because he knew the pattern of her interrogation. He knew too, she never really expected him to answer. Instead, he perched himself on the second riser of the staircase and undid the shoelaces from his Converse. He lit a cigarette, took a long draw and slowly exhaled through his nostrils. On finishing the cigarette, he flicked the stub into the nearby flowerbed, gathered his shoes and went inside. He greeted his mother with a cordial greeting poured himself a huge glass of iced water, consuming it in one gulp.

"Ma yuh eat anything today except mango chow?" Fitzroy enquired with some concern.

"Yeah boy! Elsa was here and she buy some Phoulorie and two Sahena wid ah nice Pommecythere chutney. I leave some fuh yuh."

Fitzroy looked out into the back yard, observing one of the hens pecking on the ground before flying onto the orange tree.

"Go wash yuh hands boy and come eat some food. Ah make some curry fish and rice today."

Ma Draper chuckled and adjusted her head tie, her finger caressing her itching scalp.

Fitzroy stopped to smell the bowl of chow on the kitchen table. Tipping his head back, he

Screamed, "Oh jeezzz! Ma dis t'ing smelling real fiery."

Ma Draper laughed heartily as she spooned a fish steak into the plate, "Take de chow on the table."

"Ma yuh should listen to dese people yuh know! Make dis t'ing and sell it." Fitzroy suggested, half joking at the idea but also with an aura of seriousness. He shook his head slowly, tickled by the fact that he agreed with those who suggested the enterprise to Ma Draper.

The commotion of the late evening traffic had ceased, the bats were no longer visible and the cries from Dhanraj shop had long faded away with the last golden beam of sunlight that tried desperately to fight off the twilight. The streets fell quiet too, only to be punctuated by the fierce barking from the mongrel next door.

Fitzroy looked at his mother as he scooped a spoonful of fish and rice into his mouth. He selected a portion of mango chow into his plate and chewed noisily. Ma Draper gave him a look, he fanned his mouth after swallowing and continued eating.

Ma Draper reached across the table and smacked his wrist, "Stop eating as if yuh chewing bricks nah."

Her words fell on deaf ears. Fitzroy looked up at her, asking, "Ma, how Elsa. Is a lil while now I eh see she?"

"Elsa good yuh know." She replied, stabbing at the fish on her plate.

"Yuh say dat as if somet'ing wrong Ma."

"Boy ah have to talk straight," Ma Draper spoke in a firm tone. "I know yuh have ah crush on dat Elsa since yuh goin' to school. But Elsa not interested in you."

Fitzroy laughed, trying to keep the food in his mouth. He touched Ma Draper's arm and said, "Take it easy Ma. Elsa have ah fella, she goin' to have ah baby…and before yuh go mad. No, I am not de fadder."

"So yuh know dis ahready?"

"Yeah! Ah see Elsa in town about ah month now and she give me the low down. Is ah nice fella, yuh go like 'im. Ah big boy policeman from Tunapuna. Ah hear they goin' to make him Superintendent."

Ma Draper looked puzzled and picked at the food on her plate. Classical music chimed from the radio. She closed her eyes and started to sing softly one of her hymns. Fitzroy smiled and gathered the plates as he got up. The mongrel next door barked and gave a yearning growl as it heard the rattling of crockery, expecting food to follow.

Fitzroy looked at Ma Draper's plate, she had not eaten a single mouthful of the food. Instead, she had arranged the food to look as though she had indeed eaten. She should not have bothered. Fitzroy had sat opposite, marvelling at her clever arrangement. She manoeuvred the food about the plate in a clever deception, but it failed to fool Fitzroy. He had grown accustomed to her strategy, remembering when Mr Draper made a fuss about her eating habits.

Fitzroy, despite his concerns about Ma Draper's eating,

never allowed it to trouble him. He knew she preferred to indulge in other foods which mostly included Indian delicacies such as Phoulorie, Doubles or Aloo pies. On occasion, she had sweet bread or pone, purchased in the market during her weekly pilgrimage.

Ma Draper's eyes followed Fitzroy as he cleared the dishes from the table and proceeded to wash up. He performed the task with relative ease, pausing intermittently to brush pearls of sweat off his forehead with the back of his hands. She watched Fitzroy dry and stack the dishes in the cupboard then meticulously dry every bit of water from the sink and counter. Ma Draper called out to Fitzroy, "Boy I doh know what ah go do when you leave and go to work on dem ships nah?"

CHAPTER
3HREE

The night was dense and humid, Fitzroy fanned himself with a copy of the *Evening News* before opening the paper to peruse. He was interrupted by the front gate grating the concrete; briskly, he made his way to the front door. Fitzroy had barely opened the front door when the voice yelled, "Aye Fitzy, yuh going and bounce some ball on the court?"

Fitzroy shaded his eyes from the glare of the streetlight, "Is you Watkins?"

"Is me yes, who you expectin', Satan?" Watkins said bluntly.

They both laughed as Watkins made his way up the steps spinning a basketball on the tip of his index finger, transferring the ball from one hand to the next without altering its speed of rotation.

"Keep yuh voice down nah man, yuh go disturb de pothound next door." Fitzroy warned. No sooner had he spoken than the dog went into a frenzied barking, jumping against the iron fence that rocked precariously every time the bitch jumped against it. Watkins gave a sharp low whistle and the dog's ferocious barking faded into silence.

Watkins brought the rotating ball to a sudden stop. Fitzroy aimed a finger at him, "Guess what pardner? We have a sponsor for the team." He beamed with delight at the news Fitzroy broke to him snapping his fingers in succession. "So, who is de sponsor?"

"Aboud, de Syrian from out de road. I manage to persuade

him to sponsor the team. He agreed to support us for the rest of the season with a review. These here are just samples, the rest of the kit will come next week."

"Ah see he name big, big on the back." Watkins grumbled.

"Don't be so damn pessimistic man. At least he gave us a sponsorship. So long I begging Dhanraj, all he saying is, ah go see, ah go see."

Watkins shook his head, "Is true breds, we own people failing to support projects that keep the youths off the streets."

Ma Draper walked into the room. She had removed her head tie and taking a long stern look at Watkins, she screamed at him, "Is you here making all dis blasted frigging noise while ah trying to say my prayers?"

Watkins was apologetic, he lowered his head, tucked the ball under his arm and, with humility said, "Oh gosh mums, Tantie forgive meh, yuh know ah have ah big mouth. Ah really sorry, next time ah go talk real sorf."

Ma Draper couldn't help but giggle. She sucked her teeth, "Watkins you could never talk in a quiet tone. Even when yuh quiet yuh could be heard for miles." She turned on her heels and shuffled back to her room reminding Fitzroy to lock the front door when he was leaving.

"Yes Ma, doh worry yuh head nah." He mimicked as she disappeared into her bedroom. Watkins snapped his fingers saying to Fitzroy, "If she sees yuh, she going to break yuh ass." They both broke into boyish laughter holding up the basketball kit, inspecting the quality and texture of the fabric, "We goin' places breds. When they see us on de court, we will be dazzling them."

"For real sire, for real." Fitzroy agreed.

The dense murky night had brought rain, banging hard

on the corrugated rooftops with relentless urgency. The mounds of dried mango leaves gathered on the roof got washed away to the end of the fence, unable to escape through the small aperture in the concrete wall. The water began to rise and back up into the yard, slowly creating a small ocean of floating leaves and debris drowning the fragile flowerbeds.

Fitzroy woke up earlier than usual to have his cup of freshly brewed coffee before setting off to work. He had a temporary job down at the beer factory in Champ Fleur. Every morning before leaving for work, it was customary to perch himself on the veranda wall and sip sweet black coffee.

This morning, he folded his arms close together to keep warm, savouring his coffee and surveying the extent of the flooded flower beds. He studied the black liquid in the cup and gave it a swirl, wishing he did not have to go to work. He rolled the enamel cup between his palms before finishing the sweet coffee and spoke to himself, "Come on Fitzy get yourself in gear."

The morning sun was hidden by a thick blanket of rain clouds hanging low over the eastern sky and all the way west of the island. The grey clouds stifled the sun out of view, making it appear darker than it would be normally at this time of morning. This lack of light did not hinder Borough Council workers as they hurried along, busy collecting the refuse that had piled up along the streets.

Fitzroy looked up at the mango tree on his way out. He was amazed how many mangoes had left their stems during the night in the torrential rainfall. Yet, the tree appeared to have lost none of its fruits. He lifted his hand to acknowledge Bernard who was sitting in his van, parked in front of Dhanraj shop. No words were exchanged between the two men. Tobacco smoke snaked from the open cab window and disappeared into the cold morning air. Fitzroy dug his hands deep into his pockets and cocked his head towards the sky. The rain made an appearance again, this time, the downpour heavier than earlier. Those with umbrellas quickly opened them for shelter. Others used their morning newspapers or the sanctuary of the shop eaves to shelter themselves from the cold rain that eventually drowned the beams of sunlight that had managed to penetrate the grey clouds.

Water hurried along the kerbs and into the manholes. Pedestrians skipped across puddles with relative agility to negotiate their way through the now busy main road. Men hoisted their trousers above their ankles, while some walked without a care or concern for the rain. Taxis honked their horns for passengers as they sheltered under the eaves waiting to be picked up. On the pavement, under the shelter of a fabric store, a stout Indian woman busied herself, assembling her food stall. She was methodical in constructing her stall making herself ready for the day's trading.

The rain didn't let up, pouring down like crystal spears from the sky, dissolving into ripples on the road surface before disappearing into the drains, taking with it, the grime of the dirty streets. The stout woman shouted across the street to a refuse collector, "Good weather for ducks eh Boysie?"

"Yes macumere, dis is de right weather for ducks." The refuse collector bellowed above the pouring rain, scooping up a pile of soaked cardboard boxes and dumping it into the truck. He waved in a saluting motion and hurried behind the lorry that disappeared into the distance.

Bolts of lightning divided the sky, followed by the

crack of thunder and then another charge of electricity raced towards the earth in a frenzied electrified dance. The crack of lightning and thunder had stirred Ma Draper. Another bolt of lightning brought her alert, she sat up and peered through the curtains, "Oh gorm, it rain fuh so yes! Fitzy, Fitz." She called waiting for a response.

Ma Draper whispered a prayer as she searched for her slippers with her feet. Finding them, she secured the soft slippers on her cold feet before briskly making her way to the kitchen. She warmed the coffee that Fitzroy left her and poured herself a generous cup. Fiddling with the radio, she selected her favourite station. She took time to savour the aroma of the coffee before taking up her usual perch on the rocking chair. She moved gently on the chair to find a rhythm and almost automatically started humming Ave Maria, pausing intermittently to sip the hot black liquid.

She looked up over the low wall and spoke softly, "Lord t'anks fuh de lil rain we gettin' yes to wash out some of de sins in de country. Lord we t'ank yuh fuh every little blessing yuh provide...amen." Sucking her teeth long and loud, she held the coffee cup to her bosom, "Look at the amount of water in this yard nah!" Ma Draper's eyes darted about, focussing on the fallen mangos floating about amongst the leaves. The water had backed up almost to the trunk of the mango tree and continue to rise. Her weathered face frowned at the sight of the submerged flower beds. She peered scornfully at the littered flooded yard, sipped her coffee and looked up in awe at the mango tree. The rain drummed harder on the corrugated iron roof making it impossible for Ma Draper to hear the radio.

Across the road, despite the downpour, Dhanraj was

busy as usual, fulfilling customer orders. Counting his money and shouting orders down to the workers all in a single breath. By this time, he would have taken breakfast across to Ma Draper. Today he had to wait for a break in the rain. It was customary for him to bring her a homecooked breakfast twice a week – twice a week because his wife only made breakfast twice a week. He had started this practice following the death of Mr. Draper. Yvonne, his wife, would often set aside Ma Draper's breakfast and say jokingly to him, "Here, don't forget to take the breakfast for your other woman."

Dhanraj focused his attention on a young voice as he heard his name being called. "Mr Dhanraj, meh fadder sen' nine dollars fuh yuh."

He looked down at the boy with a curious stare, counted the last few notes and directed to the boy, "And who is your fadder, son?"

"Jagdeo. Jagdeo is meh fadder," the boy replied.

"Oho yes, I remember," touching his head with his index finger.

The rain had eased to a slight drizzle. "Rolaaand." Dhanraj yelled at the top of his voice, "Rolaaaand."

Roland appeared at the huge hardwood door that separated the warehouse from the front of the shop. He stood there without answering. Dhanraj looked up, exasperated, upon seeing Roland. Dhanraj sucked his teeth loudly, "Could you take that bag on the table for the Draper 'oman please?"

Ma Draper took a sniff at the bag and laughed. "Heh, heh, heh. Yvonne dey home today! Ah mus' pick some green mango fuh she yes!" Taking a deep breath, she opened the bag and smiled, "Is meh favourite yeah, oui. - Tomato choka and float."

Without breaking the rhythm of the rocking chair, she tore the brown paper bag down the middle exposing the golden floats and the flowered enamel container that kept the tomato choka. Carefully, she broke off a bit of the float and dipped it into the tomato mixture savouring the flavours of the tomatoes and various seasonings and a hint of roasted sweet pepper.

Ma Draper was always amazed at the variety of foods that Yvonne made, especially traditional foods. Yvonne's culinary skills impressed Ma Draper immensely. Every traditional dish that Yvonne made had a different twist to it. She was astonishingly bowled over when Yvonne sent over some smoked herring pelau with a lettuce and beetroot coleslaw.

Ma Draper chewed with diligent patience on the food, savouring all its exotic flavours. Once her mouth was free, she began humming, "…yes Jesess loves you."

"Mornin' Ma Draper," a voice called from the street.

"Mackie dat is you?" She replied.

"Yeah, yeah is me. Fitzy home?"

"No boy! Fitzroy get ah little wuk down by beer factory dese days! How yuh mudder, she better dese days?"

"Yeah, yeah she not too bad." Mackie assured her.

"So yuh back fuh good then boy?" Ma Draper probed.

Mackie, it was alleged, was one of many students from Trinidad who had been detained in Canada involving a fiasco with university fees. The government of Trinidad, after numerous protest marches in Port of Spain eventually stepped in, supporting the students and resolving the incident with the Canadian authorities. The arrested students were finally released. Mackie, who was a student at the university decided to return home after his graduation.

Mackie returned to Trinidad shortly after the incident and initially became affiliated with a radical freedom fighters' movement. The organisation had many factions, one of which was deeply embedded with the Black Power movement in Trinidad. The movement had strong links with the US arm of the Black Power and other Caribbean organisations.

Black Power became a political slogan; it was a springboard from which many political and cultural institutions came into prominence. The organisation maintained a strong African cultural heritage, so much so, that most of the African members had chosen to dispel with their colonial names and adopt African ones. They embraced this move as a mark of reclaiming some form of Africanisation. It was another way of shaking off the shackles of imperialism and colonial values.

Mackie, although in full support, opted to keep the name that was given to him by his parents. He wore printed T-Shirts with the word '**Liberation**' written across the front and back with an emblem of a clenched fist against a rising sun. He never incited or advocated violence by any means, however, affiliation with the organisation placed him in that category.

Mackie's political aspirations grew stronger with the new party. Not long after joining the party he was made secretary and he later headed the Eastern coordinating team. He was aptly vocal with his opinions about the government, using every opportunity and platform to criticise the regime for making it difficult for the citizens to benefit from the country's wealth. His outspoken manner had attracted a small group of dutiful followers who had started to believe in his political ideology for change. His ambition was not to change the culture of politics but to change the mindset of the people and the country. The party leaders began to see Mackie as a threat to their positions of leadership. Whenever he tabled ideas, the party dragged its feet, or would dismiss them as irrelevant to the time. They criticised his ideas and motives for not being within the parameters of the policies and protocol.

Fitzroy paid close attention to Mackie's hunger for politics, the new ideas and vision he saw for a developing nation. He encouraged Mackie to distance himself from the present organisation and form his own party. He warned him that his policies and forward thinking clashed with the radical nature and the present political angle of the organisation that he supported. Mackie wasn't in favour of founding a new party. He outlined the difficulties he would face, not to mention the lack of national support from the electorate. Fitzroy then played his ace card. He convinced Mackie that it was in his best interest to become an independent candidate,

"There's a local election coming up soon for Mayor of Arima. This is your perfect opportunity to display your political ambitions in a confined locality and let the rest of the country take note."

Mackie was impressed with Fitzroy's thinking. "All these big ideas, you should be the one running for Mayor," he said to Fitzroy.

"No sar, I don't have orating ability as you do." Fitzroy envisaged a bigger goal for Mackie. He saw the mayoral campaign as a launching pad for Mackie to further enhance his ambitions, giving him greater political advantage for the future.

Ma Draper studied Mackie as he climbed the stairs, "Mackie! Why yuh leave Canada and come back to dis hard forsaken place? It eh have nutten here for young people yuh know," Ma Draper protested. "Yuh see Fitzy and Watkins? All dem do is play basketball, drink rum and study 'bout running down woman and, stowing away to Puerto Rico. Watkins, he throwaway his ambitions by leaving the army."

Her thoughts amused Mackie; he smiled inwardly, knowing there was more to Fitzroy's life than Ma Draper's assumptions. Fitzroy had craved wanting to become a seaman. He spoke about it all through his school life, he could see the world while working the high seas. It was Mr Draper's friend LaRose, who inadvertently instilled the idea of adventure in Fitzroy's head. Whenever he visited the Drapers' LaRose would tell stories of all the wonderful places he visited working as a cook on a cargo ship. Fitzroy dreamt of working the high seas for a couple of years before returning and opening a bookshop in the city. Mackie hoped that Fitzroy didn't abandoned his dreams of the bookshop altogether.

"Miss Draper I doh mean to be disrespectful, buh dis country have ah lot to offer young people, like Watkins, Fitzroy and *me*," Mackie argued. "But we can't sit down and wait for it to fall in our laps, we must fight for our rights as citizens, rights of black people, ...Indians too; an equal chance to prosper. And equally, to benefit from the wealth of this country rather than see it syphoned away by foreign companies."

"You just talking ah set a Yankee talk since you come back from Canada. The Prime Minister pay out all dat money and allyuh just ups and come back home...steups."

Ma Draper shook her head with visible impatience. She motioned with a nod of her head and an aura of authority to Mackie, "Take dat rod and pick ah few green mangoes for meh son."

Mackie stood tall, adjusted the black beret on his head and proceeded to carry out the task. He manoeuvred the long bamboo rod towards a cluster of mangoes before Ma Draper shouted, "No! pick de odder bunch next to it." She signalled with her finger. "Those better for making chow."

She observed Mackie as he struggled with the long bamboo pole and said with sudden excitement. "Yuh hear dem boys an' dem get sponsored by the Syrian from out de road?"

Mackie tugged at the bunch of mangoes and they tumbled down to the ground as water from the wet tree sprinkled him. "Yeah tantie, ah see Watkins last night and he gave me the news."

Ma Draper had expected a more animated response from Mackie. She watched him with some contempt as he gathered the mangoes from the ground and placed them in the plastic bowl she had fetched from the kitchen.

"So yuh mammy remain in Canada boy?"

"Nah," responded Mackie. "She left Canada and went to live in Boston. She did not like Canada at all. She says it was too cold."

Ma Draper took the bowl with both hands and thanked Mackie.

"Tell yuh granny ah say hello when yuh go home. Ah doh even see her in de market no more."

"Okay Tantie," he replied politely and waved to her making his way out of the gateway.

She watched him disappear along the narrow sidewalk, nodding her head she found a hymn in the corner of her mind and started to sing softly.

CHAPTER
4OUR

The trees stood motionless, for a moment, even the traffic seemed to have paused. The place was quiet and devoid of human din, a peaceful tranquil flourished for a few seconds, even Ma Draper's rocking rhythm had ceased, adding to the quietude. Rising early to absorb such serene moments of the day had always been a passion with Ma Draper. She closed her eyes, inhaling the newness of the day- a renewal of life.

Suddenly, the stillness was shattered by the bellowing of young man on the back of a flatbed truck, shouting. "Ice, Ice, get your cold ice. Ice, Ice, get yuh Ice! Get your nice cold ice." For a small man he had a thundering voice that reverberated above the rumble of the vehicle's engine. The green Bedford truck drove slowly along, loaded with huge slabs of ice, covered with hessian matting to secure it from melting away quickly. The shouts of Ice, Ice! drew no interest from the street as the lorry disappeared in the distance, faint shouts of Ice, Ice! could still be heard.

Rocking back and forth in her chair, Ma Draper picked up a copy of *The Watchtower* magazine from the floor beside the chair and fanned herself, "Mama yo! dis rain bring out ah heat yes. Ice man will do good business today."
Next door in Hendry's yard, the mongrel yelped happily - Ma Draper knew instantly that it was feeding time for the dog. She could hear the bitch gulping at the food, growling at anything that moved near her feeding bowl. Sita was an excellent guard dog she was unchained at

nights, free to patrol the grounds of the yard, now that the gates were secured. The mongrel had twice bitten people. Once when someone jumped the fence and tried to steal breadfruit. The other was an unfortunate morning when the front gate was left opened, and a basket vendor wandered in. The basket vendor attempted to stroke the dog as it approached him. "Is ah nice dog yuh have, is ah mixed bree...?" Before he could finish his sentence, the dog had ripped his wrist and started to attack the vendor about his body with its deadly jaws. "Sita", Hendry shouted; throwing himself at the dog to prevent any further injury to the basket vendor. There was blood everywhere as the basket vendor screamed in pain shaking his hands violently.

Hendry shouted at the basket vendor angrily, "Hold yuh hand up man, and keep it up." He rushed the vendor quickly to Casualty Department at Arima District Hospital. The vendor received several stitches to his wrist and given a Tetanus inoculation before he was discharged.

Ma Draper tilted her head to one side and listened, she could not hear the dog anymore, normality had returned. She had positioned herself in her comfort chair to engage with day's passing parade.

The news bulletin on the radio reported that the Caroni River had burst its banks, flooding the low-lying agricultural plains that surrounded the river. The newsreader elaborated that farmers had lost thousands of dollars' worth of crops such as tomatoes, lettuces, cabbages and other vegetables. "Also," commented the newsreader. "there has been reported loss of livestock as two goats and a cow were swept away by raging waters. In other news..."

Ma Draper shook her head, a motion she conducted to acknowledge every incident, whether it was good or bad. She would shake her head three to four times before verbalising her thoughts. After she had performed the head shaking ritual, she grumbled to herself, "More life lost in de place…. Ah know is only animals but is life too."

"Miss Draper, hold yuh dog meh mudder send somet'ing for yuh." A youthful voice shrieked from the front gate.

She eased herself off the chair, half sitting and standing to see a young boy about eleven at the gate holding a large brown paper bag in his hands, "A, A child, is you? Ah eh recognise yuh nah, yuh getting so big," she mused. "Come, come, me eh have no dog, is de neighbour dog yuh does hear barking all day."

The boy, his legs covered in dust, hurried to the house holding the bag with both hands. He spoke immediately as his feet met the steps, his eyes diligently searching for signs of a dog, despite Ma Draper's assurance that she did not own a dog. "Heh! mammy sen' some paynuse fuh yuh. De cow make young one nah, so she make *paynuse*."

His brown eyes continue to scan the house and about his legs. She smiled with him, said thank you, touched his shoulder, and commented, "But look how big yuh get eh boy. Is Sanjay yuh name yes, what school yuh going now?"

"I started Holly Cross last September nah. Is ah good school, ah like it. From up dey yuh could see all down Caroni an' ting yes!"

Ma Draper was amused by his observation. She motioned with her head inside the house, "Go in de kitchen yuh go see some mangoes in ah bowl, leave three and take de rest for yuh mammy."

The boy dragged his feet gingerly and inched his way through the living room and into the kitchen. Suddenly the mongrel next door started a frenzied bark, jumping against the iron fence. Sanjay ran franticly screaming at the top of his voice as he dashed out of the house. The bowl with the mangoes landed on the floor, leaving the fruits strewn about the kitchen floor. Sanjay did not look back; he was out of the house in a flash, making for the front gate before Ma Draper could make any attempts to placate him. With a blink of her eyes, she saw his shirt disappear into the empty street. She smiled mischievously and whispered, "Dat boy eh bet he dotish nah...tell yuh mammy ah say thanks."

High above, the sun's rays nudged away the dense grey clouds, allowing more sunlight to filter in, adding diamond sparkles to the wet leaves on the trees. Petrol and oil on the wet roads created pools of colour spectrums on the tarmac. The roads reeked of a sickly fresh smell that stuck to the back of your throat; you could almost taste the stench.

Petula Clark's *Downtown* was being played on the radio. It was the signature tune for a morning magazine show, popular with housewives. Ma Draper hoisted herself from the rocking chair, clutching the brown greasy bag with one hand and steadying herself with the other. She walked with cautious steps into the house, turned the volume up so she could listen to the programme, without having to strain her ears. Slowly, humming along to the tune, she inched her way to the kitchen. Her nimble fingers searched and felt for a spoon in the deep drawer. She buried the spoon into the bowl of *paynuse*, scooping out a heaped spoonful. She savoured the sweet aroma of nutmeg, ginger and cinnamon before putting the spoon to her mouth.

The sweet pulpy, buttery delicacy melted in her mouth. She sighed with utter contentment, commenting, "My goodness dis t'ing nice. Rookmin could turn she hand good." Carefully, she exacted several spoonfuls of *paynuse* and indulged with each spoonful as she did the first, licking her lips with every mouthful of the sweet indulgence.

"Oh God oh! Ah better leave some for Fitzy yes. He love dis t'ing too bad." She smiled and dipped the spoon deep into the bowl and gingerly put it to her mouth. She secured the lid back on the bowl and patted it gently.

Out in the back yard, all the plants and trees had an emerald glow from the rays of sunlight bouncing off the wet branches. Banana leaves reached out their long arms to touch the sunlight, the small breadfruit tree with its solitary fruit hanging from its strong stem looked ripe and ready for harvesting.

Two blue jays sat on the pepper tree and randomly pecked away at the red chillies. They paused and peered curiously at Ma Draper, tilting their heads from side to side in a robotic motion before resuming their fiery menu.

Ma Draper smiled at the birds. They seemed comfortable with her and carried on pecking away as she stood at the open doorway. She bent down and gathered the mangoes that were scattered on the kitchen floor. Selecting three firm ones, Ma Draper put them into a bowl and washed them. From a basket filled with various seasonings and accoutrements, she gathered all the ingredients she needed for making chow, reviewing a check list in her head. She preferred to use the peppers that had been picked earlier, rather than fresh from the tree. Ma Draper placed all the ingredients into the bowl and sang in a low voice. *"ah little more oil in my lamp keeps it burning, keeps it burning till the break of dayyyyy..."*

CHAPTER
5IVE

Market day brought a vibrancy of colours, freshness and bustling with traders and Saturday shoppers. The pavements, carparks and open areas around the market gave way to vendors plying their trade. Stalls brimming with fresh produce, haberdasheries, clothing, footwear and exotic flowers brought the market to life with its living colours. Vendors shouted from their stalls beckoning customers to examine and purchase their produce and products.

A short, dark-skinned Indian boy with skinny limbs chorused at the top of his voice. "Come and get yuh freshhhh ochres, straight from the tree to your basket." Without hesitation, a woman put her basket forward and said, "Put $2 worth in there."

Further, into the dense crowd of the open market, a grey-haired man stood flanked by two huge circular bamboo baskets. They were filled with black wriggling fish, tied together with long, grass stems. He stood with an unlit cigarette in his mouth and gazed at people as they walked by, staring at the wriggling fish. A stocky Indian woman with her hair wrapped into a bun and held together with two small varnished sticks, enquired, "How yuh selling the cascadoo?" The old man looked down at the fish in the basket, shifted the cigarette with his lips to the other side of his mouth, "$10 ah dozen."

She made a face at the fish, lifted a bunch scornfully, examining the size. She sucked her teeth and continued her way, clutching a canvas bag under her arm.

Ma Draper loved the ritual of Saturday market. She often referred to Saturday market as a gathering of communities. A place teeming with vibrancy, togetherness and gossip on this weekly pilgrimage. A place where she got news that would never reach her, unless she visited the market. 'The market was the lifeblood of any community,' was her favourite expression. Here, on a weekly basis, friendships got renewed and new ones formed. News of deaths, marriages and births were relayed in the chaotic bustle of market life. Joy, sorrow and the replenishment of food for the week ahead all played an integral part of the market ritual for Ma Draper and others who performed the weekly pilgrimage.

On a Saturday morning after having her coffee, she would grab her straw basket with a floral bouquet motif emblazoned to one side and head off to the market. She was keen to get there around 9am, and she never liked to hurry market shopping. Every stride was a calculated manoeuvre; stopping to have a chat with those she met on her way. She visited some stalls as matter of courtesy and others with customary routine. Sometimes, if she went by without stopping at a stall, the trader would shout out, "Aye Draper, we vex oh what?" There was a courteous giggle from Ma Draper with the refrain. "How I could vex with you? Meh mind far this morning."

Her first rendezvous was always at Miss Duncan's delicatessen. Here, Ma Draper indulged in a good helping of gossip and to quench her dry throat, a glass of Miss Duncan's special Mauby, with a slice of homemade coconut cake. She loved nibbling at the small chunks of coconut in the stiff cake. Burping loudly, having finished her cake and glass of Mauby, she would playfully say to Miss Duncan, "Gyul yuh save ah life today yes, as you do every

Saturday."

They both giggled and gossiped like two schoolgirls as Miss Duncan continued to attend to her customers. Their sessions would normally last for about an hour before they kissed each other farewell.

Miss Duncan waved her index finger in the air and chimed, "See yuh next week tantie. God bless and mind how yuh go."

Ma Draper replied. "Same child, same, tell yuh mammy hello eh." Adjusting her head-tie, she continued through the market admiring the abundance of fresh produce displayed all around. Taking a deep breath, she inhaled the freshness of the market. The smell of cooked food, herbs and spices, fresh meat and fish all added to what she loved about market life.

The aroma of the market and the vibrancy never failed to awaken Ma Draper's enthusiasm for the Saturday morning jaunt. She often recalled the enjoyment she had as a child from going to the market with her parents. The thrill of waking up before the sun came up and even before the cockerels started to crow. She loved the feeling of the cool morning air against her face as her dad drove to the market in Sangre Grande. A smile gathered at the corner of her lips as she remembered her father boasting that Sangre Grande had the freshest and best produce of any market in all of Trinidad.

Such pilgrimages created a cultural socialising bond with market life for Ma Draper. She often had the premonition that they could have had a stall in the market, but Mr Draper was against the idea from the moment the thought entered her head. He often joked with her, saying. "What you want stall in market for? You too upmarket for that." She was content with her Saturday morning trek and never hankered on about acquiring a market stall.

A vendor holding a small cardboard box over his head walked briskly, shouting, "Razor blades, camphor balls. Dollar ah pack. Razor blades, camphor balls... Minor Blades." An ambulance, siren screaming, picked its way through the human traffic drowning the shouts of the vendor's cry. Pedestrians cleared the roadway to allow the ambulance to inch its way through the street crowded with Saturday morning trading. The ambulance quickly disappeared, its siren fading in the distance.

Amidst the crowd, an outstretched hand stuck out above the sea of people and at the tip of a finger, a rotating basketball inched its way towards Ma Draper. Watkins tucked the ball under his arms and greeted her. "Mornin' Tantie. Fizty still sleeping?"

She shook her head and muttered, "He come home dis mornin' ah doh know if went to work or fete. But yes! He home sleeping, getting his beauty sleep chile."

Watkins offered to take her basket home, she chuckled and turned the basket upside down, "Boy I eh buy ah single t'ing yet. When yuh go tell Fitzy to come and meet me by Lau Chen to take de basket home."

"All right Tantie." Watkins stabbed his long arm into the air and continued to rotate the ball on his finger as he found a path through the crowd of shoppers.

Ma Draper's next stop was Dulcie. She referred to Dulcie as Radio Trinidad; it was here she would digest another weekly quota of gossip and news. Dulcie had one eye and wore glasses. She was a direct descendant from the Caribs, most of whom lived on the northern part of Arima near Calvary. Dulcie had been a market trader for as long as Ma Draper cared to remember. She occupied the same spot in the market since she began trading.

Dulcie earned the name Radio Trinidad because when it came to broadcasting news, no one was more efficient than Dulcie. Whether it was local news, international news or pure bachanalistic gossip, Dulcie was the source of all information. Ma Draper would learn who got married in America, who get arrested in Baltimore and in Toronto, Canada. She knew who was pregnant and who the father was and what month the baby due. She knew whose child got christened, who is godmother and godfather and who get indefinite visa for America; when they are leaving, and who they will live with in the States. She could point out all the wajangs in Arima and who sleeping with who husband. *Encyclopaedia Britannica* would have done well consulting Dulcie on Trinidad affairs, according to Ma Draper. Sometimes, Ma Draper spent over an hour listening to Dulcie, interjecting only to say, "Ehehh! is true gyul." Or she would clasp one hand to her mouth and gasp in awe, shaking her head or moan softly, "Young people today eh. Dey eh know dey born."

Dulcie never allowed Ma Draper to purchase anything from her stall. She would wrap slices of cake, pone and sweetbread or doubles and shove it into her basket. Ma Draper with her tenet would always fold a bill and hand it to Dulcie. Each time the action was met with a mouthful of cuss that flowed like poetry.

"We is family gyul, when I starving, I know where to get ah plate of food if I turn up at yuh door. Money is not everything yuh know."

Ma Draper never argued with Dulcie, but often felt she should be allowed to at least make a small purchase. On the days when Ma Draper would avoid her stall, Dulcie made a small parcel and sent it to Ma Draper with anyone she knew, who was passing her way.

After a good hour gossip session and a rundown of the weeks local, regional and international news with Dulcie, Ma Draper bid her farewell. She wandered off to her brother-in-law's stall to get a couple of christophenes, cucumbers, lettuce, carrots and beetroots. She sat and had coffee with him from his flask, spent another half hour chatting before going over to the fishmonger. Next stop was getting her plantains, pumpkin, sweet potato and dasheen from another vendor. She was very particular who she got her ground provisions from. She knew the vendors who had good quality and gave them her custom. When this was all completed, she browsed about the open market area getting odd bits and acquainting herself with old friends. She chatted and browsed until her arms ached from carrying the heavy basket, then made her way to the poultry shop.

Lau Chen, the poultry vendor, unusually tall for a Chinese man, was a gentle, soft-spoken man with jet black hair. He always came out from behind the counter to personally greet Ma Draper, often addressing her by first name. He attended to her order, knowing exactly what size broilers she required. Ma Draper would sit on the long wooden bench, painted in a bright post-box red. She waited there patiently while Mr Chen's employees prepared her order.

The live chickens were stacked in wire cages at the front of the shop. Customers would select a desired bird or would simply order by weight. The attendant would come from behind the counter, thrust his hand into a cage, and select a bird, stuffing it into a cone-shaped scale pan. At the narrow, open end of the cone, the chicken's head was exposed, eyes surveying, not knowing its fate. The poultry worker then secured a string with a small metal plate onto the feet of the chicken giving the customer a plastic disc with a corresponding number. When customers returned to collect their purchase, it could be easily identified by the corresponding number on the chicken.

Watkins and Fitzroy strolled nonchalantly into the poultry shop with a leisurely gait. Watkins greeted Ma Draper with a courteous smile and quickly pulled the neck of his T-shirt over his nostrils to mask the stench of the poultry shop. He tucked the basketball under his arm and took hold of the basket from the bench. Fitzroy was dressed in a printed cotton vest and a pair of shorts he fashioned from an old pair of Wrangler jeans. He waited for Chen to put the broilers in separate bags before handing over the plastics discs, collected the chickens and bid Lau Chen, adios.

"Chinee," A young man on a bicycle called. 'wha' mark yuh playing today?"

Lau Chen waved him on saying, "No todayee. Chen no dream, no feel luckeee."

The young man on the bike looked at Ma Draper; she fished a dollar from her beaded purse and said, "Play fowl, 26."

"Ma doh bother to cook today," Fitzroy exclaimed! "Miss Rookmin send one set ah food, dey had their Hindu puja today."

Watkins joined in with a remark, "Tantie de food nice too bad. I had to eat twice." Ma Draper shook her head, surveying Watkins from head to toe, "Dey didn't feed yuh properly in the army or what? De way both ah you carryin' orn, people go believe allyuh never eat food yet."

The thought of food brought her mind to the piece of cassava pone Dulcie gave her earlier. She could almost smell the aroma of cinnamon and nutmeg wafting from the basket dangling off Watkins long arm. She whispered in her mind, "I will have dat pone tomorrow yes!"

Laid out on the table were several plastic containers, some with the words *Dorina* margarine printed on them. The smell of curry permeated the air with its pungent mouth-watering spices. She lifted the lid of one of the containers, revealing curried masala mango. Tilting her head with curiosity, she mulled with the thought, where did Rookmin get mango, "Why she never asks meh for any mango?"

Ma Draper did not allow the thought to linger. She carried on investigating the other containers with dhal, curried channa, chataigne and pumpkin. In a brown piece of cotton, she could see the words 'National Flour Mills' printed on the edge. Rookmin had fashioned kitchen towels from the used flour bags. Carefully, Ma Draper unwrapped the cloth, the warm aroma of ghee rose to her nostrils exposing the soft warm fluffy roti. She tested its warmth with the back of her hand, pinched a piece and put it to her mouth, she chewed gently on it.

The taste was addictive, she broke off another piece dipping bit by bit into every bowl before reaching into the cupboard for a plate. Scooping generous helpings of the food onto the plate, she headed for the comfort of her rocking chair on the veranda. Settling herself on the rocking chair, she chewed and hummed a hymn to the rhythm of the chair.

There was a loud crash on the roof. A mango rolled off the corrugated iron, hitting the hard ground below. Its ripe pulp exposed where it had split with the impact on reaching the earth. The bitch next door let out two sharp yelps before settling back into the kennel, nestling her head on her front paws.

Ma Draper lifted her head surveying the fruits on the ground. The yellow juice had already started to stain the earth. She shook her head and whispered. "Dem blasted mango go give me a heart attack yes!" She rocked gently on the chair, reflecting on the food on her plate, picking at it gingerly and chewing slowly.

Fitzroy had picked four plump semi ripe mangoes and left them on a metal tray on the veranda for Ma Draper. She looked at the mangoes, shook her head and adjusted her head tie before getting out of the chair to inspect them. Taking the largest fruit from the tray, she held it to her nose and inhaled its aroma, savouring the scent. She groaned from the aches in her leg, massaging the spot with her fist, she sighed. "Jezess Lord, what is all dis pain?"

A voice from the street called out, "Mornin' Tantie." Ma Draper, in a whisper responded. "Mornin' child, how yuh mammy?" She broke off a small piece of roti and dipped it into the curried mango, again chewing her food slowly.

Across the road, Dhanraj shop was busy with Saturday morning customers. She could barely see Dhanraj sitting behind his huge wooden desk. His desk was a picture of chaos but Dhanraj could put his finger on anything he needed, with ease and accuracy, even with his eyes closed. He seldom left the desk, just on the odd occasion when he did leave for the toilet or to skip over to Ma Draper for a bowl full of her sumptuous mango chow.

Dhanraj stood just over six-foot tall with broad shoulders and a slight paunch. He had a full head of hair with grey patches to the front and sides. He wore short sleeve shirts with khaki shorts and kept a loaded revolver in his right pocket. He was a licensed firearm holder and kept the gun for protecting himself and his business. Sometimes, for a show, he would take the pistol out of his pocket and place it on the desk. Curious customers would pause to have a good gaze at the snub-nose 38 revolver.

Armed bandits had made many attempts to rob the store; on two occasions, Dhanraj had shot and wounded one of the bandits in the process. He was a crack shot, who at one time represented Trinidad and Tobago in rifle shooting and other shooting sports locally and at internationally as well.

Behind his oak desk, in a small glass cabinet, he kept some of the trophies, medals and shields he had won over the years. Next to the small cabinet, an antique frame displayed a newspaper clipping of him accepting a medal from the Governor General of Trinidad and Tobago. Alongside a family portrait, hung in a larger more ornate frame was a photograph of him posing with a high-powered rifle.

Competition no longer played an active role in his life, he served as president of the Association for Rifle Shooting and various other clubs around the country while offering tutoring sessions for young rifle enthusiasts. Many of Dhanraj customers had dubbed him 'John Wayne' because of his shooting skills.

Having satiated herself with Rookmin's food, she burped and patted her stomach. Ma Draper proceeded to prepare her daily chow with the mangoes that Fitzroy had dutifully picked for her earlier that morning. Today, however, instead of sealing the plastic bowl with a lid, she collected three jam jars from her cupboard. She sniffed at them and proceeded to fill each jar with mango mixture. In each bottle, she added seasoning and pepper in varying quantities, periodically sniffing at the jars again, adding more pepper until it had the right aroma. Securing the lids on the jars, she shook them gently, then carefully she tore off a bit of the brown paper that was used to wrap the pone. Making two equal folds, she divided the paper into three sections, roughly tearing the paper along the creased lines. Adjusting her head tie, she glanced up to the iron roof and a song came to her. *"He come from the glory. He come from the glorious kingdom. Oh yes believe...."*

Having secured lids on the jam jars filled with mango chow, she inspected them and smiled. The result pleased her. She gave the jars a little tap before placing in the cupboard in numbered sequence and continued singing *"believer, oh yes..."*

CHAPTER
6IX

Ma Draper could hear the continuous din of a bicycle bell at the front of the house. It was Duncan. He was on his daily routine visiting punters, enquiring what *whe whe* 'mark' they wanted to play that day. Coming to the verandah her eyes avoided Duncan's, "Why you making all dis racket out here?" She screamed at him. Selecting a dollar bill from her purse, she said, "Put ah dollar on whatever crab does play for." stretching her hand over the low verandah wall to give Duncan the money. She had a dream Fitzroy had secured a job on a ship. The ship was teeming with crabs, very large crabs so, playing the mark, crab seemed the logical thing to do.

Duncan protested, "Tantie crab is 33, same as spider. Yuh throwing away a good dollar boss lady." He encouraged her to play 18, 'water boat,' explaining the dynamics of the game to her. Ma Draper was having none of it and stuck with 33. She cast a pitiful gaze at Duncan. "Dis man eh bet he farce nah, and he bold-faced too." She watched Duncan ride off on his bike, his open shirt flowing at his sides as he pedalled briskly out of sight.

Her dream lingered on her mind all morning as she sat rocking in her chair. There was an abrupt pause to her motion. She got up with a thought and verbalised it, "Ah wonder if Fitzroy working on ah ship fuh true and didn't bother to tell me?" Ma Draper went over to his room, the curtains were drawn, and a strong smell of liniment rose up to her nostrils.

The first thing that caught her eye was that a family portrait was missing. Next to the bed there was a bulging duffle bag with a neat pile of clothing with a basketball resting on top. "But what is dis meh lord, you mean to say he really get ah job and eh tell me nutten?" Her heartbeat raced, tears welled up in her eyes, she was angry and sad, her tears flowed. She clasped her hands and buried her head into it. The aroma of the *shadon beni* was still fresh on her hands. Tears emerged at the corner of her eyes and traced their way down her weathered cheek. Her face sullen and her heart started to pound in her chest with a million thoughts racing through her mind. She opened the curtains to allow some light into the room, picking up the basketball as she sat at the edge of the bed. Her eyes roamed, mapping the room to see what else was missing. It dawned on her that apart from new paint, not much had changed in the room. Everything appeared to be as it was when Fitzroy was a teenager. She spotted the missing portrait at the side of the wardrobe next to his ProKeds.

Ma Draper did not hear Fitzroy enter the room. The doorway framed his physique as he stood looking at his mother for a few seconds.

"Ma, what yuh doing in here crying?"

Fitzroy's voice stunned her.

"Nutten boy, nutten." She stammered, quickly wiping the tears from the corner of her eyes.

Within a few seconds, she had composed herself, adjusted her head tie and shouted at Fitzroy, "So, mister man, yuh packing up yuh ass an' leaving here without ah word?"

"Ma yuh better calm down ah lil bit. Ah leavin' but not to go on no ship to work. I get a job down South with ah oil company. It makes no sense travelling to and from South all de time so I will stay in quarters down there."

Ma Draper eyed him suspiciously.

"I was going to tell yuh this evening."

She allowed emotions to take control and threw her arms around him sobbing, "I thought yuh get ah wuk on ah ship and yuh going to leave and never return."

Fitzroy was stunned by her reaction; the emotional display by his mother was never seen before. He had never seen her openly express, such emotions. Ma Draper seemed saddened that Fitzroy had gotten a job and moving out of the house too. He expected his mother to be happy for him, yet she seemed absorbed with the notion that she would be neglected.

Reflecting, he wondered if she was happy when he returned from the docks, week after week, disappointed of not finding work on a ship.

In her eyes, he could anticipate the question she was about to ask and interrupted her thoughts. "Don't worry, Elsa has already agreed to come and stay with you." Fitzroy tenderly dried her tears with his T-shirt. Her emotions were still swirling as she pounded his chest with her fist.

She aimed a finger at the basketball kit, "And what about all dis basketball business then, yuh leaving dat behind too?"

"Doh worry, Watkins brother Mikey taking my place on de team, he real good, better than me even. Mackie would have been ah better choice, but he is running for Mayor."

She picked up the kit, waving her hand at Fitzroy, "Dat boy is trouble I tell yuh. He involved with dem Freedom Fighters people and de Black Power."

"Ma, Mackie is ah good fella, he eh involved in dem kinda ting, trust me."

"Boy it frightens me with all these killing going on and, is ah set ah young people. Yuh eh see how police killing dem gorillas and dem left right and centre. One mistake and is bow! yuh ded, ded wid ah police bullit."

Fitzroy was amused. He laughed loudly at Ma Draper's pronunciation of guerrilla.

"What you grinning yuh teeth at then?" She grumbled.

"Ma is not gorilla, is guerrilla!"

Ma Draper let off a loud steups, shouting at Fitzroy, "Look boy doh play de ass with me yuh hear, I doh care ah monkeys what dey calling demself, just keep away from dem."

"Ma yuh does worry too much. Is not only in Trinidad tings bad yuh know. All over de world is de same ting. We lucky we have some petro-dollars to spread around. You see what happening in Chile where they overthrow the government? The virus of revolution spreading, Trinidad get ah taste but it eh over yet."

Fitzroy patted his pocket and smiled, "Me eh looking for no wuk on ships again, my strategy has changed. Oil companies paying good good money, better than working on the ships. You wait and see; in two twos I will be making enough money and yuh would not have to worry about anything."

He clicked his fingers in quick succession and boasted, "In ah year's time, you watch and see, I go be sitting back easy, easy with the amount ah money rolling in."

"Boy yuh jus' fooling oui. If tings eh work out come back home. I taking all yuh advice, ah going into de chow making business so yuh go be alright anyway." Ma Draper said aiming her finger at Fitzroy with an authoritative flair.

"Ma yuh eh going into no chow business," screamed Fitzroy. "Sooklal, ah doubles man come dis morning and ask to buy de mango. He said he would pay $200 for de whole tree. Yuh go be sitting down cool, cool now. You doh have to worry about mangoes falling on the roof all the time and making yuh jump out yuh skin."

"Oh, gorm Fitzroy no! What yuh tell him?"

"Is for de best Ma. Yuh eh have to pick up mangoes everyday and jump out yuh clothes every time ah mango hit de roof."

Ma Draper was quietly furious, cold and silent. She gazed upon Fitzroy standing in the doorway, his head almost touching the top of the doorframe. She stood up from the bed and dropped both hands to her side. Her silent pause was deafening as she studied Fitzroy's lanky frame in the doorway before her voice erupted again.

"Is who give you de authority to sell de mango and dem? Yuh never consult meh one frigging bit. Ah know is only ah hog mango tree but is my tree Fitzy, my mango tree. Ah can't fathom to think what you have done, yuh shame meh bad."

Fitzroy's lips parted to speak but was quickly silenced. "I sure Mackie put yuh up to all dis blasted nonsense. Dat boy is no good, but yuh eh listening. Is like stick break in yuh ears."

"Ma take it easy. Mackie eh put me up to nutten and if yuh should know Mackie eh in no Black Power business. All Mackie do is play basketball and go ML disco. Mackie eh meddling in no revolution business. He has a vision, a good one, and we should support him rather than all dem tiefing people in de Council."

Fitzroys' attempts to defend Mackie did little to convince her; she shoved past Fitzroy shouting at him, "You mark my word, and, mark it good mister man. Dat boy go end up with ah police bullit. Potow, pow and he dead, den yuh go hold yuh head an' bawl saying, Ma was right,

Ma was right."

Fitzroy sucked his teeth loudly and stood his ground screaming back at Ma Draper, "Is people like de Black Power who fighting for the rights and integrity of the people of dis country, young people fighting for everybody, ole, young and even dem tiefing buggers too. We should be grateful instead of condemning and, criticising people who want betterment for our Borough and de country, to make ah difference for everyone, for the future."

He hurried after her as she walked towards the kitchen singing; *Glory, glory halleluiah* on a higher tone than she would usually. Fitzroy stopped. He knew once she started singing there was no way of having a meaningful conversation with her.

Ma Draper gave a fleeting glance over her shoulders to see Fitzroy with basketball, kit and his duffle bag strung across his shoulder, making his way out the front door. Her singing ceased when she didn't hear the scrape of the front gate. Fitzroy left, leaving the gate ajar. Ma Draper shook her head, whispering under her breath, "Young people today eh! dey eh know dey born." Pondering on the silence, she picked up the verse again and continued singing, *Glory, glory halleluiah…*

Ma Draper was preoccupied. She did not hear Elsa come in; her mind was distracted with the birds on the pepper tree, busy pecking away at the ripe red peppers. A steady stream of tears danced across her cheeks as she stared out of the open back door. Her heart was sore thinking about Fitzroy and his new job in the oilfields. She dreaded the day when he would leave; she knew the house will be feel empty without him. Just like it felt empty when Mr Draper died. She wasn't ready for Fitzroy's leaving.

Nothing could ever prepare her for such a moment. The thought of the mangoes being sold to a Doubles vendor weighed on her mind. The thought of a bare mango tree frightened her too.

Her vision was of hundreds of jars stacked on the table, with Elsa busy sticking white and red labels with small text that read, *Draper's Mango Chow*, made in Arima, Trinidad. The concept was now a blur as her thoughts played havoc. She kept her focus on the back yard, looking at nothing of any real interest. The Blue Jays looked up at her and flew to the orange tree, they appeared to be smiling with her.

Lost in her thoughts, she was unaware of Elsa's presence. She didn't even hear the scrape of the front gate on the concrete. Elsa touched her gently on the shoulders, "Mums yuh okay? Yuh never answered when ah called out. Why yuh crying?"

Ma Draper hugged Elsa, resting her head delicately on her shoulders. A steady stream of fresh tears soaked into her flowered cotton dress. Elsa could feel the dampness of the tears as it absorbed into the fabric. She held Ma Draper and allowed her to release her anguish.

"Come, come and sit down." She coaxed Ma Draper to one of the dining chairs and sat her down. Elsa filled a glass with iced water from the fridge and watched Ma Draper sip it slowly. There was an eerie silence, Ma Draper dried her eyes and took another sip of water. She looked up at Elsa and rested the glass on the table.

"Elsie yuh not going to believe dis, Fitzy get ah job down in some oilfield. And what he do? He gorn and sell all de blasted mango to some Doubles man name Sooklall." Ma Draper complained.

"Mums, yuh know Fitzy only do it for you to have peace

of mind, is nutten more. Fitzroy doh want yuh picking up mango every mornin' and making chow for ah living. All he wants is for you to relax and take tings nice and easy."

Ma Draper directed her gaze into Elsa's eyes, "Well miss lady, ah suppose yuh go tell meh how you goin' to look after meh too eh?"

Elsa laughed and kissed Ma Draper gently on the cheeks, "Dat is where yuh wrong, we going to both look after each other." They both erupted into delightful laughter, hugging each other. Ma Draper rubbed Elsa's belly and asked, "How de baby?"

"Everything alright yuh know." Their laughter continued, Ma Draper's tears had faded, her sullen face was now beaming with a renewed happiness.

Elsa walked over to the kitchen table and gasped in surprise, "But wait! Mum yuh eh making joke, yuh bottling chow now?"

"Yes, my child ah experimenting with ah few diff-rent varieties for allyuh experts to taste." Ma Draper said, giving a short laugh, "Try de one marked number two, it have ah secret ingredient in dey."

Elsa laughed, "Imagine I graduate now, official mango chow taster."

She ignored Ma Draper's request and peered through the open back door into the garden. The birds had had their fill of peppers and flown off yet, like the mango tree, it glowed with the abundance of the red fiery bulbs. The *shadon beni* plants seem to spring up everywhere in the back yard among the many weeds shading them from view in the undergrowth. "Yuh need somebody to come and clean up de back garden." Elsa suggested.

"Yes girl, ah will get Rookmin son to come an' do it. Dat good-for-nutten Fitzroy doh like gardening at all. When he home all he doin' is eating, smoking weed an' sleeping."

"Mum yuh have coconut water in de fridge?"

"Yes! Fitzy full up about three bottles yesterday."

"I could take on ah nice whisky and coconut water now." Elsa mused still looking at the back yard and the various fruits, vegetables, shrubs and flowers flourishing without much tending.

Ma Draper laughed at Elsa's request, pointing to the cupboard, "Fitzroy have ah bottle of Johnnie Walker in the bottom cupboard, help yuhself."

"Mum yuh mad? Ah cyar drink no grog wid dis child in meh belly." Elsa protested, patting her belly and making circular rotations with her palm. She turned to look at Ma Draper, her face much happier now, it made Elsa happy too.

"Ah tell yuh what mum, if I did not have to work, I would have gone market with yuh tomorrow because Fitzroy not here to bring yuh basket home."

"Child, I know you would. Yuh like the daughter ah never had."

"What yuh talkin' 'bout lady? You is my mammy!"

Ma Draper smiled; her finger found an itchy spot under her head tie. She felt a tinge of excitement knowing that Elsa was coming to stay with her.

After completing her schooling, Elsa had moved back with her parents. Somehow her visits to the Drapers never ceased, it felt like she was at the Drapers more than at her own home. Her job at the property agent in Arima meant she could visit the Drapers during her lunch time and on an evening. She also worked as a part time receptionist on Saturdays at a hotel. Ma Draper lifted her head towards Elsa, indicating with a hand movement, "Yuh know where everything is, when yuh ready to fix up de room how you want it. Or use your old room in de back."

Elsa nodded attentively. She surveyed the house as if it was her first time.

"Ma, not much has changed in this house since I used to live here."

"Gyul, what I go change? Everything suits me, the way it is. Fitzroy paint it up every year, apart from dat, nothing eh wrong with it."

Ma Draper beckoned Elsa close to her and began to impart motherly advice. She listed many items Elsa should have before the baby came and things she would need to care for the baby once it was born. Elsa nodded her head in agreement to every suggestion that Ma Draper proposed and spoke only when she offered to purchase a crib for the baby.

"Mum yuh doh have to do dat yuh know. De man done buy up all dem t'ings ahready for de child. Yuh think it easy with him. Yuh would swear he is the one carrying the child in his belly."

Ma Draper held her hand gently. "It looks as though yuh find yuhself ah good man. Nowadays all dem man an' dem want to do is full-up young girl belly and leave dem."

Elsa groaned at Ma Draper's comments adding, "Is so true yuh know, dey want to jump from one bed to de next, but all dem man and dem not so. It has a few good ones out there still and, I find one."

Motioning with a head movement, she said to Elsa, "Dat bag there is yours."

Opening the large plastic bag, Elsa found vaseline, baby powder, cloth diapers, gripe water, red lavender liquid, vicks, 2 baby bottles with latex nipples, 2 pairs of knitted baby booties, a pack of baby vests, a small wool blanket and a gold and jet bracelet.

Elsa grabbed Ma Draper, hugged and kissed her all over her face and head. "Thank you. Mum you are just the sweetest person ever."

Ma Draper cupped Elsa's face in her hands, "I am so proud of you."

"It is nice to have family, Elsa said with a tear in her eye. "if you see the amount ah things mammy and daddy buy too. Fitzy was right, I do have four parents."

Ma Draper looked upon Elsa; her eyes surveyed the ceiling and the walls around her. Ma Draper's gaze, at random, focussed on the calendar hanging from a nail on the wall. There was a picture of the *Dial* which portrayed a busy and bustling pedestrian environment, without any automobiles.

"I remember dem days when yuh coulda walk de road without fear of being knockdown by some madman driver. Is just so sudden, sudden, we have ah set ah cars here in Trinidad. Oil money gyul, it have people totool-bay fuh true yes."

Her gaze carried from the calendar and again to Elsa. Elsa noticed her stare and with curiosity, questioned her fixation. "Is why yuh looking at me so?"

"I jus' t'inking," Ma Draper reflected. "what happen with you and Fitzroy? De two ah you were going good, good then vaps allyuh done."

Elsa nestled beside her and cupped Ma Draper's hand in hers, peering into her eyes. "Listen! I eh know where you and other people get dis idea dat Fitzroy and me, was an item. We are almost like brother and sister; you should know that more than anybody mum."

Ma Draper looked at her suspiciously, staring at her with compelling eyes, as if daring Elsa to be truthful. Ma

Draper gave a long burp then claimed, "Dis gas troubling meh for so man." She kept her stare at Elsa.

"Yuh know you is not the only person who has asked me dat question." Elsa said, sounding annoyed.

"I doh know why yuh getting yuhself in ah state for gyul. Yuh hear people talkin' but I did ketch two ah you kissin' in de bedroom, remember?"

A broad smile crept across Elsa's face and she laughed, cupping her mouth to prevent her from laughing out loudly. "Ma, we were only twelve years old then. And is me who kissed him. Fitzroy didn't even know his lips from his ears back then. I was just practicing on him."

Ma Draper held her side and let off a long burp and again, complained of gas. Lilting her head to one side, she motioned to Elsa and said. "Is de *whe whe* man, see what dat miserable little man want."

Elsa greeted the small, insipid man on the bicycle, "Good day Mr Duncan. How yuh goin?"

"Buh what crosses is dis meh lord. Child is whey yuh come out?" Duncan beamed, "Long, looong time I eh see yuh gyul."

Duncan, leery eyes cast a curious glance at Elsa, studying her physique. With a coy smile on his face, he asked boldly, "So, who full up yuh belly then?"

His crude comment wiped the smile off Elsa's face. She sucked her teeth and gave Duncan a stern look that erased the smug grin on his face. Lowering his head, cowering into himself, he stretched out his hand and gave Elsa a wad of single dollar bills. Muttering under his breath, hardly loud enough for Elsa to hear, "De ole lady win spider."

Elsa grabbed the notes from his hand, turning away without giving him a second glance, ignoring when he said, "Allyuh playing any mark today?"

She raced inside waving the wad of notes about with a glee on her face, screaming, "Yuh hit the big times gyul. Yuh win de mark!"

"Yuh lie!" Ma Draper stared in shock.

"Is ah good ting I follow meh mind oui. De damn fool telling me play *waterboat,* but I dream ah whole set ah crabs."

"And yuh only play for ah dollar?" Elsa groaned, disapprovingly.

"Child! Ah dollar is my limit, de little win is enough to see meh through the week, and I might even play ah mark again tomorrow."

Ma Draper folded the money and cupped it in Elsa's hand. "You keep dat and buy de baby somet'ing."

"No Ma, ah cyar do dat. You do plenty ahready"

"Look child doh argue wid yuh mudder, take de money."

Elsa stood up briskly, tucking the wad of notes into her jeans pocket. She continued tidying, adjusting the chairs around the dining table. She smoothed out the oilcloth on the table with the palm of her hand, sweeping the crumbs from the table with her hand onto the floor. A practice Ma Draper despised immensely.

Looking out the kitchen window, taking a deep breath of fresh air, Elsa gazed towards the blue sky. Smiling, she remembered the day she had kissed Fitzroy full on his mouth. He hastily wiped his mouth and Elsa kissed him again when Ma Draper walked into the room and screamed. "What in de lords name you two little wretches doing in here?"

They both wiped their mouths, staring at her with total innocence. Elsa could not contain herself, erupting into an uncontrolled fit of laughter as she raced out of the room. Fitzroy followed her timidly. Ma Draper smacked the back of his head as he went by.

The memory of the event held her smile and brought a twinkle to her eye. She reminisced on the good times they had enjoyed in their childhood. On many occasions she had gone to the Grandstand with Mr Draper to watch and cheer Fitzroy whenever he played basketball or cricket.

Often, both Elsa and Fitzroy would go to the cinema on Sundays and every Easter, she felt privileged, when invited along to Manzanilla beach with the Drapers. Mr Draper rented a beach house where they spent the entire Easter holidays. There she would help Ma Draper pick up buckets-full of chip chip, a small shellfish that was abundant on the beach that time of year. Ma Draper saved the shells to decorate the flower beds. Mr Draper had even fashioned a vase from the shells one year.

There were fond memories too, of Mr Draper when the house was under construction. He would, like Ma Draper, often sing a hymn throughout the day as he went about his duties. She remembered the one hymn that Mr Draper would always sing and started to sing it softly...*I have a sword in my hand, help me to use it, lord I have a sword in my hand. Help me to use it, lord, I'm goin' away to watch an' to pray, never to come back 'till the great Judgement day...*

She recalled Mr Draper vividly saying one day, his voice strong and powerful. "De soil in dis yard would forever produce food and whoever should live here, will never go hungry...amen."

Elsa sighed and whispered, "Amen to dat pappy." Surveying the abundance of food growing in the yard that included huge banana trees, their purple flowers attracting a swarm of busy bees, pollinating, orange, lime and breadfruit trees, peppers of many varieties grew without cultivation, sugar cane, shadon beni in abundance, soursop, tomatoes, a moringa tree with its crop hanging from the thin branches like giant green needles and of course, the mango tree. How true his words were; the yard was never without a variety of fruits and vegetables at any given time of the year. Hendry, the neighbour, used to always refer to the Drapers' yard as the garden of Eden.

Mr Draper showered Elsa with paternal affection, treating her as his own daughter when she was adopted into the home as a young girl. Elsa's parents lived in the countryside, managing a farm east of Arima. There was limited transport available where they resided making it difficult for Elsa to attend school in Arima. Her father paid a taxi to take and fetch her each day, creating a strain on their financial resources. Elsa's parents face the dilemma of removing her from school or continuing to struggle financially.

The Drapers had suggested to her parents that Elsa could stay with them during the week and return on weekends. The suggestion presented a solution to the predicament they were up against. Elsa's mother was relieved that her daughter did not have to give up school. She didn't want history repeating itself in her family. As a young girl, she was forced to quit school because her parents could not afford the books and uniform for her to gain an education. She wanted a better life for Elsa; one where she had choices and was not limited to farm life and domestic work.

Elsa often reflected on her younger days with the Drapers, she cherished the fond memories that had helped to shape her morals and upbringing. Fitzroy often said to her that she had four parents. And she would laugh and say. "I am a lucky girl."

Elsa knew that without the intervention of the Drapers her chances of an education would have been zero. Her family wasn't poor, but it had been a struggle to enable Elsa to attend school and continue into secondary education. The Drapers ensured that she had a comfortable home and a good environment to pursue her studies. They never took over as Elsa's parents but made sure that her education needs were catered for.

A gentle breeze blew across Elsa's face at the kitchen window. The cool wind opened an invitation for her to venture, barefoot, into the damp yard. She surveyed the garden, overgrown with wild bushes. Tall spears of lemon grass and sugar cane stalks populated the garden and wild vines plaited themselves around the trunk of the banana plants. She watched as an army of small black ants marched in regimental chaos, up and down the purple sugarcane stalk, up to its arrows and back down into the earth below, carting away pollen stuck to their legs.

To the front, the central part of the yard blossomed with roses in a variety of hues. Exoras, heliconia, marigolds, poinsettias, perriwinkles and various flowering shrubs creating a hub for happy butterflies, hummingbirds and bees. Jump-up-and-kiss-me bloomed merrily, buzzing with insect life, At the centre of the garden stood a verdant *zebapique* vine. On the vine Ma Draper had tied a blue, Milk of Magnesia bottle, to protect the vine against *maljou*. She had learnt this method from her mother, who used it to protect her garden from envious eyes.

Every time one of the neighbours experienced abdominal pains or had a cold or fever, they would run to Ma Draper and beg for some *zebapique* leaves. The orange and lime trees that Mr Draper had planted along the fence stood laden with young citrus fruits. The mango rose tree stood resplendent as the sentinel over the entire garden.

Mr Draper had carefully dug the wilted looking tree from the middle of the plot and replanted it near the edge of the fence. The architect had cautioned Mr. Draper about the dangers and proximity of the tree to the property's foundation. Mr. Draper would not hear a word of it and cautioned that the only way that mango tree was going, was over his dead body. No one expected the mango tree to thrive, Mr Draper himself had doubts, but encouraged Elsa to water it regularly and to ensure parasites didn't attack the plant.

She felt proud of Mr Draper's stance on the mango tree; a frail little plant, no more two feet tall with about six leaves – she had watered the plant dutifully each day. She lifted her head and gazed upon how majestic and prominent the tree had grown, its strong branches like outstretched arms, supporting the huge bunches of mangoes. She was disappointed when it turned out not to be a Starch Mango tree as Mr Draper had professed. He had examined the leaves and had no doubt in his mind that it was Starch Mango. They didn't have the heart to cut it down after discovering it was mango Rose.

From the yard, Elsa could hear Ma Draper singing a hymn. She strained her ear to recognise the hymn but without success. She sucked her teeth for no apparent reason, sighed, half rubbing and patting her tummy to ease her discomfort, then spat in the undergrowth.

The air was humid and only the hum of traffic on the main street could be heard until the piercing scream of the siren at a textile mill, shattered the stillness. The siren signalled it was 5 'O' clock. The factory siren alarmed three times a day on weekdays. Seven in the morning, mid-day and five in the evening at the end of the working day. It was a good marker for time keeping across the borough as the siren could be heard from miles around. Elsa looked up at the mango tree and verbalised her thoughts. "Let me go an' make somet'ing for de lady to eat eh." Gently massaging her belly with one hand while supporting her back with the other, she spat into the bushes.

The television illuminated the room as Ma Draper sat motionless on the couch, looking at the television. She sighed and sucked her teeth, then spoke. EEh eh! Elsa, yuh eh hear on de news? Police looking for ah man from Arima! Dey say he sportin' ah Rasta hairstyle." She waited for Elsa's response but there was none from her as she stood behind Ma Draper looking at the television screen. The only sounds in the room came from Ma Draper's heavy breathing and the TV set.

Ma Draper tilted her head back to look up at Elsa. "Yuh well quiet my child, something bodderin' yuh?"

"No Ma! Everyt'ing fine yuh know."

Ma Draper sensed Elsa's quietness. She had grown to know many of Elsa's traits and knew she was not one to be silent for long. Elsa would always find conversation material, engaging Ma Draper in many debates.

"How yuh quiet so gyul?" Ma Draper said without taking her eyes off the television.

"Nutten nah, meh mind just drifting at the moment." Elsa rested her hand on Ma Draper's shoulders, assuring her that everything was okay. They both watched the rest of the news in silence.

After the news and weather report, Ma Draper sat on the

couch massaging her aching knees pounding them with her fist intermittently. Elsa went to the kitchen to prepare dinner. After preparing the meal they both sat at the table and ate heartily. Ma Draper smiled at Elsa.

"Yuh does make ah nice coconut bake oui."

Elsa knew that Ma Draper loved coconut bake and tried to make it whenever she had the opportunity. She looked up from her plate at Ma Draper, "Yuh want some more?"

"Nah gyul, I full up now."

Ma Draper retired to her room after her dinner. She sat at the edge of the bed grooming her hair. She opened her Bible, scanning the scriptures as she brushed her soft grey hair. Elsa nestled down on the couch. She stretched her legs out on the chair and gave a long sigh. She massaged her tummy gently as she eased herself into a comfortable position.

In the background she could just about hear Ma Draper harmonising a hymn in her room. Elsa caressed her tummy in circular motion and chuckled, recalling a remark that Ma Draper made about her belly. "De way yuh belly plump and round like ah ball, I sure, sure is ah boy child yuh making."

It had surprised her too, Marlon professed with some surety, that she was having a girl. Most men always favoured a boy as a first child. Elsa herself had no gender preferences, wishing only for her baby to be born healthy, and without complications. Already, other women who bore children were giving her stories of eight-hour labour and describing childbirth pains, in detail.

She continued massaging her tummy allowing her thoughts to roam. The atmosphere in the house had changed since Fitzroy moved out. The house no longer had that jovial mood she had grown accustomed to in the past.

Darkness consumed the daylight quickly, swallowing the final glow of the sunset completely, bringing different dynamics to the town. Clothing and haberdashery stalls on the busy sidewalks disappeared and were replaced with a couple fruit vendors selling apples, pears, grapes, bananas and watermelons. Further down the street, hotdog stands, coconut vendors and an oyster seller gave rhythm to the nocturnal streets. At the corner of a crossroad, a vendor selling home-roasted peanuts cried at regular intervals, "Nuts, Nuts...sallllt and fresssh. Nuts, Nuts...sallllt and fresssh."

The vendor's bike was painted red, green and yellow - Rastafarian colours. The bike was fitted with a huge metal box that housed a gas burner to keep the nuts warm. Across the front and sides of the metal box, sign-written in bold red letters were, 'IN JAH WE TRUST, IN MAN WE BUSS'. Smaller letters underneath read, 'Absolutely NO Credit' in a calligraphy style. These words were purely ornamental for you could regularly hear customers say 'Ras gimme two pack ah nuts until tomorrow?' Or, taxi drivers would slow their cabs and the Rasta always knew what the driver's preference was. They would drive off making a circular motion with their hands, a signal that meant they would pay later.

People would congregate around the nuts vendor and their debates would centre on a range of topics from politics, the economy, unemployment, the Caribbean, world issues and the current local election. This evening, the discussion was centred on the young mayoral candidate, Mackie. Since the election campaign began, the debate focused on central issues pertaining to the borough.

Arguments ensued about who was best qualified to lead the Borough over the next four years. It was common talk across the borough, in every shop, rum shop, market stall or taxicab, people were talking about Mackie. He was a new sensation in local politics. His presence created a buzz and he had an aura of new perspective wherever he went canvassing. The people loved the vibration he brought and the unity he ignited among people of every age with his new approach to politics.

"Allyuh forgetting that this young man you guys so highly rating was arrested and deported from Canada." The smartly dressed gentleman in a pencil grey pin stripe suit said with an air of authority. "And dat make de bredren ah criminal sar?" The Rasta snapped.

"No, not at all my friend, I am merely alerting your attention to a fact that most people in this society seemed to have forgotten, conveniently too, if I may say so."

"But you know as anybody else in dis lan' dat bem boys and dem never do anything."

"True, true." The small crowd chorused.

A small man dressed in work wear, who may have been a builder added, "Tell meh something pappy, you from Arima?"

The man in the suit looked bemused as he observed the small man tossing peanuts into his mouth. "I don't see the relevance with the point I'm trying to convey onto you?"

"Well yuh see breds, we are Arima people and, we like de brother. De man come to serve a purpose, a mission and a vision for this place, for de grassroots people. Is people like allyuh who want to install tiefing politicians in suits to bring down de country, but we not going to allow it anymore."

"Short man, yuh have lyrics boy!" Someone in the crowd chanted, encouraging debate. The debate continued with constructive heated sessions as the Rasta dived in and out of the arguments to serve his customers. Car horns honked as they drove by either to acknowledge the Rasta or to get his attention for packets of nuts. Others honked vying for passengers. As the evening aged, the chaos subsided, and the night was now less fraught than it had been a few hours earlier.

Across the road from the vendor, the Indian lady was packing away her stall into boxes and stacking them into a small van. Its doors were half rusted away, and the bonnet held together with a piece of electric cable with a two-pin plug still attached to one end. The back windscreen was replaced with brown packaging tape, making visibility through the rear window, zero.

The Rasta shouted above the roar of the traffic, "Aye allyuh cut out all da nonsense 'bout politricksters an' buy some nuts nah!" Laughter erupted and the man in the suit quietly left. The Rasta and a stout man in the wheelchair were the only two left discussing the mayoral elections, pausing only to serve the odd customer.

The Rasta vendor had many phrases for his customers. He would say to taxi drivers. "Okay make ah turn" or, for regulars he would make a fist and touch hands saying "Rastafari" and for the unknown customer he just said, "Salt or fresh." He also used terms such as Indian, Creole, Blackman, Dougla, Syrian and Spanish to greet people of different ethnic origins. There was one person, a Venezuelan *panyol*, who the Rasta always addressed as *Trini Jesus*. The man had a fair complexion, sported a blond beard and long hair, and he was always dressed in khaki clothing with a cutlass sheathed in a brown leather case.

CHAPTER
7EVEN

Across the Caribbean, a paradigm was taking place. People were voicing their dissatisfaction with governments in the region, forming organisations to protest and unite in favour of resistance and change. The populace supported any organisations that showed solidarity for working-class citizens. Many of those in political positions began to wear African attire to perpetuate an 'Africaness' a celebration of their African identity - a trend that was resonating rapidly across the region.

Almost every Caribbean island began percolating a black consciousness objective, seeking to rid itself from the clutches of colonial and imperialistic stagnation. Campaigners of the Black Power movement from America and Britain lent their support to their Caribbean counterparts. While many of the islands pursued and gained independence, they continued to be stifled by the claws of colonial remnants. Role models such as Malcolm X, Mohammed Ali and Stokely Carmichael were regularly quoted and emblazoned in publications and posters were aimed at perpetuating black consciousness, resistance and the liberation from narrow logic.

This paradigm attracted Fitzroy's attention. He abhorred the mentality of being independent, yet beholding to the so-called mother country, England. He welcomed the pride that people took in themselves and praised those who stood up for what they believed. Though he did not agree with the Freedom Fighters movement, he owned a copy of Carmichael's book, *Black*

Power: The Politics of Liberation and a copy of the Malcolm X autobiography. Mackie was astonished to find these publications on Fitzroy's bookshelf. Books that he himself had not read.

Mackie's political ambition fuelled a desire in Fitzroy to promote, develop and market Arima to such an extent, that it would attract people from all over the country and the Caribbean as a sporting hub. Fitzroy was many things: a theorist, a sage, an organiser and activist, a young man who possessed excellent persuasion skills, but he didn't see himself as a politician. He saw a politician in Mackie.

He drafted a manifesto through years of research, calculations and observation then presented his vision to Mackie. It took Mackie a couple of days to read and digest the contents of Fitzroy's work. "I never knew that Arima was a Royal Chartered Borough," he said to Fitzroy. "More so, I didn't know it was the only one of its kind outside the United Kingdom. This could present so much marketing and investment capabilities for the borough."
Pepe, sitting on the bleacher next to Mackie said, "Yes, de Queen give we dat when she had her carnation up in England." The rest of the team chorused, "Coronation boy! Coronation."

Mackie shook the document at Fitzroy, "This is excellent stuff. Imagine if the government get their hands on this?"
He thumbed through the document with curious admiration. Pointing at a section in the portfolio, Mackie asked, "Were did you get these figures and more importantly, are they achievable. If I am to present these to the voting public, I have to back it up with hard evidence my brother."

Fitzroy wagged a finger at Mackie, "You are the university graduate, not me. All the evidence and information you need are presented in that document, it's up to you how you analyse and use it to formulate victory."

Mackie was steadfast in his campaign; he followed Fitzroy's manifesto, vowing to abandon the rum and roti politics that was fast consuming the island and its political parties. His campaign was conducted with stringent policies for the betterment of residents and workers in the borough. He was disillusioned by politicians and the empty commitments they made to the people at every election.

His manifesto pledged cleaner streets; a municipal police force that would go beyond the boundaries of the Town Hall and market. One that would complement, the borough's growing policing needs. Creating employment locally was a major issue as well as and facilities for young people to develop skills, not just recreational, but for the enhancement of their future. He outlined plans for development that would see new schools, industry and housing to meet the challenging needs of the borough.

The local press, the opposition and government all tried to tarnish Mackie's image from the onset of his campaign. They continually focussed the electorate on Mackie's time, in Canada and his affiliation with the Black Power movement. The slander from all sides did little to deter or divert support for Mackie. If anything, Mackie's campaign grew stronger and stronger with every scathing criticism the press, opposition and government levelled against his private and political life, manifesto and policies.

The media, despite their best expert analytical efforts,

could not produce enough evidence to discredit the manifesto. In spite of the continued barrage of negativity, the press failed to deter support for Mackie. The young electorate could not be persuaded to sides. Their unwavering support was an extraordinary turn around in the electorate.

Mackie and his campaign team never allowed any negativity that was thrown at him to obscure the focus of the election campaign. Mackie himself never paid much attention to the bad press. He was impressed with the professionalism of his campaign manager and her team. Their ability to turn negative reporting into a positive and proactive vibration was remarkable. His one regret throughout the campaign was having to quit the basketball team. He resisted the inevitable decision for as long as he possibly could. Eventually, with some persuasion from teammates and his campaign manager he relinquished his place with the basketball club. Doing so gave him more time to concentrate on his political journey. He was now free and committing all his energy into his mayoral pursuits.

Elsa perused the daily papers scanning for any articles about Mackie. Since his campaign began, she bought the two daily papers each day. She collected all the articles into a neat pile in order of publication. Humming a random song, soft and low, she contemplated for a second or two, before saying to Ma Draper.
"Dey eh have ah single article in de papers about we boy today." Elsa complained, her voice filled with disappointment. The lack of news on the election drew a comment from Ma Draper, "I doh know why allyuh muching up dat Mackie boy for nah, he eh no good. That boy is trouble for this place, he is ah Black Power."

Elsa moved with quick assertiveness to defend Mackie, "Ma, Mackie looking to the future of this place, not the past. Youth is the pillar for the future society. People like allyuh set the foundations for the future and it is for people like Mackie and the younger generation to ensure that the groundwork for our children and their children to be secured now, rather than later."

Ma Draper's ideology was unwavering; she refused to be convinced about Mackie's integrity. She diverted the conversation from politics to plans for Sooklal. She knew that missing Saturday market was not something she was prepared to do. There was a long pause, before she looked up at Elsa, "It goin' to be sad to see all dem mango just gone from de tree yes."

Elsa clasped Ma Draper's hand in hers and tried to bring a sense of reasoning to her. "Ma dis is de best ting for you, dem mango is just ah nuisance. Nobody eh eating the mango and everyday yuh must clean this place all by yourself. Fitzy make de right decision by encouraging you to sell the mango. At least yuh could enjoy the money from de sale, look on de brighter side Mum. Yuh could even take ah holiday to Tobago and see aunty Delphina."

Ma Draper laughed, "You know I starting to miss de blasted mango already."

Elsa shook her head from side to side, a smile creased her face, "Ma you not easy nah." She scanned through the newspapers a second time just to ensure that there was nothing she had missed.

Ma Draper anticipated the dawn of each Saturday morning. She cherished the ritual of going to market, allowing nothing to hamper her, not even rain. The thought of not being at home while Sooklal harvested

77

the mangoes worried her. She had concerns about him destroying the plants, she hoped also to secure a few of the mangoes for making chow. She knew it was impossible not to go to market, she knew too, Elsa would not be available to stay in. Her Saturday job at the local hotel meant she wouldn't be at home.

Elsa was keen on taking on the job to earn some extra cash for when the baby arrived. Knowing once the baby arrived it would be months before she was able to work, she snapped up the opportunity when it presented itself.

Marlon, despite all his reasoning failed to convince Elsa that there was no need for her to continue reception work at the hotel. Elsa insisted, dismissing his, and Ma Draper's concerns about working, well into the final trimester of the pregnancy.

Darkness crept in suddenly, silencing the roar of the evening bustle. Bats darted about the sky in a choreographed frenzy, seemingly racing into each other and suddenly ricocheting in a tangent, like fighter aircraft, engaged in aerial combat manoeuvres. Ma Draper could hear the Hindi music from Rookmin's radio on the next street. Above the din of the radio, Rookmin could be heard singing along to the famed Indian singer, Lata Mangeshkar.

Ma Draper lifted her head, looking directly at Elsa, "I always say that girl should go on Mastana Bahar but she husband protesting. He eh want she go on TV."

"Is ah shame, I could never tell if is, the radio or Rookmin who singing." Elsa commented as she continued sweeping the kitchen floor without looking up. She brushed the pile of rubbish close to the door and unlatched the metal clasp.

Ma Draper's head perched over the low back rest of

the sofa and said gently, "Doh sweep the rubbish outside eh." Elsa sucked her teeth loudly but without disrespect, "You still wid all dis superstition foolishness?" The old lady laughed and sighed, "Is dat what have dis world corrupt today, we are leaving all ah we values and picking up western idioms."

"Oh Gorm, mum! Yuh hit meh with ah lexicon dey gyul." They erupted into a raucous laughter. Elsa carefully swept the small mound of rubbish to the side of the wall and secured the broom in front of it. They both listened attentively to hear Rookmin's singing in melodious harmony, interrupted by shouts to Sanjay. "Boy go and wash yuh blasted foot before yuh go inside de house. Yuh parading yuhself whole damn day all over de place and yuh want to go inside wid yuh dutty foot." The singing resumed with its same melodious tone.

Complete darkness had consumed the daylight, the dog next door had ceased her endless barking and, in the distance, Rookmin's singing could be heard no more. The radio fell silent too. Inside the house, moths and geckos gathered around the yellow light bulb on the ceiling. The perfectly camouflaged lizards waited patiently for their winged meals that the electric glow attracted. On the odd occasion, the gecko would miss its target and land on the table below with a thud, only to scramble up the walls again, where the safety of the rafters gave it protection from Elsa's slipper.

Elsa shook her head disapprovingly as the gecko scurried up the wall. "One ah dese days dem blasted gheckos go fall straight inside yuh food yuh know! I tired tell yuh to shift de table from under de light."

Ma Draper stuck her finger under her head tie and in a whimpered tone muttered. "Well gyul, yuh better fix de table how yuh like."

The oilcloth on the table was littered with gecko droppings. Elsa looked at it, sucking her teeth as she wiped it clean with a bleached cloth. After she had cleaned the table, she readjusted the position of the table from beneath the ceiling light.

On completing the task, she grated a generous helping of solid cocoa, nutmeg and a stick of cinnamon into a pan of simmering milk. She stirred in all the ingredients and allowed it to simmer for a few minutes more before taking it off the fire. The aroma of the chocolate wafted across the room, arousing a comment from Ma Draper, "Elsie dat smelling just like yuh daddy Draper used to make it."

Elsa smiled and replied, "I followed his recipe, just like he showed me. I used to enjoy this drink whenever he made it for us, especially when it rained and the place damp and cold. Back then, all yuh wanted to do was jump into yuh bed and listen to the rain making music on de galvanise."

"I know," Ma Draper laughed, "you and Fitzy used to snuggle up with us on the same bed, giggling for hours when it rained. I miss him not being here."

"Don't worry about Fitzy, he going to be just fine and, tobesides, he going to write yuh and come up on his days off."

Ma Draper groaned as she eased herself out of the sofa and ironed out the creases on her

long floral skirt with her hands before adjusting her head tie. She rubbed her tired eyes and yawned. A bout of tiredness had come over her. "It get dark quick, quick today man." She remarked. Elsa agreed, adding, "Is de rain, all dem heavy, heavy rain clouds making de place look dark and later than it really is."

The expectation of rain prompted Ma Draper to massage her knee. She rubbed it slowly with both hands commenting, "Is why dis knee giving meh pressure so?"
"Dem weather forecasters should consult you for a true weather report yes." Elsa chuckled playfully. She would tease Ma Draper about her aches. Whenever she said to Elsa that is was going to rain, sure to her word, it would rain. "Gyul, when you see this knee start up, bet yuh bottom dollar, rain coming. Is only ah little spray with WD40 does ease it yes." She massaged the knee vigorously, knocking her fist on the offending joint several times. The action seemed to bring some comfort to the troubled spot. Ma Draper joined Elsa in the kitchen helping her with the food preparation.

A huge crowd had gathered for the political meeting in the car park outside the basketball court. The floodlights inside the courtyard gave some illumination to the agitated crowd eagerly awaiting the key speaker of the evening, McKenzie Brown. Some people held up placards that read 'Vote Brown for Change'; others read 'One Arima one People'. At the front of the platform, a long banner held together with nylon ropes and painted in bold red roman letters, read 'Unity for Opportunity'

The crowd applauded as Mackie made his way to the small platform and took the microphone in his hand. He held his hands in the air and beckoned the crowd to a silent murmur. Placards were held high into the air as the gathering awaited Mackie's word.
Seeing the enthusiastic crowd reminded him of his days at university, addressing the students' union of which he was president. His thoughts journeyed to the first time he stood to petition the students rally. The rush of adren-

alin he felt then returned and he beamed with enthusiasm. Mackie was a natural at public speaking, his heart pounded, fuelling his adrenalin. He lifted his hands in the air with folded fists.

Mackie tapped the microphone once and began his oration, "Ladies and gentlemen, Arimians, the day of reckoning is upon us. There are too many vagaries from national and local politicians that are stifling small, important thriving towns such as ours. It is time we made our voices heard. Not just from the street corner or rum shop debates, but in the corridors of government." The crowd erupted in a chorused cheer, Mackie waited for them to settle, then continued. "We must show the central government that we can perpetuate change for our society, locally and with opportunities in, employment, social development and a legacy for the future in the place we live and work, for today, tomorrow and beyond. So, when you vote, *vote* for the future of your community. It's *your* Borough, *your* vote, so when you vote, vote for unity and opportunity. Vote for the future of Arima."

Mackie waited for the energised crowd as they cheered and applauded on his every word. "People, I urge you forget Black Power, colonial power, Indian power or African power and focus on one thing and, one thing only, and that my brothers and sisters is People Power. There is strength in unity, and if we stand unified, we can move mountains."

The crowd roared in jubilation, they hoisted their fists into the air and shouted, "Mack is the man, Mack the man."

Elsa quietly lifted a clinched fist into the air and shouted, "Power to de people Brother Mackie." Her voice drowned out by the chants from the crowd. From the platform edge, Mackie's eyes met hers, and above the jubilance, he acknowledged Elsa's response with a nod of his head. The excited crowd cheered and surged forward to greet Mackie. At the back of the crowd, he looked on as a huge banner was unfurled with his portrait. It simply read, 'Mackie for Mayor'. There was an echo of applause as Mackie raised his hands in the air to acknowledge the unfurling of the banner. He jumped off the low platform and began to shake hands with people in the crowd. He touched Elsa on the shoulder and smiled, "Not long now eh." She gave him a friendly smile and replied, "One week, one week and you will be Mayor."

"Tell Fitzy I sorry 'bout not coming by, but you know how it is with this election business. Meetings after meetings, seems nonstop sometimes."

Elsa held Mackie's arm, "You know Fitzy gone to the oilfields to work?"

Mackie tilted his head and gave a puzzled look, "What yuh mean he gone to work in the oilfield?"

"He got ah job with one ah dem foreign oil companies."

Mackie shook his head in disbelief as he continued to shake the hands of people who mobbed him, squeezing his way through the friendly crowd, greeting his supporters. The turnout pleased him, the confidence people displayed for him motivated him and gave a renewed energy. He felt magnificent among the people, they cheered, and some even fist bumped him.

Mackie began to believe, victory was now inevitable, yet he could not allow himself to become complacent. Voting day was always the crucial decider. It was when most people make that precise decision on their final choice. Being new in the political arena and an independent candidate did not scare him in the least. He savoured every moment of his campaign. The journey proved a valuable learning ground for him. He rose to every challenge that presented itself, conquering every adversity and learning immensely from meeting the electorate. Quite clearly, Fitzroy had done his homework when producing the manifesto. More importantly, his campaign team adhered to the details that were set out.

The national newspapers had him in their polls as a clear winner by a majority. However; Mackie did not allow himself to be strangled with the misconception of newspaper polls. He knew only too well that such polls could be deceptive. He campaigned vigorously to bring the message of his manifesto to the constituents of every village, avenue, road, trace and squatter settlements. The press too, had done a U-turn and started to champion Mackie's policies for local government. Having scrutinised his policies and projections they could find no flaws in his forecast for development. Local businesses warmed to his concept and pledged their support when he took office.

The Mayor's election campaign began with four candidates vying for the position. The hopefuls were; one from the opposition party, one from the ruling party, another independent candidate and Mackie.

Midway through the campaign, the other independent candidate withdrew herself from the election, without giving a clear reason for doing so. A media campaign by the ruling party against the opposition candidate backfired and it emerged that the government's choice for mayor had a tarnished record for misappropriating funds at a leading Credit Union where he was a Trustee on the board. The revelation brought about his resignation as a potential candidate and ended his political career.

In a statement, Mackie said, "Elections are always a controversial time. We undertake a path in public life without stopping to reflect about the road behind us. It is a tragedy that my fellow candidate has fallen victim to this lack of reflection that his past would come back to haunt him. However, it is reassuring, that these issues have come to light publicly, before the disease of corruption found its way into government offices at any level."

The slander worked in Mackie's favour. Most of those who supported the government's candidate had switched their support to Mackie. Despite the swing, Mackie was not complacent. He knew that the opposition candidate had powerful financial backers and the support of most of the local businesses in the Arima district.

Contribution for Mackie's political campaign was funded by Mackie himself with assistance from his mother in America. A few of the smaller businesses supported him and his vision. One of the Trade Unions also provided some financial backing for Mackie's campaign. They welcomed his approach to community values and the need for encouraging the younger generation into politics. Mackie's greatest asset was the people themselves. The dedication and enthusiasm displayed throughout the campaign was one of a unified community, moving with a common objective. Local printers donated banners and bunting free of charge for the campaign and a car rental firm agreed to lease vehicles for getting voters to polling stations on election day.

A Grenadian businessman pledged, should Mackie become mayor, to donate the cost for the restoration of the town's iconic landmark, the *Dial*. For many years the clock ceased to function, for reasons beyond anyone's intelligence. Efforts to repair the clock had been ineffectual, despite many endeavours and soaring costs to the council's coffers.

The clock had been a gift to the citizens of Arima, back in 1898, from a former mayor. It is believed to have been operated by a mechanism powered by water from a nearby stream. The stream, through geographic developments had been diverted, and the clock never functioned after the diversion. The ornate timepiece became a silent sentinel, standing at the centre of the crossroads at the heart of the town.

Mackie was aware that having the local businesses on board was crucial to many of the projects that needed to be implemented and without the overall support of the business community the road ahead could be a steep hill to climb. What Mackie did have in his favour was the younger generation of the Syrian, Lebanese and Portuguese business fraternity. The tabloids too, began to work in Mackie's favour. They no longer saw him as a delinquent deportee, but as an astute thinker and a visionary for the future. People were beginning to understand the projection of his manifesto and the vision for the borough.

Elsa gazed in awe as the crowd enveloped Mackie. Each, wanting to shake his hand or hug him. She looked at her watch, sighed heavily and let her mind drift. She cursed herself silently for agreeing to work, wishing she had opted out when given the opportunity by the manager of the hotel.

Gently, she caressed her belly and thought of Marlon wondering where he might be and what he was doing or where he was working. Her thoughts were never without him, she would often wonder where he was posted and what dangers he faced.

Working undercover prevented him from divulging his duties even to Elsa, though he had utmost faith in her. He knew he could tell her anything and the information would stay with her. However, Marlon decided it was best that his duties remained within the protocols of the police service.

One thing he did alert Elsa to, was the ongoing surveillance of Mackie by Special Branch. Mackie was put under observation because of his affiliation with a certain political party that the present government deemed a political threat to democracy. Although his affiliation with these former political allies had waned, he was still blacklisted as a potential threat by the government.

Elsa demonstrated her loyalty, although she had known Mackie since their childhood, she kept the information to herself. In any event, there was no need for her to divulge the information. Fitzroy had informed her that Mackie was now under police surveillance. "How do you know that?" she quizzed Fitzroy. There was no need for Fitzroy to explain further, she knew the campaign team had a solid group of individuals who were well connected in all areas of the government and the private sector. "Through my understanding," Fitzroy said, "it was your man who passed the info to somebody on the campaign team."

Worrying about Marlon's safety was not unfounded. Twice he had been in gun fire exchange with armed criminals. His skill and rapid evasive actions saved him from being shot. He was also no stranger to the press. His heroic duties kept him in the national news constantly.

Generally, for his effectiveness in solving complex cases and for receiving commendations for his services in and beyond the line of duty.

The night was warm and buzzing with activity as Elsa strolled slowly home, leaving the public meeting before it had ended. Small crowds gathered around food vendors, jostling for service. She held her tummy and spat in the open drain. Under the lights of a closed rum shop, a coconut vendor chopped green coconuts with lightning fast accuracy, standing on the back of a pick-up truck - his cutlass razor sharp.

Further along the street, the peanut vendor sat on his bike smoking a marijuana joint under the dim streetlamp, without care or fear of the law. The awnings from the shoe shop on the corner gave the Rasta shelter from the elements. In the window, huge colourful posters advertised back to school footwear at discount prices. The Rasta called out to Elsa, "How was the meetin' sista?"

Elsa paused, spat on the ground and answered, "It was good man, really good. I think we boy going to win by a landslide. De people like him too bad! Next Monday we going to have a new mayor, mark my word."

The Rasta tossed his dreadlocks behind him tucking the matted hair under his huge colourful knitted hat. He touched clinched fist with Elsa who had crossed the road to greet him. They conversed for a short while before Elsa bid him farewell, continuing to drag her feet at a slow pace, down the quiet, dimly lit street.

The huge mango tree created a silhouette in the darkness and in the background, the living room light extended a glow through the glass panes of the windows. Seeing the lights, she assumed Ma Draper was still awake. It was unusual, but she saw the flicker and the glow of the television screen every time a sequence or frame changed. She knew Ma Draper did not watch late television. Her viewing ended with the news and weather report, before retiring to her bedroom. She would brush her hair, pray, read her bible verses then settle into her bed.

The metal gate grated along the rough concrete and again when Elsa secured the gate shut with the iron clasp. Next door, Sita was alert and barked knowingly at the noise of the gate. Elsa snapped her fingers and the dog fell quiet again. Dragging her feet without urgency, she gazed up to the clear sky, brightly dotted with twinkling of stars. The sight of the celestial objects triggered her memory and caused her thoughts to drift to Fitzroy.

Nights like these reminded her of the times when they would sit out on the front steps of the old house gazing into the galaxy. She would quiz Fitzroy about his knowledge of the constellations. She smiled, recalling how he knew the names of every cluster of stars in the night sky. Mr Draper would stick his head out the front window and shout. "Go to bed you little scamps. You have school tomorrow." They giggled mischievously to his stern command and in the background, they could hear Ma Draper with a hinting 'ahem! It was a clear indication that it was time to retire to bed. They would giggle scrambling up the steps before climbing into bed.

Elsa made a quiet entry into the house from the back door. She was surprised to find that Ma Draper had left the television on and was sound asleep in her room.

With a tiptoe, Elsa avoided a loose floorboard in the kitchen, being careful not to wake Ma Draper from her sleep. A quiet breeze rustled the leaves with a gentle caress. The mango tree swayed with the breeze and stillness returned as quickly as it had disappeared. Only the distant traffic on the main road disturbed the quietness. She sat gracefully on the couch, kissed her hand and started to rub her tummy.

Quick flashes of Marlon sitting in a police car increased the rotating motion in which she massaged her tummy and then, an abrupt halt. Elsa mopped a tear drop that had gathered at the corner of her eye. She looked at the headline on the paper that lay on the couch beside her. *'Deported Student set to Become Mayor.'* Her gaze at the newspaper created a yearning for Fitzroy to return home for the election celebrations. In her heart, she knew that Fitzroy wouldn't. He would not have the slightest inclination to return to engage in any such celebrations.

Mackie had pleaded with Fitzroy to join his campaign, pledging a post would be available for him to raise the profile of sport in the community. The grandeur of the post was not enough to persuade Fitzroy to follow Mackie into the political arena.

Elsa shifted the paper with an uneasy trait before picking it up and placing it on the table directly under the light bulb. She looked up at the yellow light and saw that two geckos had perched themselves on the rafter, calculating their strategy for the next meal.

A muffled thud pierced the silence of the room. Elsa was not moved. She had grown accustomed to the sound of the mangoes hitting the hard earth or dropped on the galvanize roof such that they never startled her, even in the middle of the night.

Sita, the dog next door seemed to have grown accustomed to the disturbance as well. She lifted her head with a curious look and settled back into her kennel. In the distance the scream of a police siren shattered the silence of the night once again, Elsa shifted uneasy on the chair, trying to get comfortable.

Two more days and the wait will be over she thought. The election had everyone agitated. It brought vibrancy to the borough, something that had never been experienced during an election, general or local. People of every colour, shape, size and race were wearing black T shirts with the slogan 'Mackie is de Man'.

Mackie himself had brought three campaign jerseys for the Drapers. He said to Ma Draper, "Ma yuh vote count too yuh know!"

Ma Draper gave Mackie a measured look, squinting her eyes before she spoke, "What you know about politics son? It seems just de odder day you leave and gone Canada and now vaps, outta de blues you know what bess for Arima. What right and experience you have, to govern Arima? Just now yuh will be telling we how to run the country."

He tried to engage with Ma Draper, but the attempt was muted. She resisted him to the point, confessing, "I for one will not be voting for you so, yuh bess hads take back your jersey."

Elsa chuckled to herself remembering the conversation between the two. The irony was, Ma Draper wore the jersey around the house while doing her household chores.

There was nothing about Mackie on which Ma Draper could inherently form a negative opinion. She quite simply equated Mackie with the scandal that erupted in Canada with the Trinidadian students. Although she never fully grasped the context of the fiasco, she saw Mackie as a direct link with the events at the Canadian university. It was enough for her to label Mackie and associate him with delinquency.

Mackie had been at the university at the time but was not part of the group of students involved with the affray that had unfolded there. On his return to Trinidad, the press hounded Mackie for a story, he refused to be interviewed by the newspapers and never sought to refute the matter or absolve himself from blame.

He used the media coverage of the incident to his advantage, which in turn benefited his publicity so that he gained favour with the majority. Fitzroy, Elsa and Watkins all knew the truth. Watkins had persuaded Mackie to keep quiet about his non-involvement with the scandal, claiming it would eventually generate publicity that could work in his favour if he ventured into politics.

Elsa let her head down on the couch, remembering how they all sat in Fitzroy's room, a bowl of mango chow in the middle of the bed trying to convince Mackie that he could be the next mayor of Arima. Mackie laughed at the idea with a mouthful of mango chow motioning his hands, with disapprovingly, "I am not qualified to be no mayor. Look Watkins there, let him go for it. He is the one qualified with all at least three university degrees and who spent two years up in Sandhurst, England training with the SAS. Let him run, he could make a real difference, not me."

Fitzroy snapped his fingers and shouted, "Man yuh mad or wha? Watkins could just about play a game of basketball. You want him running for mayor? Dem degrees he have is burns, first, second and third degree."

The room erupted in laughter. Watkins selected some chow with one hand and spun his basketball on the index finger of the other. He sucked his teeth chewing the mango pieces before aiming his finger at Mackie, "Breds, you are the right man for this mayor business. Ever since we were at school you had an interest in politics and, where best to start than in your own backyard?" Watkins turned and waved his clenched fist at Mackie and said, "You will be mayor Bro, just believe. We know you can do it."

Mackie lifted a clenched fist at Watkins and gave a fleeting glance at the others in the room. They all stared at him with approving glances. He smiled, took some mango chow from the bowl and shook his head. "Allyuh mad no ass yes."

Elsa looked at the headline on the paper again and with a clenched fist whispered, "Yes, Mackie for mayor." She rolled over on her side, cradled her belly with one hand and allowed her eyes to shut, dimming out the light from the ceiling. She felt herself drifting into slumber.

CHAPTER
8IGHT

The full moon hung majestically in the clear night sky, its reflection soft and subtle on the calm ocean below. As far as the eye could see, the lunar glow followed the sea sending rippling light back to Fitzroy. He adjusted his hard hat and looked at the paper in the moonlight, smiled and looked at the tabloid again before folding it with great care, securing the paper into one of his pockets. He clutched the rails with a firm grip with one hand punching the air in exuberance with the other and shouted at the top of his voice, "Yes Mackie, you will be Mayor."

Cautiously he surveyed his surroundings making sure no one had heard his animated outburst. Seeing no one, he relaxed with his own company, looking up at the huge luminous biscuit in the sky. He drew in a huge gulp of sea air and sat down on the damp iron floor. Below him, he could hear the sea lashing with a fury against the rig and the chorus of the machinery as it tunnelled the seabed extracting crude.

Fitzroy gazed at the moon as a solitary cloud drifted slowly, obscuring its view. For a moment there was a yearning to be back in Arima, to participate in Mackie's victory, to savour the taste of a well-deserved win. He could picture Elsa jumping and screaming clutching Ma Draper and shouting, "We done it gyul, we done it." Ma Draper would be expressionless and would probably say, "Dat election was ah shambles, what ah young boy so could do for this place?"

Fitzroy was comfortable in his new job. Within a couple of weeks on the rig he was promoted to supervisor and then project foreman. His colleagues were amazed at the rate at which he progressed. They remarked that it would normally take a person six months to become a supervisor. The comments pleased him, and he thanked them for the support and encouragement and for accepting him so readily when he joined as a mere rookie on the rig. Fitzroy demonstrated an excellent, can do ethic that pleased his superiors.

Although he was glad to have avoided the election campaign, Fitzroy was looking forward to progress and to see his ideas take shape. He strived for Arima to become a commercial and sporting hub, and a more affluent town, attracting people to shop and enjoy sporting events. Already, a new industrial estate was taking shape along with, a major car plant and a world class horseracing facility. He envisaged other sporting arenas in the borough such that cricket, hockey, tennis and football could play an integral part with facilities of professional standards, just like the new velodrome.

Education centres too, where young and mature people could embark on vocational training and shopping facilities that could rival the city were all part of his dream. There was no doubt that Mackie's victory could make these visions become a reality.

In Fitzroy's search for better personal prospects and tranquility, he found both in the South of Trinidad. Within a few short weeks of moving to Pointe-a-Pierre, he had already amassed a considerable amount of savings. He rented a plot of land with a small wooden building consisting of one room. He used it when he came to shore, stocking a minimum amount of foodstuff and valuables in the dilapidated structure. The building was surrounded by tall fields of sugarcane to the back and the expanse of the oil refinery complex to the front. The sprawling maze of the refinery and its complex network of pipes thrilled his imagination.

The small structure had the necessities of running water and electricity. On the light blue walls, a single page calendar with a picture of a nude Caucasian woman sitting on a purple satin sheet, wearing high heels, hung from a nail. His working timetable was blotted out with a black marker pen. Two blackened pots stood in the corner of the room on a small table with a green enamel two-burner gas cooker. In a straw basket, some onions and potatoes were the only signs of foodstuff in the room. A convoy of ants scurried across the floor and up the wall on the other side of the room like a crazy mob, disappearing out of sight. On the floor, in one corner, a plastic bowl was set to collect water from the leaking roof when it rained. A roll of *Flashband* lay on the table, bought to repair the leaking roof. It sat in the same spot since it was purchased. In the other corner of the room stood a small table and two chairs with a storm lamp. It offered ample light for the small room when there was a power failure.

Fitzroy spent most of his time in San Fernando. There he opened a bank account with a Canadian owned bank, and deposited most of his earnings, withdrawing only enough to see him through his time on shore. He regularly sent money for Ma Draper, enough so that she could live comfortably. The waterfront was where he spent most of his spare time. He would sit for hours on the shoreline writing in a small grey, marbled notebook. He noted all the things he had done since leaving Arima. He made projections of what he intended to achieve while his employment on the rig lasted. San Fernando afforded him the solitude he craved. He had a job he enjoyed and all the comforts he needed for his own relaxation. Everything existed in perfect tandem for him, and while he missed the adrenalin of the basketball court, he was quite content with writing his thoughts and adventures in his diary.

Fitzroy adopted the attitude of a physician who studied himself, noting all his activities in precise detail. Although not as detailed as the physician he noted his entries very concisely indeed. He avoided elaborating on work but was careful to detail all his activities while on shore. Writing about his work life never transpired into his notebook. He once wrote in his book, 'working life had no adventure, it's just a required routine' and drew two solid lines under the remark. There were days when he recorded how long it took him to walk from the waterfront to his favourite restaurant in San Fernando.

His first entry into the notebook read, Monday: bought one notebook, a newspaper, sat by the wharf - fishermen had a bad catch. Inside the book, he also kept a collection of clippings from the daily newspapers about Mackie's election campaign, compiling them in chronological order of publication.

On the High street, everything and everyone appeared to move at twice the pace as Fitzroy. He showed no enthusiasm to be anywhere for any given time or purpose. In contrast, people around him hurried by in purposeful gait. Those trying to catch stores open before they shut and those jostling the evening rush hour for taxi and bus services to get home. Street vendors shouted their wares at the top of their voices. Curious people stopped and handled the goods while some walked past without a glance. One vendor sternly said to a customer, "Lady, doh squeeze up de zaboca nah." The customer paid no heed and continued to inspect each avocado, testing its ripeness by pressing her fingertips into the fruit, much to the annoyance of the vendor.

Fitzroy paused to digest the cry of the vendors, remembering his Saturday morning trips to the market. He had only ever gone to the market to bring home the heavy shopping basket for Ma Draper, after she had done her shopping. He was never one for the market, especially disliking the smell of the poultry depot. If there was one thing he did miss on a Saturday, it was the aroma of Ma Draper's cowheel soup. She had made it every Saturday for as long as he cared to remember. He remembered too, the fun times Watkins, Elsa and himself enjoyed at Love Mist discotheque on a Friday and Saturday night.

Something struck Fitzroy and he jolted back, shifting quickly. He discovered it was a bit of newspaper whipped up by a gust of wind. He dusted his shoulder and meandered towards his favourite Chinese restaurant. This was his chosen place to eat in San Fernando. He wrote in his notebook that the restaurant reminded him of Kong's, a Chinese restaurant in Arima.

The waitress at the restaurant had grown accustomed to Fitzroy and his fascination with being seated at the same table every time. The spot, unknowingly to her offered him a good view of the main road. Here, he took great pleasure in watching people go by, sometimes making notes on people he had seen more than once.

The waitress came over and set the cutlery on Fitzroy's table. She scribbled his order on her note pad. He watched her swinging her slender hips as she walked away from him. She slipped the order over to the short Chinese woman behind the counter who shouted the order to the chef, "One portion flied One-Ton, one chicken chow meein and half flied chicken."

Fitzroy hardly ever altered his menu when dining at the restaurant. The waitress had grown so accustomed to him, she wrote his order before he could sit down. From his vantage point Fitzroy sat and read the *Evening News* and completed the crossword puzzle while his meal was being prepared.

The restaurant offered Fitzroy the right amount of privacy to read, make entries into his diary and to observe the outside world from his favourite table. The space was perfect for reflecting on his day. Here he would do most of his planning before his meal arrived.
The restaurant was also beautifully decorated with lively oriental art.

Colourful paper umbrellas hung from the ceiling alongside lanterns adorned with Chinese calligraphy. A waft of incense filled the air as Oriental music played low in the background.

Traffic roared outside, horns blared, and vendors bellowed to attract potential passing trade. A group of women conversed in a raucous manner outside the restaurant, causing many of the customers to peer through the window with a hint of interest in their gaze. Before long, they had moved on, Fitzroy could smell his food. He folded his paper neatly and looked up to see the young lissom woman bringing his meal over. She passed him a complimentary smile before setting the food before him. He could smell her perfume as she leaned towards him. It had crossed his mind to ask what perfume she was wearing but decided to leave it as a thought.

The golden hue of the evening had long disappeared,

the street outside now glowed under the yellow rays from the streetlamps. The darkness had silenced the vendors and the heavy roar of the traffic outside. People walked less briskly along the dirty sidewalks that now seem abandoned by the crowds earlier.

Fitzroy cleared his plate of its contents and patted his lips with a paper napkin. Before he could lift his hand to get the waitress's attention, he noticed she was making her way towards him. Fitzroy smiled at her efficiency. His eyes followed her, admiring her physique, and the easy movements of her hips as she negotiated her way to him. Instantly, he was attracted to her and tried desperately to mask his admiration.

He paid the bill and gave her a generous tip. With a thankful nod, she flicked the note with her index finger. With a smile, she tucked the grey note into her bosom, patting it gracefully. She pursed her lips and mimed a kiss to him. Fitzroy saluted her with his paper and left the restaurant. Putting the pen to her lips, she followed Fitzroy with her hazel eyes until he disappeared down the narrow avenue from her sight.

The night was musky and dank, on the streets cockroaches and rats scurried about without fear or interference from humans, the night belonged to them now. Below, in the valley leading to the sea, the lights from ships in the ocean twinkled like stars in the sky. On the other side of the road, a small crowd began to congregate outside a cinema. Fitzroy swaggered over to the cinema studying the large posters for both cinema viewings. He contemplated at length on which movie he should choose. Both cinemas were adjacent to each other. One cinema played only Indian movies, the other, Hollywood movies. They were aptly known as Cinema 1 and

Cinema 2. Fitzroy studied the posters and made a clear choice. The film playing at Cinema 1 was a Hollywood war movie he had seen at least six times in his lifetime. Quietly in his mind, he decided that the new Indian blockbuster would be the one to watch. Ironically, the Indian movie *Sholay*, was a remake of the famous *Magnificent Seven*, a western classic.

After the movie, the streets grew deserted as rapidly as they had filled up with cinema patrons. Fitzroy stood at the top of the hill, looking in both directions and then, down to the seafront. His brain wanted to take his feet down to the seafront to sit there until the dawn arrived, looking out onto the open ocean. In the distance, he could see three faint human figures disappearing into a nearby street. The sound of barking dogs was the only noise that disturbed the night as a cool fresh breeze swept his across his face.

Holding up his hand to the light, he checked the time on his watch. He rubbed the face of the watch with his shirt-sleeve, looked at the watch again before making his way through a narrow alleyway.

The alleyway stank of stale urine, in the doorway of a department store, a vagrant casually stacked pieces of discarded corrugated cardboard to form a mattress on the cold concrete. Fitzroy cupped his mouth and nostrils with his hand and hurried along the alley that eventually led to a wide street. The street, surprisingly, was busy with a hub of activity. Under the awning of a shop, an Indian man sat behind a small wooden table with a flambeau burning brightly. The table was lined with small glasses at one end, each with a measure of small oysters sitting in water. On the other end, stood bottles filled with various concoctions of delectable looking sauces.

To the left of him a woman lazily fanned a coal-pot with a folded copy of the *Evening News* as fresh corn on the cob roasted on an iron grill. The aroma of crackling coals and corn rose to greet Fitzroy. Nostalgia consumed him; he remembered Ma Draper roasting corn on a similar coal pot in the back yard near the breadfruit tree.

At the doorway to a club stood a burly looking man with a boyish face, his head clean-shaven and arms folded together. He greeted Fitzroy with a friendly nod. Fitzroy acknowledged him with a kind of unwritten code. Above the door, a sign painted in bold black san serif letters read, 'Members Only.' Next to it was another sign stating that the premises were licensed to sell 'Spirituous Liquor' and named the licence holder.

Inside, there were two billiard tables and three pool tables. A lanky grey-haired man was leaning across the billiard table with his cue trained at the pink ball. Before making his shot, he shouted, "Alright Fitzy?" Fitzroy acknowledged him by raising his hand. Blue chalk dust settled on the table as the tip of the cue struck, sending the pink ball hurtling across the green felt table and slamming a red ball into the centre pocket. Beyond the tables, there were small private rooms. Groups of men of varying ages drew heavily on cigarettes as they played poker. On the card table a mound of cash awaited the winner. Fitzroy lingered at the poker table studying the cards in the hands of two players from his vantage. He tried to calculate the amount of cash on the table. He estimated there must have been over one thousand dollars on the table made up of twenties, tens and five-dollar notes. Surreptitiously he reached into his pocket and produced his notebook. He wrote in bold letters, 'OVER ONE THOUSAND DOLLARS ON TABLE-guesstimate.'

A buxom young lady, her cleavage thrust up and wearing tight-fitting denim shorts that looked two sizes too small, brushed against Fitzroy as he wrote in his notebook. She smiled, surveyed him, flicked her hips and said, "Sorry sah." With a cunning eye, he studied her as she made her way over to the bar carrying a tray stacked with empty bottles and glasses, casually wiping the empty tables as she went by. Her hips created a calypso rhythm as she went by.

Fitzroy sat on the balcony studying the abandoned sloping streets that stood quietly under the yellow glow of the streetlights. He sat on one chair and put his feet up onto another. He caught the attention of the young woman and ordered two beers. She returned with his order and set the bottles before him. Fitzroy gave a toast with the two beers, "To Mackie, the new mayor of Arima." On the balcony, he sat alone drinking and saluting Mackie, touching both bottles together and taking alternative sips from each bottle.

The poker room was now deserted. The winner of the card game had collected his winnings and departed for the night. The deck of playing cards lay neatly stacked on the green felt table, ready for the next set of players. The room reeked of stale tobacco as the ceiling fan circulated the stale air, disturbing the cigarette ashes from the ashtray and littering the felt with every oscillation.

There was a calm silence in the club, far from the earlier commotion and now, the only sound the shattered the quietness was the crack of billiard balls colliding. The two men played all night and as dawn crept in to erase the darkness. They showed no signs of going anywhere. Below the balcony, the streets began to come to life with council workers busy sweeping and clearing away the piles of refuse heaped along the sidewalks. The street-lights flickered, then went off. It wasn't long before the area began its chaotic cycle once again. Taxi drivers hooted their horns to attract passengers and newspaper vendors enjoyed a brisk morning trade. Lorries roared along the narrow streets making deliveries.

Fitzroy fished out his notebook and wrote; *Last night drank a toast to Mackie. 5.30 am San Fernando is alive again. 5.32 am leaving club.* Why he had found it necessary to make this entry was not clear to him either. Looking at the emerging chaos below, Fitzroy realised that it was the first time he had paid any attention to the morning commotion. For a prolonged period, he stood in awe gazing at the urgency in which people went by. He was amazed to see that people had the same urgency in the morning as they did at evening rush hour. The only vendor out this time of morning was the newspaper seller. Almost everyone stopped to buy a paper and it seemed she knew them all, greeting them by name as they grabbed their daily newsprint.

Ma Draper stood over Elsa and observed her as she slept on the couch. Elsa cradled her tummy as she slept. Ma Draper walked softly to avoid waking Elsa from her slumber, she crept into Fitzroy's old room and fetched a blanket. She tenderly draped the blanket over Elsa, taking great care not to arouse her. Clutching her bible, she moved stealthily back to her room where she sat on a small chair that Mr Draper had made her. She turned the pages with gentle care until she reached Psalms. Studying the pages, she nodded to herself before turning another leaf. She perused the scriptures silently.

The night was humid, with grey clouds obscuring the moon from view, while a gentle wind rustled the trees outside with a delicate sway. Ma Draper waited for a mango to hit the iron roof, but the sound never came. Her eyes were full of pain as they carried to a painting on the wall, of Mr Draper and herself. She smiled a half smile at the memory of having the painting done, recollecting fondly the Saturday evening they were sitting at the front of the house. A polite young man walked straight into the yard and asked. "Can I paint you?" Mr Draper looked at the lanky youth in a small afro hairstyle and freckled face with some guarded scepticism before asking. "Young fella! yuh gone mad or yuh smoke ganja?" The young man was apologetic, he smiled and spoke in a clear polite tone, "No sir, I am an artist and I looking for people to draw or paint and, you look the perfect couple for me to paint."

Ma Draper looked the young man over and said, "Boy we would love for yuh to do de painting but we cyar pay for dat kinda ting. Dat is rich people business."

"Oh yes! We doh have any money." Mr Draper agreed.

"No, no!" Pleaded the young man. "The painting would cost you nothing! I am doing it free of charge. It is all practice for me to build my portfolio."

"Port-who-folio?" Screamed Mr Draper, as he stood up, revealing his muscular physique, rigid and straight. His stance reminded the artist of an actor, Kirk Douglas standing proud and showing off his dominance. He seized the opportunity and interjected before Mr Draper could speak, "You see what I mean! You have the perfect poise and your muscular physique is just the kind of subject I am interested in capturing. Both you and your wife would do justice to my paintings." Mrs Draper shook her hands at Mr Draper and conceded, "Okay man, let de boy do de painting nah, we eh have to pay and dat is de most important thing."

Mr Draper looked at the young man and asked, "where you from young man?"

"Blanchisseuse." He replied with a smile.

The painting had many pleasant memories for Ma Draper, and she adored it from the moment it had arrived. The instant the painting got delivered, she ordered Mr Draper to hang it in the bedroom. Mr Draper protested, saying it should be adorning the living room, but Ma Draper insisted it should be in the bedroom.

The picture hung on the southern wall at the end of the bedroom next to the doorway. The portrait had only been hidden from view once when Mr Draper passed away. She had covered the picture with a small towel until he was laid and to rest only after about a week, did she remove the towel to reveal the painting.

As a young girl, she had observed her mother covering, or turning the frame so the photos faced the wall in the house, when her grandfather died. Instinctively, Ma Draper followed the tradition. She never really understood the significance of the ritual, neither did she question the purpose. She walked slowly towards the painting and touched Mr Draper's face. In a low voice she said, "Yuh know Fitzroy was always a free spirit. We could never keep him here, but now I t'ink we lose him forever."

Ma Draper stared at the painting with a look of anticipation, half waiting for a response. She sucked her teeth and returned to her bible, smoothing out the crease where she had marked the page. Patting the bible, she whispered a prayer, keeping her gaze at the painting. She nodded and said, "Yes I know Fitzy would be home one day. He just wants all dis election ting to settle down."

She consoled herself with her prayer before nestling

into her bed listening to the gentle rustle of the trees out-side as they danced to the music of the wind. It wasn't long before sleep had taken hold of her.

CHAPTER
9INE

Voting had commenced at 6am and already hundreds of anxious voters were queuing to cast their votes. Two young police officers stood guard outside a polling station. One armed with a standard issue 303 rifle and the other a riot stick and side arm. They chatted amicably as voters casually registered their votes. They emerged after voting, proudly displaying a red, inked-stained index finger, indicating that they had voted - a colonial practice introduced to prevent any fraudulent voting at elections.

Across the Borough, polling stations began to see a huge turnout of the electorate, especially amongst the young voters. There was a vibrant buzz with everyone as people shuffled to and from Polling Stations across the wards casting their votes. Police squad cars made frequent patrols at the various polling stations as the day progressed.

There was a steady, peaceful flow of voting with a significant rise in young first-time voters. The island always had a peaceful election process however, the police were on high alert. It was the first local election after the failed coup attempt in 1970 and the authorities, although not wanting to seem heavy-handed, were taking precautions to ensure that their presence didn't go unnoticed.

At one polling station, Mackie turned up to vote. The press and a small crowd mobbed him while the police stood by casually, taking no notice of the commotion surrounding Mackie. The melee did not pose any danger warranting intervention from the officers. The crowd merely wanted to shake Mackie's hand and congratulate him, prematurely. He was only too happy to oblige, before taking time to be interviewed by the press.

The crowd was joyous. They joked with the police as Mackie emerged from casting his vote, lifting his hand to show the reddened index finger. Two men lifted him onto their shoulders and carried him off down the street hailing him as the new Mayor of Arima. The Indian lady, plying her trade under the haberdashery store, waved her hand showing her inked-stained finger, and shouted, "Yuh had my vote."

Mackie signalled the crowd to set him down, he shook their hands and they dispersed, some heading to the nearby rum shop. A highly polished Toyota saloon pulled up alongside, and waited for Mackie to get in. The car drove away at a slow pace down the main street. People walked along and tapped on the car, some stuck their heads into the car window and shook Mackie's hand. The driver cautiously brought the vehicle to a halt whenever they did.

The mood in the town took on a celebratory chord, championing Mackie as the winner of the election by mid-afternoon. Most people who turned out to vote were between 18 and 30, and, most had voted for the independent candidate, Mackie. There was almost an eighty percent turnout from the young voters who fuelled the early speculation. It was difficult to judge the older voters and the die-hards. While they themselves did not openly support Mackie, neither were they overtly in support of the current councillors. Many of the older voters simply voted for those who were already there, revealing - better the devil you know.

The council had been plagued with widespread corruption over the last couple of years and had seen the resignations of at least six councillors over mismanagement and fraudulent allegations. Despite the allegations and some resignations, no one was subject to any investigation for the alleged offences of corruption. Mackie promised a full investigation into all corrupt allegations as part of his manifesto, attesting to do everything in his capacity as mayor to bring those responsible to answer for their actions. Making this promise to the people had helped to swing voters during the campaign.

The administration was openly criticised for the mismanagement and corrupt councillors. Yet nothing prevailed regarding the miscarriage of public office and monies. Confidence in Mackie's camp swelled as the day unfolded. Campaign managers and those involved all knew it was just a matter of waiting until 6pm when the ballots closed for counting to commence. Outside the Town Hall, a small press gathering waited eagerly. There was a small team from a press agency in Canada that had also assembled. They donned university sweaters, distressed jeans and wide brimmed straw hats, drinking from green coconuts with straws.

In Port of Spain, at Police headquarters, an emergency meeting was taking place with top high-ranking Flying Squad officers. A tall lanky Superintendent enquired. "Where is Detective Corporal Marlon Dudley stationed?" "We are checking that right now sir." A reply came from an adjoining room. It was not long before a response was relayed to the Superintendent. He looked at the piece of paper handed to him and screamed, "Who de hell put dis man on election duty? This is one of our top Detectives and we have him on a local election assignment, but this is arseness without reason."

Another officer interjected, "Sir I understand that he was assigned to watch over the mayoral candidate."

"Why wasn't I brought up-to-date with this information?"

"Don't know Sir."

The Superintendent contemplated, "That may be so, radio Arima Police Station and let DC Dudley know that he should report here for an operations briefing at 1900 hours today, election or no election, this is priority."

The details were quickly scribbled onto a piece of paper and passed to the adjoining room. The officer radioed for a direct relay to DC Dudley who at that moment was sitting in a patrol car outside a polling station.

Marlon listened to the dispatch as it came over on the police radio. He shook his head and sighed, "Man, these people think I am a robot or what? I've been working three days non-stop. They want to kill me or what?"

The officer sitting in the driver's seat, drummed on the steering wheel and laughed at Marlon's comments, "Doh worry sir, they probably calling you in to notify you of a promotion."

"Promotion my arse," Was Marlon's response, "you know how long I working as a Detective? Five years man! I spent one year in St Joseph and then this Super pick me out for the Flying Squad. This election posting has been a cushy number for the longest while."

"Well yuh cyar have it easy on your way to the top now, can you?" The constable chuckled.

"You from these parts constable, what you think of this new guy for Mayor?"

"Well for ah start, he has my vote. The man is ah young visionary, the people like him and that is important. What more can you ask?" The constable showed Marlon his stained finger confirming he had voted.

"How long you in the force constable?"

"Eighteen months next Tuesday. It's not a bad job and I prefer it up here in my hometown."

"Are you a good driver?"

The constable looked at Marlon with curious suspicion and drummed on the steering wheel with both hands. "I want to think I am a good driver my Sergeant never complain yet."

"We need some good drivers in our department you know! I could put forward your name and see what happens." Marlon extended his hand to the young constable and they shook hands.

"I am going to speak to my Superintendent and recommend you for a driving position. We could use a man like you on my team."

The young constable looked at Marlon and shook his head approvingly, extending his hand again to Marlon. "Thank you, sir."

The Polling Station was far quieter than it had been earlier in the day. Many voters who had already voted mingled outside the polling station in small groups debating the possible outcome of the election. The irony was, most of the people had already resigned to the fact, Mackie had won the election - by a landslide.

Marlon, on receiving the message radioed the police station for someone to relieve him at his post due to his pending arrangement at police headquarters.

Amidst the small gathering, Marlon made eye contact with Watkins who had a basketball spinning on the tip of his index finger.

Watkins looked Marlon with an emotionless stare, brought the ball to a halt with his middle finger and thumb. He lodged the ball under his arm and made a pistol gesture at Marlon with his right hand.

Marlon tapped the constable on his leg. "Yuh know dat fella with de ball?"

"Sure man! Everybody know Watkins. He is one ah de best basketball players we have in the Eastern region, probably even in the entire country."

"Yuh sure about dat? You never see me play."

"Where you from man? You have to go and watch ah ball game to see real quality."

"I think I will," replied Marlon. "So, what else does he do besides play ball?"

The constable cast a curious eye at Marlon, and shifted in his seat, he cleared his throat.

"Ah not being funny here Corporal but is like yuh fishing for something."

Marlon placed his hand on the officer's shoulder and said, "Not all my brother, I just wondered what he did for work, nothing wrong with that, is there?"

The constable shrugged his shoulders nonchalantly; there was a short pause before he responded, "Ah don't think he employed anywhere nah! The last thing I heard he left de army. He went England, trained with dem SAS army people. When he came back, he left the army just like that."

"Is ah real waste though, the country invested a lot of money on this man because they saw potential in him, and he just threw it away just so." Marlon looked at the constable for agreement and was shocked when the young officer disagreed.

"Dat is all well and good for you to sit there and say sir, but the army eh have no prospects for these people, he better off sweeping the road."

Marlon was flabbergasted, he shook his head slowly took out his ID and showed it to the constable. "Yuh see dat? It is service to your country. Just like ah soldier, it is the problem with our society. No respect. It will be the downfall of this place if it continues."

"What you talking 'bout respect sir? People don't have respect for the police or army, because people like us are seen as bullies man! De people don't respect we, de fraid we. Most police today are drunkards or wife beaters and they refer to these soldiers as potato peelers."

Marlon laughed at the constable's remark, securing his identification card into his pocket. "So, tell me, which of those categories do you fit into my friend, wife beater or drunkard?"

"None! I eh marrid and ah doh drink."

"Well then, you should not label everybody with the same tainted brush that you carry around in your back pocket."

"You know what ah mean though, you've been in the Service ah long time, ah sure yuh share my views."

"Not at all, I have to disagree," Marlon defended. "there are a lot of good policemen and policewomen out there, and most of them doh beat dey wife, or husband for that matter." There was a moment of laughter, the young constable nodded to an extent of agreement with Marlon, but not in a whole-hearted way.

"You know I am going to be a dad soon, a girl from your town too." Marlon remarked.

"Yuh making joke, what is her name? I probably know her."

The radio crackled and they stopped to listen to the bulletin, but the radio fell silent again. Another police car pulled alongside the officers acknowledged each

other with a nod. A plainclothes police officer disembarked from
the vehicle carrying a submachine gun and a holstered revolver.

Marlon shook hands with the young constable and reminded him of his intention to put his name forward as a driver to his superiors at head office. He stuck his head back into the car and said to the constable, "Elsa! Elsa Nurse is her name and I am sure you don't know her."

CHAPTER
10EN

The afternoon sun showed no mercy, the lack of breeze intensified the humidity in the atmosphere. Trees that lined the roadside stood rigid like giant sentinels, offering some solace of shade. People walked lazily to their destinations, some employing the use of umbrellas to shade themselves from the onslaught of the scorching heat. The sun was so ferocious that even in the comfort of her veranda, Ma Draper felt lethargic. She lacked the vigour to replenish the mangoes on the tray with fresh ones as she normally did on an afternoon. She fanned herself with the folded newspaper and gazed at the small crowd gathered outside Dhanraj shop. There was the usual din of the afternoon customers as they placed orders and talked among themselves. This time, however, most of their conversation centred around the election.

From the kitchen, Elsa bellowed, "Mama! Yuh eh goin' and vote?" Elsa smiled, she knew the answer to her question and half regretted she had posed it to Ma Draper. However, she had presumed that on the day, Ma Draper would have changed her mind and voted.

Ma Draper's attitude towards Mackie was unwarranted and unwavering, despite his popularity and though she knew within herself that the candidate she supported had not a glimmer of hope of ever being re-elected. When asked why she didn't like Mackie, she would always respond by saying, "My blood eh take him."

Convincing Ma Draper to alter her morals and vote for

Mackie was a magnanimous task. Elsa decided that the matter was best left as it were, rather than hinging on a hope. She knew only one person had the capability of convincing Ma Draper otherwise, and that was Fitzroy. Elsa sighed heavily and wished Fitzroy was around. Not for the sake of swaying Ma Draper's vote but to share in the experience that he put into motion.

"Is like allyuh don't give up nah," Ma Draper mumbled under her breath. "I would never vote for dat boy, he too wotless and, besides, me and he mudder doh see eye to eye." She looked up at the mango tree and sighed. The tree seemed to have lost none of its fruits, birds fluttered about feasting on the soft yellow pulp from the ripe mangoes. Elsa sniggered with the thought. What not seeing eye-to-eye with his mother got to do with her voting for Mackie? Her thoughts did not linger.

The dog next door let off a sharp howl, followed by a long pitiful groan. Ma Draper scraped at her head with her fingernails, looked up at the mango tree again and whispered, "Lord Jezess! Dat eh sounding good at all nah, somebody going down." She pondered for a moment, searching her mind for people she knew who were unwell. Quietly she began a hymn in a sombre rhythm. Her pupils darted about as her mind searched for those relatives or friends who might be seriously ill. Ma Draper paused in her hymn and prayed, asking God to make better, those were suffering and in poor health.

Ma Draper's memory reverted to her childhood. She recalled when the dog they had let off a pitiful groan and a prolonged howl, like a wolf. Her father muttered under his breath at the breakfast table, "Hmm! Like somebody kicking the bucket today!" At the time she didn't understand the term. Without fail, later that day, news came that an elderly neighbour three doors away had passed away just hours after they had heard the groan from the dog. She remembered her father saying, "Dogs, they know when death coming." Ma Draper knew only too well the extent of her father's words and the cry of the dog next door frightened her.

Her quiet interlude was shattered by a small man on his bike as he rang the bell vigorously, yelling out to Ma Draper from the front gate, "Playing any mark today Tantie?"

"No boy! not today, ah dream too much foolishness." No sooner had she finished her sentence the bicycle had disappeared with just an echo of the bell in the distance.

Ma Draper allowed her thoughts to drift back to the eerie sound that Sita had made. A worried look enveloped her face, she gave a long sigh followed by a hymn. *"Yes, Jezess loves me, yes Jezess loves me..."* There was a long pause and she did not resume her singing. A worried spell had her bewitched her. She was suddenly saddened and tearful.

Elsa pondered on the extended pause and called out, "Mama, you okay?"

The rocking chair moved back and forth but there was no answer from Ma Draper. Elsa dried her wet hands on the hem of her dress and went out to the verandah.

There, coursing its way down Ma Draper's cheeks was a stream of tears. Elsa gently brushed the tears away with her fingers. She knelt and cradled Ma Draper. "What yuh crying for now mama?" Elsa held her close and gently allowed her to cry quietly.

Ma Draper looked up at Elsa, her face wearing a frowned, distressed gaze. She spoke in a low, soft tone, as if all the life in her body was drained, "I so worried about Fitzroy, is two weeks now since we hear from him." The rocking chair stopped briefly. "Dat dog pitiful cry is the messenger of death. Fitzroy out there in the sea, anything could happen to him and we wouldn't know. Lord Jezess, why de ass he find himself out there? Lord have mercy yes!"

Elsa kept a comforting embrace on her. "I am sure that Fitzroy is fine. If anything had happened, I am sure we would be notified by the company." She patted Ma Draper's damp cheeks with the end of her floral dress. "If it makes you feel any better, I will go up by the telephone exchange later and give the company a call. That way your heart and mind would be at ease."

Ma Draper shook her head disapprovingly, "Nah leave it, he must be just spending longer out at sea."

Elsa grinned, "Or maybe he hook up with ah nice South woman that making him happy."

"Is true gyul, all kinda t'ing going through meh blasted head since dat dog howl." Ma Draper sobbed. They both chuckled and hugged each other.

The wind ceased and everything appeared motionless. The leaves on the trees no longer rustled and the dark ocean quietly crept to the pebbled shoreline. Fitzroy gazed out into the darkness, punctuated only by the spots of light on the passing ships in the distance. He patted his pocket, reassuring himself that his little notebook was still secured in its place. There was a compelling urge to take it out and write his thoughts. The darkness deterred that urge. He folded his arms around his knees and allowed his eyes to follow a lone seagull in the darkness. The gull floated over the quiet sea before silently landing on an anchored fishing boat. Fitzroy buried his head between his knees, and before long he had drifted off into a slumber.

In the distance he could hear Ma Draper's voice, she was beckoning him to shut the door behind him. Fumbling in the dark, he yelled back to her, "Ma I can't see no door to shut."

The sound of seagulls drowned out Ma Draper's voice, he could hear the ocean, alive again. Ma Draper's voice urged him again, "Turn on the light boy!"

Fitzroy opened his eyes and rubbed his face with both hands. The glare of the dawn light dazzled his eyes and the emerging tide was almost upon him. He scrambled to his feet to avoid getting his shoes wet. Seagulls fluttered franticly above some small fishing boats navigating their way to the shoreline.

A small crowd of rugged looking youths assembled, ready to heave the vessels in. The crisp ocean air had revitalised Fitzroy. He watched the young men, their muscles tensed and rippling as they heaved in unison to bring the boats to the shoreline. Licking his dry lips, he raised a hand to acknowledge the youths. Many of them he knew from his frequent trips to the waterfront. They would sometimes come over, sit and converse for hours on end with Fitzroy, sharing stories about their life, while he shared his experiences of working on the oil rigs and growing up in Arima. Every time the fishing boats came in, they would offer him free fish, but Fitzroy always declined. On one occasion, he accepted and took the large kingfish to Petra at the restaurant.

Fitzroy rubbed his face vigorously to wipe away any sign of sleep and dusted the dirt off his trousers from where he sat on the ground. He patted his pocket feeling for his notebook. Having established it was still in its place, he carefully took the book out and unfolded one of the newspaper clippings that he had kept. Fitzroy absorbed the headline. '*Arima set to welcome the youngest Mayor in the country.*'

He recalled the days when Mackie would come around and they would make fish guns using bicycle tubes and metal spokes for spears. They would then go to Valencia River to shoot fish. Getting to the river was always full of excitement for them. Passing the orange fields, they could not resist the urge to pilfer some oranges to satiate their appetite. They used their T shirts as bags, tying the sleeves together to carry off their hoard of oranges.

Mackie and Fitzroy had always been the best of friends throughout their school years, and into adulthood. Fitzroy was amazed how their friendship blossomed since Mackie returned to Trinidad. During Mackie's stay in Canada, Fitzroy would often go down to Tatil building, in Port of Spain and send telegrams whenever there was important political news which he felt might be of interest to his friend. In a roundabout kind of way, it was Fitzroy who enthused Mackie on to a political path. Today, Fitzroy seemed pleased with himself. He had persuaded Mackie to engage with the challenge of running for mayor. The outcome pleased him, Mackie was about to create history, and he was extremely proud of his friend.

Fitzroy kept his head down, he strolled along the gravelled area dragging his feet on the loose stones as he walked. A stray dog wagged its tail vigorously at him. He stopped and patted the dog on its head, snapping his fingers he motioned to the fish stalls and said, "Off you go Phantom." The dog dutifully obeyed and scuttled off towards the shoreline.

The once quiet streets of the night had transformed into bustling boulevards heaving with pedestrians, vehicles and vending stalls. People weaved between traffic darting across the busy roads going about their daily business. Drivers honked their horn violently as pedestrians stepped out in front of slow, moving cars, without care or concern. Fitzroy crawled along without care or haste. He had traipsed through these streets so often he was confident it was possible to shut his eyes and let his feet deliver him to a desired point. Above his serene composure, the cries of the early morning vendors could be heard intermingling with the din of the traffic. He meandered through the chaotic streets to a jewellery store. His feet had taken him to where he wanted to be and then they paused, like a driver selecting the parking gear, bringing the vehicle to a halt.

Fitzroy made a visor with his hand and peered into the huge glass window, his eyes selecting items of jewellery randomly. Inside, the assistant smiled at him, he responded with a smile to acknowledge her. He knew too, it was an invitation to come in, and he willingly accepted. The jewellery store was an upmarket establishment with three branches in the country, one in Port of Spain one in San Fernando and the other, a smaller branch in the Duty-Free lounge at Piarco airport. They advertised regularly on national television and all the major newspapers, magazines and radio. As Fitzroy walked gingerly on the carpeted floor his feet seemed to sink into the plush carpet with every step. His nervousness was obvious as he casually brushed his face with his moist hands.

"Good morning sir! How can I help?" The polite young assistant behind the glass counter smiled, offering her assistance. She was quite beautiful with an olive complexion and oval face and stood nearly six foot tall. Her teeth were exceptionally white and her smile and grey eyes captivated him. Fitzroy stammered, "I...I err, looking for ah nice ring, something special."

The assistant smiled again. This time her smile made him comfortable and relaxed. She fiddled with some keys from her pocket, looking at Fitzroy from the corner of her eye, "Is it a present or for yourself sir?"

"No, No! I am going and....well not exactly. I am going, I want to ask somebody, I mean, a girl... to... get married."

The assistant beamed a smile at Fitzroy, clasped her slender hands to her face and said, "Wow! that's so romantic. Well sir, these here are not wedding bands you know. Come over this side and I will show you the wedding bands. You want diamond or just plain gold bands?"

Fitzroy eased himself over to the other side of the store where the assistant produced a purple velvet tray with a beautiful assortment of rings arranged on velvet mounts. His eyes sparkled with excitement then fell into a moment of despair.

The assistant studied him trying to read his emotion, then in a soft voice asked, "Is everything okay?"

"Yeah, I was just thinking, what if she says no, and I eh even know she ring size."

There was a broad smile on her face, she touched his hand gently and said reassuringly, "Mister, a handsome man like you will never get turned down. Just one look at this ring, she bound to say yes; especially if she knew, where you bought it."

"As a woman, which of these would you recommend?"

The young lady smiled, looked around cautiously then whispered, "We are not at liberty to make choices for the customers you know, but as the saying goes, diamonds are a girl's best friend."

She removed a diamond-studded ring from the velvet

mount, placing it in Fitzroy's palm. He trembled as the assistant placed the ring in his hand. He picked it up gently fearing it would break in his tough hands. He examined it for a moment and returned it to the assistant allowing her to secure the ring back into the tray.

"I much prefer that one with the three diamonds. It looks nicer and I think it will look good on her finger too." Fitzroy beamed a boyish grin, feeling at ease now with the assistant. He brushed his face continuously, tapping his pocket, reassuring himself that the notebook was still secure. He sighed heavily, brushing his face again. The assistant looked at him, smiled and said, "Mister, you don't have to make your mind up now you know! You could make a deposit to secure the ring and think about it. And, you could choose another design when you come back, if you don't like this one."

Her kind words made Fitzroy feel at ease. He looked at her and said, "Can I see your hands?"

The assistant obliged and Fitzroy asked, "Can you try that ring, pointing to a ring on the tray. Very kindly, she removed the ring from the velvet tray and slipped it onto the selected finger. The assistant tilted her hand modelling the ring at all different angles for Fitzroy to examine. Almost, without any hesitation he was satisfied with his choice, "Okay! I'll have that one."

Carefully she removed the ring from her finger and secured it into a small beautifully crafted black box, lined with a fuchsia velvet fabric on the inside. She presented a view to Fitzroy, he nodded approvingly. She snapped the box shut offering a gently smile as she did.

"It is a beautiful ring," the cashier commented, "there are only two of its kind made so you are making someone very, very happy with this ring."

The assistant and the cashier both smiled broadly with Fitzroy and wished him the best of luck for the future.

CHAPTER
11VEN

Behind a wide heavy oak desk, the Superintendent looked up at Corporal Dudley who was standing to attention. "At ease Corporal." The Superintendent motioned as he spoke, offering Marlon a seat. Nervously, Marlon sat on the stout leather chair as his senior shuffled through some files on his desk before separating them into two neat folders. Marlon searched through his mind for a reason behind this official meeting, trying to anchor in his thoughts any precise motive.

He strained his eyes to catch a glimpse of what was stamped on the front of the files and could barely see the letters URG written in red on one of the folders. The other folder was totally obscured.

"No need to strain your eyes Corporal, this one's for you." the Superintendent quipped as he relaxed in a lounge position on his chair.

Marlon could now see the file was stamped URGENT in bold red letters and in smaller black text, *For the Attention of Superintendent M. Dudley.* He picked up the file and surveyed the contents ignoring the smaller text on the front of the file marked, Superintendent M. Dudley.

Inside the file, he saw a photograph of a young man. He studied the photograph, trying to recollect where he had seen the young man before. The Superintendent lifted his voice and held up another file, "You have been recommended to take up my position here as Superintendent, with immediate effect. If you accept; are you ready for the challenge?"

Marlon nodded with some reluctance, "No sir, but I am willing to give it my best."

"Signing this document will be the last role I officially conduct in this office. I am moving to Southern Division in the capacity as Acting Commissioner."

"Congratulations sir." Marlon extended his hand to the Acting Commissioner.

The Superintendent surveyed Marlon, "Son, you've been an exemplary officer under my command and I know that you will execute your new role with the same vigour, sincerity and professionalism as you have always done throughout your career in the police service. However, this is a bigger challenge, and many will expect you to fail. You have my personal recommendation on this promotion. I can think of no other deserving officer for this post but yourself. But that is just my opinion. Others may disapprove. Luckily, I have the final say where this is concerned."

Marlon stood to attention. "No need, at ease." He walked around the desk offering his hand to congratulate Marlon. He motioned him to the chair on the other side of the desk and cautioned, "These halls are filled with entities wishing to cut you down and hinder your progress, especially an officer of your stature, rising through the ranks as you have. There isn't anything that I can tell you, except to be on your guard."

The two men shook hands firmly, Marlon watched as his senior left the room. He settled his hat on his head, tucked his cane under his arm and walked through the doorway without looking back, leaving the door behind him open.

Marlon stood silently as the Acting Commissioner disappeared down the corridor. He loosened the top button of his tunic before lounging in his new chair. He surveyed the cardboard boxes stacked neatly in the corner of the room, secured with brown packaging tape. He assumed they belonged to the new Acting Commissioner and upon examining the labels, his assumption proved to be correct. They were all addressed to the Southern Police Division headquarters in San Fernando.

Making himself comfortable, he studied the folder marked URGENT. He scrutinised the photograph of the young man again, still puzzled. Pacing his mind, he tried to recall where he had seen or, met the young man in the photograph. There were no names or details attached to the photograph, making it odd that is was attached to the file. Taking a felt marker, he drew several question marks on the back of the photograph and another to the front before fastening it to the front of the folder with a paper clip.

He perused the logistical details of a covert operation to apprehend a notorious gang, who presently were terrorising the country with a spate of armed, aggravated robberies. The gang had carried out several successful armed robberies across the country and so far, not a single arrest or breakthrough had been made in the case. The only information available to police was that the suspects sported Rastafarian hairstyles.

During two of the robberies there had been fatal shootings. The police had come under extreme pressure to apprehend those responsible for these heinous crimes at all cost. What puzzled Marlon as he studied the notes was why wasn't the Flying Squad involved in this case sooner? Giving the severity of the crimes, he had expected that such a case would be given top priority. He studied the papers carefully spread out on the desk again.

Sitting back in his chair, he tapped at his lips with his index finger, "I see! He whispered to himself. This mess has been passed to me on a platter so I can become a scapegoat when it fails miserably. What a wonderful parting gift Mr Acting Commissioner."

Superintendent Dudley's promotion meant he was now head of the operation to bring an end to the current crime spree in the country. Looking through the files it dawned on him that his department included the entire northern division Flying Squad. The magnitude of the promotion frightened him. He was assuming control of an entire division as well as the responsibility of capturing and bringing to justice those perpetrators responsible for the spate of daring robberies across the country. He began to sweat as he poured over the documents repeatedly, double checking and, counter checking intelligence details. The more he looked at the files the more he noticed the lack of vital investigative material. He assumed they were either omitted or not done or, purely an oversight by the intelligence gathering officers.

Marlon was curious to know who compiled the report. The tactician responsible for the operation had missed vital information needed for the scope of such a national operation. The precise details were outlined for specific divisions and the number of officers drafted for the operation fell considerably short of what was needed. The plans and recommendations submitted to the departing Superintendent constituted, in Marlon's opinion, a shambolic mess. As head of the division, he dismantled the existing operational plans by marking a big red X across the document and confining it to the bottom drawer of his desk. Pressing the buzzer on his desk, a young curvaceous WPC, in uniform, entered the room.

He looked up seemingly surprised and handed her a piece of paper. "Can you get me that officer as soon as its humanly possible. He's stationed in Arima presently?"

The WPC saluted. "Yes sir. Congratulations on your appointment." She left the room clutching the paper between her fingers, a faint smile on her face, leaving her perfumed scent behind.

"Thank you." Marlon said and he continued redrafting a new operation plan. He was flabbergasted with some of the inadequate measures that his predecessor had drawn up for the covert operation. Given his experience in the field, he could foresee the proposals would have been catastrophic from the onset. He shook his head with a disapprovingly sigh. He held high regard for the former Superintendent and was puzzled how he could have allowed such flaws in a major police operation. Marlon mused, calculating that perhaps he had not read the draft, knowing that he was handing over the reign to someone with great competence in the field.

Marlon pondered for a moment on his promotion to Superintendent and that of the Acting Commissioner. There were officers who were far superior in their experience to occupy his position and likewise the role of the Acting Commissioner. The thought troubled him. Why was I promoted? he thought, drumming a pencil on the desk with no apparent rhythm.

Marlon knew he had an exceptional record since his promotion to Detective and then to Detective Corporal. Joining the Flying Squad had catapulted him into an area where he enjoyed tremendous success. His rate in solving cases and apprehending criminals had been exceptional in his division. His prominence put him in the public eye with the press continually following his progress. He was the recipient of many commendations and awards for his efforts in the line of, and beyond the call of duty.

His current promotion was a giant leap in his career. No other officer had moved through the ranks and been given such a portfolio of responsibility so quickly. Marlon was uncertain whether he would be successful in executing his new duties with the same precision and effectiveness that he had grown accustomed to as a Corporal. The promotion carried a new level of responsibility, at magnitudes he had not had until now, and did not envisaged. The strain now levelled at him, weighed heavy on his shoulders. He abhorred the weight of the administrative duties that came with the promotion. But he could not wait to break the news to Elsa.

By the end of the night, Superintendent Dudley had finalised his operation plan. He had drafted in fourteen new officers who he knew had impeccable records and removed two from the original squad who he suspected of falling short of their expected duties. While no hard evidence existed, alleged compromise of the morals of the police service was questioned. Officers in his command would need to abide explicitly with the law and carry themselves such, that they have the confidence of the public behind them.

Marlon stuck to the original course of him undertaking the Eastern leg of the operation and left the Northern unit unchanged. They were all specialist in their quarters, and he did not wish to disrupt anyone's working pattern, especially when it had produced results. He had drafted in the young constable from Arima making a total of eight in his squad and three cars for his unit, rather than the four-man unit that was originally planned. He switched the operation stations and kept it secret until the night of the operation. With a squad now bolstered to twenty-eight including Eastern and Northern Divisions, he was confident of cracking the robbery cases and bringing to an end, the freedom of those responsible for the crime wave across the country.

There was a rap on the door, the young WPC walked in without waiting for a response. "Sir, PC Beckles went off duty earlier, but I have asked for him to be summoned here as soon as he is notified."

"Thank you, officer ...?'

"WPC Murphy, sir."

"What's your first name?"

"Michelle."

"Officer Murphy, can you get me the marital status of these officers please. I want to know if they have kids also. Is that possible by tomorrow evening?"

"Yes sir, that is possible."

Marlon flashed a warm smile at WPC Murphy, she responded with one of respect as she turned and made her way out of the room.

It had been a long tiring night for Marlon. He had not anticipated working this late. Looking at his watch, Marlon knew it would be too late to visit Elsa and give her the good news. He stretched his arms as far as they would go into the air and yawned lazily. Squeezing his fist tightly his knuckles made a crackling sound that echoed in the empty room. Shuffling his files together, he thought, I need to get a briefcase now. He jabbed his finger on the buzzer. WPC Murphy emerged, again without knocking.

"Miss Murphy, can I have a large envelope to put these files please?"

"Sure! gimme ah couple ah minutes okay?"

Michelle returned later with various selection of envelopes in different sizes, tucked under her arm. She presented them on the desk for Marlon to choose from.

"Would that be all for tonight sir?"

Marlon studied the envelopes then looked up at WPC Murphy, "Sorry constable, yes that would be all. Apologies for keeping you back later than expected."

"All part of the job sir." WPC Murphy responded.

"Indeed, it is." Marlon gathered his files, hesitated for a bit, then wrote a note to himself. Get a briefcase.

CHAPTER
12ELVE

Fitzroy gently removed the covers and quietly got out of bed. He looked at Petra lying on the bed; her shoulders exposed and fast asleep. Walking over to the window, he looked out into the distance, observing the calm ocean with small boats sailing across his view. He never really took the time to appreciate the wonderful view from Petra's apartment. Outside, the dawn light was enough to see the lone tomato plant that attached itself to the metal rails. There were several ripe fruits hanging from its delicate verdant vines, ready for harvesting. Across the room, he watched Petra as she slept. Clutching the velvet box in his hand tightly he opened it intermittently to admire the jewellery inside.

He had taken his eyes away from the bed and not realised that Petra was awake. It startled him when she said, "You're up early! What's that you got there?" looking at Fitzroy curiously.

Fitzroy smiled, not looking at her directly, "It's a wedding ring."

Kneeling on the floor beside the bed, he held out his hands exposing the ring and said, "Petra Miles, will you marry me?"

Petra was speechless. She held her breath for a few seconds before she spoke, "You are not being funny are you Mr Fitzroy Draper?"

"I will, understand if you said no." Fitzroy said hesitantly.

"I would love to be your wife Fitzroy Draper. I never expected this. Never thought…, well never thought anyone would ever propose to me; least of all you." Tear drops crept about her cheeks. Fitzroy kissed them dry.

He climbed into the bed and placed the ring on her finger. She held her finger up to the light and admired it.

"Are real these diamonds?" She asked with a smile.

"Yes 'oman is real diamonds and real gold too, before you ask. You think I would buy you Mickey Mouse ting?"

They were both jovial, their laughter echoing in the quiet room. They embraced each other as she constantly admired the ring on her finger. Fitzroy could see the words forming on her lips, he placed his finger on them. "You don't need to know how much it cost, just that it was especially made for you."

Petra squeezed him and they snuggled up closer, looking out as the dawn began to paint a promising new day.

Petra remembered fondly, the first day Fitzroy walked into the restaurant. She could tell he was not from San Fernando. The way he walked, hesitantly, every step, unsure of where he was going and what he was about. His peculiar habits intrigued her too. She figured him to be a policeman but after a few visits she became aware that he wasn't, not the way he tipped her. After a few visits, her impression of him changed. When Fitzroy did make conversation with her, his voice was smooth and mellow, like that of a singer. Somehow, he sounded different when ordering food. Petra was quite surprised by his forward manner when he first asked her on a date. "Sorry," she said to him with a straight smile. "I am married."

Fitzroy said nothing more to her whenever he dined at the restaurant. She continued to serve him with the same courtesy as when he first came in. Sometimes she even nudged him with her hips as she went by, turning to give him a provocative smile.

Some weeks later, he walked in with a single red rose and presented it to her, again, saying nothing. Petra smiled and accepted the gesture with a pleasant thank you. She processed his order as usual and continued to wait at the tables without giving him a second glance. Settling at his customary table, he took out his notebook and placed it neatly beside him. He was about to make an entry when Petra appeared. She laid a piece of paper in front of him, turned on her heels and proceeded to serve another customer. He watched her attentively as she attended to the other customers. He examined the piece of paper she had left him. In neat calligraphic letters, she had written. *I finish at 8 tonight.*

As Fitzroy held up the note, she glanced over her shoulders to see his reaction. He folded the note neatly and placed it into his notebook. His face showed no emotion. In the notebook, he wrote; 'a date tonight.'

Their lips met, lingering as they enjoyed a long kiss. She grinned, admiring the ring again in the light that filtered through the windows. She wondered if he had kept the note that started their dating.

"So where are we having this wedding then Mr Fitzroy Draper?"

"What yuh mean? Right here in Sando." He said without having to think about it.

"Your parents don't mind coming down to San Fernando?"

Fitzroy picked at his fingers pushing back his cuticles with his thumbnail.

"Not really," he replied looking into Petra's eyes. "I was hoping it would be just you and I, then somewhere exotic for honeymoon."

Petra tilted her head to one side trying to make sense of Fitzroy's actions. "Don't you want your family with you there? If my parents were alive, I would want them to come."

There was a long pause, it brought a deafening silence to the room. Fitzroy dusted his hands and said without looking at Petra, "My dad is dead, and I don't really want my mother to make a fuss. Maybe it's stupid, I just wanted it to be us, no crowd. You could invite anyone you want though."

"Are you worried about your mum accepting me?"

Fitzroy look her fixed and said, "I haven't told my mum about you and just feel it isn't right to just spring a wedding on her."

Petra twirled the ring on her finger, her eyes studying the grey sky. It was as difficult now, as it was when she first met Fitzroy, to analyse him. She was no good at psychoanalyzing, but she knew in her heart he was a good man. His quirkiness had attracted her to him at the restaurant. The mystery about him and his solitary habits had intrigued her. Now she was beginning to have those feelings again. She yearned now to know more about Fitzroy, yet he never divulged a great deal about himself to anyone.

Petra never envisaged she would be lying next to him and, more intriguingly, proposed to by him. His proposal had stunned her, filling her with joy and an untold amount of happiness. She was enthused by the gesture and longed to share it with someone. Her nearest relative was her cousin Bertha, who lived in San Fernando.

Marriage had not been in Petra's immediate plans but, Fitzroy's charming personality and his warmth had thrilled her. She was fond of his weird sense of humour and his quiet demeanour. Nothing seemed to agitate him.

Fitzroy eased himself out of the bed and paced the room. He knew that Petra was uneasy about his plans. They had unsettled her. She sat quietly on the bed, twirling the ring on her finger. Fitzroy knelt beside her on the bed with apologetic eyes. "I am sorry if my plans don't fit with yours for the wedding. I should have discussed it first."

In the back of his mind, he realised neither Petra nor himself, had ever confessed their love for each other. And yet here he was, in her bedroom, rain beating a rhythm on the roof as he proposed to her. He clasped his hands in hers and looked her in the eyes, "Petra Miles, I have not said it before, but I want you to know that I love you. You have given my lonely life a purpose. I want to marry you and spend the rest of my days with you, to make you happy, to share your sad days, to share your happy days and to hold you when I feel low. For only you can lift me to that happy place in life that I ever long to be."

A smile appeared on her face; she fixed her eyes on Fitzroy without uttering a word. Lifting her finger, she touched his lips, "I love you too Fitzroy Draper. You have brought a great deal of joy to my life, and I like it. No one has ever made me feel respected and happy at the same time. No one has ever treated me the way you have treated me."

He stopped her from saying anymore, "Please don't compare, you've given life to my existence. Before you came into my world I existed only on the rigs and the streets of San Fernando, the sea front and nightclubs."

She smiled, "And the restaurant." Petra continued twirling the ring on her finger as they lost themselves in each other's eyes.

"Well Mr Draper, we will have our wedding in San Fernando. The two of us and my friends as witnesses, then we will zoom off to your exotic place...I will call it Tobago."

They laughed in each other's arms and watched as the promise of a sunny day turned to rain. The heavy droplets drummed against the surfaces, composing a melody. Fitzroy studied the heavy down pour as it lashed against a tomato vine on the balcony rails, its fruits being drenched by the crystal clear, rain. In his mind, he could see the water backing up against the red brick wall with the fallen mango leaves blocking the small aperture in the wall, preventing the water from escaping into main drain. Petra patted the space next to her and invited him back to bed.

Three Mazda model 616 police cars pulled into the station car park in San Juan, one with its police markings and the other two, mint green in colour, unmarked. The cars parked parallel to each other at the far end of the car park.

Marlon alighted from a green car and addressed the seven assembled officers. "Gentlemen I have chosen you all specially for this operation based on your record and your ability to get results as police officers. This is a dangerous operation and I urge each of you to be extra vigilant and look out for each other's back. We are a team, don't forget that for a single moment. It could prove detrimental if we did."

The officers looked at each other and shrugged their shoulders. A couple of them lit cigarettes as they listened to the Superintendent attentively, "As you are aware there is an alarming concern for these armed robberies taking place across the country. Working on new intelligence, we are making a series of raids across the north and eastern divisions. Ours is at a house in Curepe." Marlon handed out stapled sheets to the officers as he spoke. A voice from the back asked. "How good is the intel sir?" "Our sources are confident that it is sound, CPL Alvin." Marlon continued. "Our aim is to apprehend these felons alive. These criminals are armed and very dangerous. They have demonstrated to us that they are not afraid to use their weapons, with total disregard for human life."

A wail of sirens shattered the quiet night as two squad cars raced out of the car park with purposeful urgency. Marlon waited for sirens to wane and continued, "Given the nature of this operation, we are, from this day on to be armed with SMGs and revolvers. No rifles." A hand went up in the darkness but was not seen. A voice followed. "Why SMGs sir?"

"Officer Clyde, these weapons are far more effective at close range combat than rifles and are easier to manoeuvre. Criminals seem far more capable at getting superior weapons than the police these days. This is our best compromise."

Marlon approached PC Beckles and patted him on the back. "Officer Beckles, welcome to the Flying Squad. Because this is your first assignment, I want you to be my driver and wear side arm only. Be sure to carry extra ammo."

PC Beckles nodded, "As you wish sir."

"All our supplies have been delivered here on my request. You will document your weapons and ammunition with the desk Sergeant and leave any personal items, except watches, with the Sergeant in envelopes provided with your names written on the front." There was a lot of chatter amongst the officers in the car park. Marlon snapped his fingers in rapid succession to get their attention, he said, "When we go into the briefing room, you will not be permitted to make any telephone calls after the briefing. Anyone who wishes to make telephone calls can use the next half an hour or so to do this."

Each officer armed himself with a Sub Machine Gun and a service revolver. The officers also ensured that they were packing extra ammunition. PC Beckles examined his revolver, removing the lanyard from the pistol and secured the weapon into the holster. Cpl Alvin signed out two revolvers and an SMG. PC Beckles looked at him wit a grin, "You expect gunfight at OK Coral?"

Marlon adjusted a camouflaged detail cap on his head and slung the SMG with its canvas strap over his shoulder. He inspected the two magazines before switching on his radio to check its battery life. The radio gave a loud bleep signalling that the battery was fully charged. Several similar bleeps echoed around the room as the others carried out the same routine checks. Marlon looked at his watch tapping the face with his index finger. The watch with its silver steel bracelet, hung loosely on his wrist. He synchronized his watch with the station clock and asked the others to do the same.

At the front desk there was a commotion as two officers dragged in a young man, his shirt ripped and bleeding from his forehead. He was handcuffed, with his hands in front of him, protesting that the police had beaten him, claiming police brutality.

The desk Sergeant tossed a bunch of keys to the officers and shouted, "Stick him in cell number two."

PC Beckles shadowed Marlon around the station while the others made their way outside to the car park and lit up cigarettes, puffing smoke into the air.

The police cell was filthy, wet and strewn with coarse tissue paper and dried blood; it reeked of stale urine and human faeces. The two officers dragged the prisoner into the cell and slammed the steel gate shut. From behind the gate, the prisoner shouted, "One ah you gone dead tonite."

Marlon stopped and listened with some concern. The prisoner shouted again, "I did not do anything. Is dat Rasta beat me up and you let him off."

Slowly, Marlon walked along the narrow corridor that led to the cells. He approached the cell with some caution. He could see the prisoner's face covered in blood and fresh blood oozing from the opened wound on his forehead, dripping on the floor.

"Sergeant, this man needs medical attention!" Marlon shouted with a level of urgency in his voice.

"What's your name son?" Marlon enquired.

"James, James Cumberbatch."

"How did you sustain that wound James?"

"Dat redman police beat meh wid he gun."

"Sergeant! Marlon yelled again, "Get a squad car and rush this man to casualty now."

A young constable hurried to the cell with a wad of tissue paper. He separated the wad of paper into two, pressing one bit onto the wound on James' forehead and handed the other bit to the prisoner.

James pressed the tissue paper hard against his wound and wiped his face with the other piece of paper towel.

"Tell me a bit more about this ordeal James."

"What de ass you care? Is yuh pardners dat beat me up."

"Please James indulge me."

"I was having an argument with my ex-girlfriend when

dis Rastaman, she new boyfriend came up and started beating the shit out of me." James mopped his face and continued. "Den dese two officers come rushing over and grab the Rasta. Next ting I know dey leave he and start to give me blows."

"Did they identify themselves to you Mr Cumberbatch?"

"They wearing police uniform man, I didn't think they were selling doubles."

The constable handcuffed James and ushered him out of the cell and led him to a waiting car, in the car park. Marlon followed taking care not to step on the fresh blood trail. The siren screamed and the car sped off in the direction to the hospital.

Inside the station Marlon was gathering information on the two officers that arrested James. He requested the Sergeant send a copy of the report to his office once it was completed. In a corner of the station at a small desk, a plainclothes officer held up a newspaper to Marlon. The headline read, '**New Superintendent Tackling Crime Head On**'. Marlon smiled with the officer who saluted him and as he made his way out to the car park, joining the rest of his squad in small talk.

"What was all that about sir?" PC Beckles asked.

"Not sure myself, but something's a bit fishy. Can't understand why a man bleeding to death is just dumped into a cell and left there with no medical attention."

"Sir dat is normal in all police stations. Is what I was saying to you, people have no confidence with the Police."

Marlon summoned his squad at the corner of the car park and announced, "Listen up everyone we will be leaving here at approximately 01:30 hours. Make sure you are prepared physically, mentally and psychologically. Check and double check your weapons, remember our operation starts the moment we drive out of this car park."

There was a resounding 'yes sir' from everyone. Once he had made the announcement Marlon made his way back inside the station. PC Beckles sat behind the wheel of his car and drummed on the steering with his index fingers. The others smoked cigarettes and chatted with each other.

The relaxed atmosphere with the squad did not last for very long. Marlon stuck two fingers in his mouth and made a loud whistle. He raised his hand and made a circular motion in the air, giving the signal to depart. Marlon pressed a button on the radio and contacted the northern team, advising that the operation was now active. PC Beckles engaged the engine, setting the car in motion. Slowly, the cars crept out of the car park and made their way along the main road.

"Have you ever been on a raid officer Beckles?"

"No saree, I haven't. Neither have I ever discharged a weapon whilst on duty."

"Tonight may get nasty so be on your guard."

"Will do sir." Beckles replied.

The cars proceeded along until they arrived at a crossroad junction. Beckles indicated left and joined the steady flow of traffic heading east along the main thoroughfare connecting east with the west.

The cars were quiet until the radio crackled; Marlon's voice echoed, "Gentlemen we are approaching our target destination soon. No sirens and no unnecessary attention to ourselves. Let's focus on what we are here for and, let's get a result tonight."

On the approach to their rendezvous, the cars reduced speed considerably and negotiated the left turn, avoiding a mob standing in the road as they flocked a food vendor. Beckles tapped the horn lightly and drove cautiously. The pedestrians clambered onto the pavement to avoid the cars. Casting a glance over at Marlon, he said, "I think cinema just finished sir."

Marlon looked around and replied, "I think you are right constable, proceed with care. A small detail I overlooked."

Along the street, most of the houses were fenced and gated with cars parked in the driveways. The gardens were well kept and adorned with an abundance of floral shrubs with blooms that scented the night air. A lone mongrel chased after the police car, giving up as the vehicle disappeared out of its reach. Up ahead, the hills stood majestic, like giant sentinels in the darkness. The road formed a junction and to the left, ended with a cul-de-sac, while to the right it followed through, leading to another side street that continued back onto the main road.

PC Beckles turned left into the cul-de-sac and parked the car near some tall grass almost obscuring it from view. He switched the engine off, and an eerie silence prevailed. The marked vehicle took up position further down the street dissecting the street to prevent any traffic from proceeding in either direction. One officer got out and stood in front of the car while the other two sat and waited.

Nearby, a lone streetlight partially gave some light to the living room of the house on the corner. The house was the police target tonight after being under surveillance for some time. It was suspected of being a drug den.

Inside the house on a small table in the living room, a yellow and blue basketball kit lay neatly folded with a *Spalding* basketball on top. In the bedroom, a lanky naked figure emerged at the window, peering through the curtains. He studied the parked car at the end of the road partially obscured by the tall bushes and a figure sitting in the driver's seat with the door opened.

He crept into the living room to get a better view and could see another figure lying flat on the grass in the front garden near the wall. He hurried back to the bedroom and quietly whispered to the nude figure on the bed, "Go back to sleep. I have to split, police watching the house." Creeping nearer the bed, he kissed her forehead and said, "Stay in bed don't get out."

In a swift action, he dragged on his jeans and T shirt, laced his Converse sneakers as quickly as he could. Making his way through the living room, he knocked the basketball of its perch and caught it before it could meet the floor. Carefully, he tucked a 9mm pistol into his waist. Outside, he could see another officer next to the car with his hands tucked deep into his pockets pacing the small area in front the car. At the back of the house, two officers had positioned themselves at the back door, with weapons trained on the door.

With great care and silence, he opened one of the windows at the far side of the house and climbed out leaving the window slightly ajar. Scaling the brick wall, he landed on some rusted corrugated iron that made a loud noise.

One officer raced round the house to investigate and discovered the window ajar. Radio silence was broken, the officer screamed down the radio, "Suspect on the run, I say again, suspect on the run."

The other officer kicked in the door with his heavy boot and stormed in. His weapon trained in front of him, hurrying to open the front door allowing the other officers in. They spread through the house combing every room. The basketball tumbled to the floor and rolled under a table in the commotion.

Two officers investigated the back of the house while Marlon and the others searched the house. Marlon gave the all clear for the two officers to pursue the target who was spotted jumping the neighbour's fence and running into a wooded area at the back of the house.

Cpl Alvin shouted from the bedroom, "Sir we have one female in the house."

Marlon radioed PC Beckles and requested the car be brought to the front of the house.

In the distance, two shot rang out in succession followed by a crackling of the radio. "Sir we have a man down. Two shots fired by the assailant, Cpl Clyde hit sir, I say again Cpl Clyde hit and bleeding badly."

As the officer lay on the ground clutching his shoulder the assailant had maintained a crouched position and trained his weapon in the direction of the pursuing officers. After a minute had passed and there wasn't any movement, he secured the safety on the weapon and continued running through the thick vegetation.

Marlon radioed the marked car, "Mobile 2, mobile 2. Can you rendezvous with Cpl Clyde and get him to the nearest casualty department?"

"Mobile 2 received, and out."

The radio crackled again. The officer gave an update on Cpl Clyde's condition, "Sir the Cpl is losing a lot of blood, had to abandon chase."

Marlon responded and informed the officer that a vehicle was on its way to their location to get Cpl Clyde to a hospital. He stressed that the search should commence as soon as Cpl Clyde was mobile and on his way to hospital.

The young lady sat up on the bed with the covers pulled up to her neck. Marlon signalled to one of the officers to stand guard outside and allowed her some privacy to change. She emerged wearing an oversized T shirt and sat with her legs crossed at the dining table. Marlon looked at the basketball kit on the table and asked. "You play basketball Miss?"

"They belong to my boyfriend." She answered dryly.

"Do these look familiar to you Officer Beckles?"

"No sir, never seen it before. I know the name of the team and the sponsor on the back but never seen this kit before."

"This is now evidence, try and not contaminate it."

"Do you have a warrant?" The young woman asked as the officers rummaged through the house.

PC Beckles held up a document to confirm that they did.

"Are you the owner of this property Miss…?"

"Gaspard. No, I am not the owner. The house belongs to my father Dr Gaspard, who I am sure you know very well."

Marlon paused for a short moment, then addressed Miss Gaspard in a formal capacity.

"Miss Gaspard, do you live here alone?"

She left her chair and paced the room pulling her oversized T shirt over her knees, "Yes, I live here alone."

"Tell me about the man seen leaving the property Miss Gaspard."

"What do you want to know? I knew him from school. We spent some time together in the past and, we spent the last two nights together, is that a crime now?"

"Certainly not Miss Gaspard. However, he has made himself a fugitive and that gives us cause for concern. Is he involved with any criminal activity?"

Before she had a chance to answer the question, PC Beckles alerted Marlon to something he found in the corner of the room.

"Excuse me Miss Gaspard."

Marlon moved closer to inspect the peculiar object. He moved it around with his boot and found it was a Rastafarian wig. Marlon tried to comprehend the meaning of what he was seeing. He picked up the hair piece and showed it to Miss Gaspard, 'Does this belong to you Miss Gaspard?'

"No, it belongs to my friend."

"I take that to mean the man seen leaving this house earlier?"

"Yes!"

"Why did he run Miss Gaspard?"

She looked Marlon in the eyes and said, "You would have to ask him that when you catch him officer. Maybe you scared him."

Marlon grabbed the radio, "Listen up officers, we are not looking for a Rastafarian, I say again. We are NOT looking for a Rastafarian. We are working on a new description... keep you posted."

"Copy that, over and out."

Marlon radioed the nearby St Joseph police station and requested some uniformed officers and a canine team. He instructed Cpl Alvin and Cpl Narine to stay at the house until the uniform officers and the canine team arrived. The radio was alive again and Marlon requested the status of the search from the officers in the field. Marlon informed them that he would be joining the search with PC Beckles as back up. He signed off with a cautious note, "Be careful fellas."

"Miss Gaspard what is your boyfriend's name?"

"He is not my boyfriend. Dean...Dean Watkins."

"Can you describe him to me?" Marlon asked.

She provided the Superintendent with a detailed description and asked, "Am I under arrest here officer...?"

"It's Superintendent Dudley. No! You are not under arrest Miss Gaspard. I must caution you however, that it is an offence to aide and abet a known criminal and to provide false information. Do you understand this caution?"

Marlon watched and waited as PC Beckles noted the caution in his book.

"Miss Gaspard I am aware of *who* your father is and, his political position. However, no one is above the law in this country. You are free to go anywhere in the country, but I must advise you to notify the police if leaving the country. Also, take note that if found to be knowingly harbouring a criminal, you will face prosecution."

"Do you want my passport?"

Marlon assured her that it won't be necessary as he had complete faith in her cooperation with the investigation.

PC Beckles removed his revolver from its holster, placing it in a recess between the passenger seats. Marlon sat in the front passenger seat with a powerful torch trained along the bushes as they drove, flooding the thick verge with light. The area plunged into darkness as the beams from the torch went out. The dipped headlights from the car provided the only illumination to the pitch-black road.

Marlon aimed the torch at an abandoned shed, he signalled PC Beckles to stop the car. They both got out, approaching the shed with caution. PC Beckles aimed his revolver in the direction of the shed. Dried twigs snapped under their feet. Marlon flooded the shed with light as they both kicked it open. The shed was empty and overgrown with vines and thick undergrowth. In the distance, both officers could hear the dogs yapping as they followed the trail from house, along the path that the suspect took.

Dean had hidden himself in a small ditch in the tall grass. He too, could hear the approach of the dogs. It was only a matter of minutes before they would be upon him if he maintained his position. Quickly, and quietly, he removed his socks and cut them into two pieces with a small knife. He tossed the four pieces into different directions. In absolute silence he moved stealthily through the bushes further away from the approaching dogs. Behind him, he could hear the dogs, they were separated from each other. He knew that his trick had confused the dogs, buying him some vital minutes to make his run. Sweat poured from his face and his clothing was wet from the dew drenched grass. His adrenalin pumped as he calculated his next move.

The skyline was shifting its hues to accommodate the approach of a new day. Dean looked at his watch. "This is a shitty way to start your day." He said to himself in a whisper. About fifty yards ahead of him, he could hear the drone of the early morning traffic. He knew, the break of day would give him more cover than the darkness. It was easier to manoeuvre among people than hide in thick vegetation.

Heading towards the hills was not an option. It would narrow his chances of escape and it would be easier for the police to request army guides and assistance to track him. They would have a significant manpower at their disposal. They could easily employ the use of the police and army helicopters to help flush him out into open area.

Dean's mind flashed back to the basketball kit left on the table in the house and the wig. How Miss Gaspard was coping with the questioning from the police was uncertain, but he knew burdening himself with that worry would do him no good at this time. Once the wig was found, Dean knew that the police would have it figured out. He knew too, Miss Gaspard would not compromise herself or her father's political position by giving false information to the police about him.

The police dogs had drawn a blank as they dragged their handlers in different directions through the tall wet grass. PC Beckles brought the car to a halt and listened to the howl of the dogs. He could tell by the sounds the dogs were making that they had found nothing. He gauged the distance of the canine team, drove along the gravel path and brought the car to a halt flashing his torch in sequence to alert the handlers of their position.

Marlon radioed Corporal Alvin requesting a sweep of the area, starting at the house and ending at the rendezvous point with them once they had completed the exercise.

To the East, the sky was transforming from darkness into a golden haze, the sun began to announce it presence. Marlon looked at the brightening sky. There was not much darkness left, he hoped that the emerging light would give them an advantage in the tall grass. He pondered on Miss Gaspard's story and somehow knew she was lying about the amount of time she had spent with Dean. It was of no relevance to him now, but his instincts told him their relationship went further than she had made out.

Dean had made his way out of the tall bushes and crouched inside an empty oil drum about fifty yards from where PC Beckles was parked and waiting for Cpls Alvin and PC Narine to emerge with the canine team.

Dean was sweating profusely, his heart pounding on the walls of his chest. The voices were too close. Making any movement now would prove detrimental. He reviewed the details of the weapons he had glimpsed and turned over the information in his head. He had not seen police carrying Sub Machine Guns before. The entire police party was armed with SMGs. It crossed his mind that they came prepared for close combat gunfire. He knew that engaging in gunfire with the police at this stage was a, no win situation for him. Instead, he was happy to conceal himself and bide his time.

From his camouflaged hideout, he could see a tall tree ahead of him with heavy branches and thick foliage. The tree would give him ideal cover since the dogs had all gone quiet. He evaluated his move and made for the tree.

Corporal Alvin and PC Narine left the house and proceeded with their instructions. Corporal Alvin pressed the transmitting button on the radio and spoke into the device, "Sir we have just learnt that this guy we are after is an ex-Army Officer. He has trained in England with the SAS at the Sandhusrt Military Academy, Mosad in Israel and with the US military service."

"Copy that Corporal," Marlon responded. The radio fell silent again, then crackled, "Be on your guard Corporal."

Marlon released his finger from the button and cursed loudly. His hands slumped to his side allowing the SMG to hang loosely from his shoulder. This is getting more and more complicated by the minute he thought to himself. He squeezed his forehead between his thumb and middle finger and looked at the officer next to him.

"Is that bad sir?"

"It complicates matters to an extent, yes! He is in his element in this terrain and I am sure he has headed into those hills."

Franticly, Marlon started to pat his pockets dropping the radio in the process. He produced a photograph of a young man. There were several question marks drawn on the back of the photo and one on the face of the photo. "Corporal, I think this is our man."

The Corporal studied the photo shinning his torch onto the picture and shrugged his shoulders. An indication that translated to mean, he had no idea who the person in the photograph was.

Marlon walked over to the car. PC Beckles sat behind the wheel, drumming with his index fingers.

"Beckles do you know where that basketball player from Arima lives, the one we saw on Election day?"

"No sir, no idea but I am guessing its somewhere near Railway Terrace."

Without another word, Superintendent Dudley radioed Arima Police and requested that two detectives be sent to ascertain the whereabouts of Dean Watkins. To his advantage, the desk Sergeant knew the address that was required, making the exercise even easier.

Marlon stressed he should be notified as soon as information became available. He warned the Sergeant that the suspect was armed and dangerous. Officers attending should exercise caution.

The rest of the Squad had all converged at the rendezvous point. Marlon gathered them for a reassessment of the situation. He briefed everyone on the developments that emerged over the last half an hour. "I am certain that our man, given his military capabilities have taken to the hills."

"I want to disagree with that sir," Corporal Alvin remarked.

"Any specific reason for arriving at this conclusion Corporal?"

Corporal Alvin searched his pockets and produced a small note pad. He sketched a rough layout of the area and pin-pointed locations that they had exhausted, "Given the width of that drain sir," he said pointing in the direction of the canal, "It is impossible for him to jump that distance, giving the heavy overgrowth. Had he walked through we would have spotted the wet trail."

"What are getting at and, what do you propose then?"

Having worked on many operations with Corporal Alvin, Marlon was confident to let him offer his views and implement a plan if he had one.

Corporal Alvin was about to speak when the radio interrupted. Marlon listened attentively to the message from the investigating detectives. Their search at Dean's address had proved futile. His parents had not seen him for over a week and, they professed it was not unusual for him to be away for long periods.

Marlon pressed the transmitting button and requested that the officers go back to the address and get some detailed information on the dates when he was away for long periods and, check it against the dates when there was a prevalence of robberies anywhere on the island.

"My proposal is that we concentrate on this area south east of here," Corporal Alvin continued. "I think he will attempt to conceal himself in the urban environment rather than confine himself in a negative environment where he is opened to the elements and without proper facilities to protect and defend himself."

"This is good thinking, well done. You can have my job." Marlon congratulated.

Corporal Alvin's finger traced along the map on the notebook as he spoke, "I think that Mr Watkins wants to give us the impression that he has taken to the hills, given his military background. What we must consider here, he's adept in any environment and, I believe he's opting for the urban one."

Marlon nodded in approval and cleared his throat, "Listen up guys, Corporal Alvin will brief us on the next stages of this operation. He has a theory and we should give it some consideration."

"Thank you, sir," Corporal Alvin said as he began to outline a new strategy.

"We are going to concentrate on a thorough sweep of this area here. He indicated with his finger. "We would have had the advantage of three vehicles. Two officers can proceed on foot, joining us later. The two police cars can circle these areas." Cpl Alvin, Marlon got into the car with PC Beckles, both went off in separate directions leading towards the main road.

The Superintendent lifted his hand as the officers readied themselves. "Please everyone! Vigilance is the key word here, this man is armed, he is dangerous and, he has demonstrated, he has all intent on killing."

The dogs became agitated again after being given the scent from Dean Watkins socks, found by Corporal Alvin and PC Narine, during their sweep. Marlon sent out a renewed request for plainclothes officers to keep watch at the Arima address. He did not believe Watkins would make such a crucial error and return to his parents' address. However, he wanted to cover all options at this time.

A progress report from the Northern team confirmed success with three arrests and the seizure of number of weapons and ammunition. A large quantity of cash and several Rastafarian wigs were also confiscated. Further searches were continuing at the premises and the surrounding areas. One suspect had escaped during the raid. The Corporal heading the assault confirmed that he did not envisage a lengthy process in capturing the suspect. It was noted too that none of the suspects arrested were Rastafarians. One of the arrested felons was identified as an ex-army private.

Marlon congratulated them for their work and relayed that they were not so victorious with their leg of the operation. He expressed delight that there were no casualties on their part, as his team had suffered. There had been no reports of the wounded officer's condition since he was taken to hospital. Marlon knew it would be sometime before any formal notification was released about the patient.

The series of events that transpired had intrigued Marlon. In his first major assignment of his promotion, the operation was not as straight forward as he had anticipated. The implication of the Dr Gaspard's daughter in connection or affiliation with this gang would attract substantial media attention. How would Dr Gaspard react to these allegations with his daughter? Dr Gaspard was an influential figure in politics. His intervention could create stagnation in any investigation through corrupt individuals at all levels including high ranking police officers and political figures in government. Marlon was weary that he now had to tread carefully and to ensure that all protocols were adhered to in strict accordance.

Spears of sunlight found their way through the morning clouds, chasing the darkness away slowly, as the night retired allowing daylight to grow. The roadways became tangled with pedestrians and motor vehicles as the grind of the morning traffic increased steadily.

The howl of the dogs gave Marlon cause for concern. They seem to have picked up a scent, but this was soon short lived with a brief radio transmission.

Marlon instructed the dog handlers to discontinue their search. He calculated that the risk of the dogs and the increase of civilians on the streets contributed a danger to the public and he did not wish to entertain the possibility of any public casualties. This would jeopardise an already fragile operation, which had resulted in one casualty and a probable ticking time bomb, in the form of Dr Gaspard.

The radio came to life, Marlon responded, "Go ahead mobile."

"Sir we are heading back your way, we've drawn a blank on our end."

"Copy that."

Corporal Alvin radioed for an updated status to the search and verification of everyone's position. He gave his concerns about the influx of civilians on the streets, highlighting the concerns that Marlon himself had already voiced. Marlon challenged his mind on the options available to him knowing fully the consequences that would befall him should the operation end in a failure and, worst yet, if there were to be any civilian casualties at the hands of the police. Already, he had one wounded officer who had been shot.

Marlon knew there had been a positive result with the

Northern phase of the operation upon which he could be build. Should they draw a blank on his end, he could use the success of the Northern leg to dispel any negativity, should it arise. The weight of responsibility began to bear down heavily on his shoulders. He looked eastwards and saw the golden hues of dawn fast disappearing, leaving a bright blue sky.

This was not good for the operation. Daylight, while it had its advantages, also presented increased civilian dangers. Vehicular traffic could prove detrimental should an exchange of gunfire ensue. Marlon was now confident that they were pursuing one man and the prospects of capturing him had renewed optimism.

Reflecting on his promotion, he wondered why he was chosen for the position of Superintendent. There were several senior officers that outranked him and, would have fulfilled the post with far more experience than he had. These officers were also far more deserving of the post than. What worried him was that many of them now came directly under his command. He was aware, however, of the new Acting Commissioner's faith in him. He had worked under his leadership at St Joseph police station many years ago before being promoted to detective.

He could not allow the distraction of his promotion to overhaul his strategy and displace his thoughts from the task at hand. Marlon tried desperately to drag his mind away from the jaundiced dilemma that overwhelmed him. Failure was not an option that he was prepared to entertain. Accepting his promotion, he vowed to deal with to the current criminal statistics tarnishing the country and to bring about some manner of equilibrium. Adding to his burden, Marlon knew there was Elsa and the baby. He had planned to propose to her after she had the baby. A senior police officer living a separate life from his child would not reflect well in the eyes of the public. He was certain the media would have a field day with such a story. Marlon's mind juggled with all these thoughts, yet he knew the present operation needed him to be fully focussed. He needed to keep his thoughts from meandering and focus on the task at hand.

The squad cars pulled alongside each other, Corporal Alvin alighted and was joined by Marlon. Corporal Alvin drew an imaginary line with his finger, indicating the areas on the sketch that they had exhausted. "I can only speculate; our man has made his way back to the main road and has more than likely eluded us on this occasion."

Marlon's eyes followed the corporal's finger as it snaked across the hand drawn map. For a moment he was inclined to agree with the Corporal. The other officers had already exhausted their trail and were on standby waiting for further instructions.

"Okay!" Marlon sighed, "dispatch the canines back to station and let us head back and debrief on this disaster."

PC Beckles brought the car alongside the soft verge to allow an approaching lorry to get through the narrow road. The lorry driver, peered into the car with some suspicion and on observing the weapons, proceeded with some caution. PC Beckles stuck his head out the window and shouted, "Police!"

The lorry driver sighed and yelled from his cab, "Well yuh better check ah man down de road, ah gunman just hijack he car."

PC Beckles quickly swung the car onto the tarmac employing the blue lights and siren. The rear wheels of the car kicked up loose dirt from the verge as it sped off in the direction given by the lorry driver.

A radio communiqué was sent to the other cars as they sped off, the siren piercing the relatively quiet morning. The car braked suddenly to avoid an Indian gentleman waving franticly in the middle of the road. Marlon and Cpl Alvin jumped out of their cars before they came to a standstill and accosted the frantic man. After getting a detailed description of the vehicle and the assailant, the officers sped off in the direction of the main road with a screaming siren.

PC Beckles relayed the updated information to the other officers, directing them, on Marlon's instructions to implement a roadblock near Curepe intersection.

Having reached the main road, Marlon knew that the driver could not have gotten far, given the estimated time the car was hijacked. Judging from the traffic congestion on the roads, his optimism was heightened.

Marlon relayed a radio message to the rest of the crew advising caution. "Let's leave all heroics for the movies. We are on the lookout for a green, I say again, green Cortina with a missing wing mirror on the left. This man has already proven his intentions with a firearm, a powerful weapon by the description, so be on guard."

Corporal Alvin and Marlon alighted from the car leaving PC Beckles and the other car to patrol the back streets that ran parallel to the main road. Corporal Alvin went along the main road heading West while Marlon headed East. Corporal Alvin voiced his apprehension about going in separate direction. Marlon agreed with the Corporal, but it was the only way to cover both carriageways.

The traffic dragged along at snail's pace, filling the

morning air with petrol fumes. Marlon coughed, inhaling the foul smell. He could almost taste the petrol at the back of his throat. He jogged along the pavement scanning every green vehicle he saw in the distance ahead. He tapped his pocket, checking for his radio, only to realise that he had left it in the car. Passersby and other drivers stared in awe at the heavily armed officers, franticly scanning vehicles as they hunted for their suspect.

In the distance, Marlon spotted a green Cortina. He took a huge gulp of foul air and saliva after he identified the Cortina with a missing wing mirror. He threw a fleeting glance to see if Corporal Alvin was anywhere in sight, but he was not. Intense fear gripped him, his stomach tightened, sweat began pouring down his face as his anxiety increased. His mouth filled with a metallic taste. "Is this what fear taste like?" he thought, looking to the heavens.

Nearing the vehicle, Marlon reached in his pocket and drew his service revolver. Proceeding cautiously, he used the other cars as cover to get closer to the Cortina. Suddenly, the Cortina swerved onto the slow, oncoming traffic, ramming the front end of the car into the oncoming vehicle, shattering the headlamps of both cars and scattering shards of glass on the tarmac. Marlon's strides became urgent as he gathered momentum. Nearing the car, he took aim at the tyre and prepared to squeeze the trigger. The car reversed, smashing into the car behind, knocking Marlon off his balance. He fell to the ground, losing the revolver as he hit the hard road surface, and suffering minor bruising. The green Cortina sped forward then braked to a halt. The driver got out, assumed a crouched position and fired two shots. The first shot missed Marlon, the second caught him on the leg and he fell over.

Pedestrians screamed and dropped to the ground, hiding behind parked cars, rubbish bins and lamp posts. Drivers in their vehicles cowered in their seats. Other bystanders watched the drama as it unfolded. Dean, without any urgency, looked about at the traffic on the main road, stuck the pistol into his waist and calmly got into the car and drove off.

Two hundred yards ahead, Marlon could see a clear path that would take Dean onto the highway where he could make an easy getaway. Marlon had no radio to alert the other officers to request backup and install roadblocks on the highway.

Corporal Alvin, alert on hearing the shots turned on his heels, heading into the direction of the gun fire. He barked into his radio calling for urgent support to be dispatched, giving clear details as he ran towards Marlon clutching his SMG.

Marlon patted his leg franticly, inspecting his hand to find no blood. The bullet had ricocheted off an ammunition magazine in his pocket and lodged into a nearby lamp post. He jumped to his feet, retrieved his revolver and raced towards the Cortina heading in the direction of the oncoming traffic. Drivers swerved to avoid smashing into the car, the Cortina rammed others out of the way. Dean could see a clear the path ahead of him, he knew it would take him to the highway. People were screaming, shouting and pointing at the wrecked vehicles and the action that was unfolding before them. In the distance, Marlon could hear the varying wail of the police siren. Keeping his sight trained on the Cortina, he heard the siren fading away. He cursed loudly, knowing that his backup was heading in the wrong direction.

The Cortina mounted the pavement to gain access to the clear road ahead but was soon blocked by a delivery van. Dean quickly reversed and negotiated his way back onto the road. On the approach, about ten metres from the car, Marlon sprayed the back of the vehicle with a squeeze of the trigger on his SMG. The car danced awkwardly and spun on the road smashing into oncoming traffic. Dean regained control, stuck his hand out of the window and fired two more shots at Marlon, who took refuge behind a parked car, the bullets shattering the windscreens. In his head he calculated six shots fired. He concluded too that this was a professionally trained person. He did not fire indiscriminately, wasting ammunition. Marlon deduced he must have just one magazine.

Marlon's heart pounded inside his chest. Blood oozed from his wound, sustained when he fell earlier. He could hear the wail of the siren once more, fear gripped him, his saliva thickened in his mouth as he gained on the car. Dean was unaware that Marlon had gained significant ground and he tried to pull the car away. Marlon was quick, he stuck his hand through the window and grabbed the steering wheel, trying to veer the car to the kerb.

In quick reflex, Dean wound up the window, trapping Marlon's arm, dragging him along the road. His SMG dangling about his body as the car sped along. Marlon kept his grip on the wheel as his legs crashed against the broadside of the car before hitting the road. Pain rushed through his body. He tried to prevent his legs from getting lodged under the car as it swerved along the road. He could feel his arm being wrenched off, but he kept his grip on the wheel. His body crashed into a metal bin on the side of the road as the car swept from side to side.

Corporal Alvin kept his pace. He was shouting down the radio for backup once more. Corporal Alvin could see the Superintendent hanging from the car. He barked into the walkie talkie again, shouting for urgent mobile backup. PC Beckles heard the urgency of the transmission. He was too far away for any form of rapid response. Corporal Alvin was unable to take aim at the tyres for fear of hitting the Superintendent. The car zig-zagged dangerously about the road and as Marlon's body crashed against the car, each impact registered a new level of pain. He kept his grip on the steering wheel. He felt faint and his body could not produce enough adrenalin to fight off the pain. Marlon could feel the energy being drained from his body and knew it would only be a matter of time before he fell into unconsciousness. As blood oozed and sweat poured from his body, flashes of Elsa holding their baby raced through his mind. He was beginning to go limp, the car stopped suddenly. Dean smashed his fist into Marlon's arm, causing him to let go of the steering wheel. He wound down the window and Marlon fell to the ground. He tried desperately to get to his feet. Dean flung open the door with a powerful force knocking Marlon back to the ground.

Dean, in no hurry, got out of the car and levelled a boot into Marlon's side. The pain was excruciating, Marlon curled into himself to prevent another blow into his middle, gripping the SMG close to him. Dean saw Corporal Alvin advancing and hurried to the other side of the car to retrieve his pistol. He took aim at the officer and fired a single shot. There was a rapid crack of gunfire and the smell of spent ammunition filled the air. A few feet away from the car, a body slumped to the ground.

Marlon looked up. The trees on the roadside stood like

giants over him, their branches like angel wings, spreading out to shade him from the morning sun. He tried to move but his legs stayed where they were, his fingers twitched and only his eyelids moved. He could see several faces looking down at him. He recognised Corporal Alvin, standing over him with two SMG's slung over his shoulder. His left arm felt numb, he could hear a multitude of voices around him but was unable to or recognise any words or conversation. Beyond the faces, he could see blue skies and he could see the reflection of blue flashing lights in the Corporal's pupils. The voices and the sounds around him were fading, he could see the Corporal Alvin lips forming the words, move back, move back. Marlon's eyelids became heavy, he could not hear the voices anymore, his world fell into darkness.

CHAPTER
13TEEN

Fitzroy rotated himself clockwise then, anti-clockwise in front of the full-length mirror, repeating the manoeuvre again. The pencil grey, pinstriped suit hugged his lean body cutting a dashing, handsome figure. His hair was neatly groomed. He adjusted his tie, looked at it in the mirror and asked, 'Merve, how do I look?"
"Like a man going to give his life away." Mervin laughed.
"Be serious man." Fitzroy said sharply.

Mervin laughed aloud, patting him on the back, "Boss you look great. That suit was made for you. You look like James Bond." Fitzroy squeezed Mervin's hand and thanked him for being his best man. Mervin was the only person apart from Petra that he really knew in San Fernando. They worked the same shifts on the offshore rig. Mervin would often invite Fitzroy back to his home on a weekend to have lunch with his family. He knew Fitzroy was a stranger to San Fernando and in some small way, Mervin sympathised with his loneliness.
"What you mean thanks for being your best man? I'm the only person you know stretching form Point-a-Pierre to San Fernando...well apart from Petra of course. How she fall for you boy, yuh wuk obeah?"

Mervin's wife, Juliette, would tease and encourage Fitzroy, saying he should find a nice South girl and settle down. Fitzroy protested he was not the marrying type. "I am maintaining a bachelor life for as long as humanly possible." Juliette would laugh in his face. "You wait, de right woman eh hook you yet and pelt ah good waist on you."

Mervin's home was always full of laughter, with a great sense of family. Fitzroy looked on at the way Mervin showered his son and daughter with equal affection. He took time to read with them both – something Fitzroy never had with his father growing up.

Although his dad had been a good provider, he was never one to overtly show his affection.

Fitzroy did not experience this emotion and so, never missed it. Seeing Mervin and his interaction with his children, he wished that Mr Draper had been more like Mervin. Mervin was good in the home too, he would prepare meals and helped Juliette in the kitchen. She would say to Fitzroy what a good husband he was and praise him among her friends.

After Sunday lunch Mervin and Fitzroy would sip cold beers on the verandah overlooking the majestic San Fernando hill in the foreground. The setting sun cast a beautiful hue on the terrain, a sight he only saw in photographs. Juliette left them alone conversing about books, cinema, oil production, politics and West Indies cricket. Mervin looked up at the lush green hills pointing to the summit. "Fitz, you think if Africa had a cricket team, we would support them rather than the West Indies?"

"Boy yuh ketch me with that one yes."

"I mean we does get vex when the Indians support Pakistan and India when they are playing, I think we might have been the same if it was Africa."

Fitzroy contemplated on Mervin's theory, "You stumped me with that one boss. We should do a survey and see what people think."

"Nah!" Mervin said, "I think people would say no, primarily because there was never an African cricket team and we can't count South Africa."

Fitzroy's palms were moist with sweat. He was nervous, the thought of spending the rest of his life with Petra thrilled him and an aura of happiness rippled through him. Juliette walked into the room carrying a freshly made rosette. She had plucked the rosebud and ferns from her garden and carefully bound it together with silk ribbons and thread. Reaching over to Fitzroy, she fixed the boutonnière unto his blazer, smiled and patted his shoulder. "There you are Mr handsome." She whispered, placing a kiss gently on his cheek.

"Petra will make a good man out of you." She teased.

Juliette was different to most women Fitzroy had known. She was an open, flirtatious yet firm, honest and serious human being. Mervin on the other hand, displayed pure vagabond tendencies which Juliette never complained about. She never seemed to mind when he was loud and obnoxious. Mervin had spent many years in the army, mostly training recruits in the latter stages of his army career. He retired after the attempted coup and mutiny in the 1970 Black Power uprising. When a director from one of the oil companies offered Mervin the position of chief engineer, he did not think twice about accepting the position.

The work meant he was closer to home, but it came with a price. It also meant he was away for long periods when offshore. Juliette was thrilled that they could spend more time together as a family when he was on shore leave.

Despite only knowing Mervin and his family for a short period, Fitzroy felt at ease with them. He trusted their judgement and heeded their advice, whenever he sought it from them. Juliette was the sister he never had, level-headed and the most caring person he could hope to know. He could not compare her to Elsa and would never entertain the thought of doing so.

"De jacket eh too tight?" Fitzroy grumbled, inspecting himself again in the mirror. Mervin sucked his teeth loudly and threw a glance at Juliette.

"You eh fine he behavin' like ah little 'omam?"

Juliette laughed, she took Fitzroy's hand in hers and squeezed it gently. He felt comforted, by her kind, warm and calming aura. He felt protected, like a frightened child safe in its mother's embrace.

"Stop babying him," Mervin said to Juliette as she gave him a hug.

Juliette cast a crude look at Mervin and yelled, "Shut up and go get dressed, otherwise we will be late. You know how you take five hours to dress. You worst than some women."

Mervin and Juliette left the room leaving Fitzroy standing in front the mirror. He put his nose to the rosette. It was perfumed. He inhaled and savoured the scent of Juliette's perfume. Juliette had sprayed it with a generous squirt of her most treasured Estée Lauder perfume. Fitzroy smiled and carefully took off his blazer putting it on a sturdy, wooden hanger. He sat at the edge of the bed allowing his thoughts to drift to Ma Draper. In his mind, he toiled with his decision not to inform her about his marriage and why he failed to invite her to the wedding. Whether he was searching the depths of his mind for self-assurance about his decision, he knew one thing for certain, it was too late to rectify the choice he had made.

Rubbing his hands together he let out a low and prolonged sigh. His mind raced, he knew it was not the time or place to be weighed down with such matters. He could not think of a single valid reason why he had not invited Ma Draper or Elsa to the wedding. What played on his mind too, Mervin and Juliette never questioned why? There was no time now for regrets and whatever his rationale, it could not be reversed.

The morning sun greeted the green hills in the distance with a warm golden kiss. The rush of traffic heading into San Fernando became a crawl. The day was maturing into a perfect one for getting married. Fitzroy thought of something Rookmin had said many years ago. "When you eat from pot, it will rain on your wedding day." In his head, he was revisiting the many times he had eaten from the pot. His thoughts were now on Petra, he wondered if she too was nervous and like him, fretting about how she looked in her dress.

Fitzroy tried to picture Petra in her splendour, her soft brown alert eyes, her dress clinging to the curves of her slender body. He imagined she would wear her hair down to accentuate her beautiful shoulders and neck features. She never wore her hair down except when at home. Her brown hair complimented her eyes. The first time Fitzroy had seen her tresses in flow, he was in awe at how long and thick her hair really was.

Suddenly, he realised that he did not know what colour dress she was going to wear. They had both discussed colours, but she never agreed on one. It wasn't intended as a surprise, just Petra's idea of adding a little twist of excitement to the day.

Her dress was ivory and tea length, with a sweetheart neckline made from satin, lace and silk with miniature rose appliqué across the bodice and one sleeve. Along the hem that dropped below her knees were beautifully snowdrop embroidery. A cascade of rose appliqués designs embellished the front and formed a twirl around the length of the dress. Her hair held back with a jewelled tiara was flowing down to her shoulders. She gazed at herself in the mirror and held back a tear. "What's the matter?" Bertha, her cousin asked.

"I just wished Mum and Dad could have been here today."

Bertha hugged Petra and gently daubed at the teardrop with a cotton pad, taking care not to smudge Petra's makeup. "Your Mum and Dad would have been very proud of you today."

"Do you think I am doing the right thing Bee?"

Bertha gave Petra a cynical look, held her shoulders firmly, "Doh be silly girl, this man come from wherever he come from, walked in...and found you."

"He's from Arima, actually," Petra said, with a smile.

"In a couple of hours all your fears will be conquered by happiness," Bertha comforted.

Juliette, Mervin and Fitzroy arrived at the small church, a stone structure tucked away in a back street, away from the bustle of the busy San Fernando commercial roads. The church yard was filled with yellow and white roses and a solitary fir tree that looked as old as the church itself. A stone footpath led to the front door where they were met by the Pastor, a small adorable man with a greying beard and fixed grin. He ushered them inside. Fitzroy greeted the owners of the Chinese restaurant with a friendly handshake and bowed. He sat beside them, adjusted himself on the bench. The Chinese man touched him on the arm and said, "No Fizzy, you sit up font, you de saclifice." Fitzroy smile and followed the instructions.

Several candles illuminated the small church giving a distinctive aroma of burnt wax. A huge bouquet of red and white hibiscus, white roses and ferns adorned the front of the altar. Along the church pews, white roses wrapped with long stems of ferns were pinned to the pews.

Mervin patted Fitzroy on the back. He wore a big smile on his face and said, "This is it pardner, the last free minutes of your life. The door is open, yuh could still make a dash for freedom. Head back Arima and live bachelor ever after." Both men laughed. Mervin patted him again and said, "You are a lucky man Fitz, Petra is a super lady, I feel sorry for her."
Juliette smacked Mervin playfully on the arm with her purse and whispered. "Stop making fun of the boy."
"Don't mind him," Fitzroy said. "I know he's trying to get a reaction from me." They all laughed and waited for Petra's arrival. Fitzroy was overwhelmed with excitement, pleasure and by the desire of holding Petra and having her transform his life entirely. He patted his sweaty hands on his trousers and picked at his cuticles nervously, looking round every time the church door creaked open.

The ceremony was short and to the point. After a short prayer, the Pastor read a verse from the bible before asking the couple to recite their vows. Fitzroy was so nervous he fumbled in saying his vows. Petra had looked him in the eye and holding his hands with confidence, she made her vows.

The pastor made a sign of the crucifix with his hand before pronouncing them man and wife. He shook their hands and wished them all the best for the future. Petra squeezed Fitzroy's hand and kissed his lips gently. Her lips tasted different today. He imagined, this was their first kiss, and was lost in her eyes. They embraced each other warmly. She mopped a teardrop from the corner of her eye without anyone noticing. Her heart was filled with happiness and imagined that Fitzroy's was too.

At the end of the church service, everyone went back to the Chinese restaurant for the reception. Bertha planted a firm kiss on Fitzroy's lips and said, "You are a lucky man, yuh better treat her good yuh know?" Fitzroy smiled, nodding to agree with Bertha. He knocked his glass with his ring finger to get everyone's attention before announcing. "Listen people, I have an announcement to make."

"O God! Don't tell us yuh make the 'oman pregnant ahreeady," Mervin shouted.

"Nah, nothing like that," Fitzroy smiled. "The company wants to send me to Scotland to pursue some studies in Petroleum science and engineering at a university in Edinburgh. Petra and I talked about it and we decided to take up the offer."

"Well, well you kept that quiet bro," Mervin said, sounding pleased.

"I wanted to tell you last week but thought I would leave it for today."

"So, when you off then?" Mervin prompted.

"We were planning to take a honeymoon to Tobago before this, but decided to take our honeymoon in Scotland instead, in a fortnight."

Everyone cheered and offered their congratulations to Fitzroy and Petra. Shaking hands, kissing on cheeks and sharing a toast.

Mervin grabbed Fitzroy's hand, shook it vigorously and congratulated him. "You deserve it man, I am glad that the company sees it fit to invest in local people rather than bring in foreigners to do these jobs."

"Shut up Mervin, yuh sounding like a politician now," Fitzroy joked.

They both toasted each other knocking bottles of beer together. Mervin nudged Fitzroy and smiled mischievously. "Aye! Yuh sure yuh eh bribe dat woman to marry yuh?"

"Shut yuh ass man. I doh know how Juliette put up with you nah?"

Mervin chuckled and took a long drink from the bottle of beer gesturing towards Juliette. "Yuh see dat woman dey? She is ah godsend to me."

CHAPTER
14TEEN

Ma Draper rose at her usual time and brewed her coffee. She sat on the verandah and enjoyed the aroma of the freshly ground Hong Wing. Studying her surroundings, rocking in her chair. Soon, she got the chair into a half rhythm before finding a suitable hymn.

This morning, her thoughts grew heavy and the air was foul. Try as she may, she could not find a flowing rhythm with the chair, she struggled with keeping time with her morning hymn, from the hymnbook in her mind. She looked to the sky and said. "Lord Jeezez, I know something's not right. I pray for your guiding strength to deal with it, whatever it is." She sipped slowly from her cup, savouring the taste of the fresh coffee.

Next door the dog appeared to be in playful mood. Ma Draper could hear Sita, her strong tail knocking against the wooden kennel. Despite the animal's excitement there was an eerie stillness to the morning; it made Ma Draper shiver.

Ma Draper looked up at the mango tree with all its fruits hanging like Christmas bulbs at the end of its branches, green, red and yellow, some purplish in colour. A gentle breeze disturbed the tree rustling the leaves for a short spell, before everything was seemingly still again. Sita too, had settled into her kennel, snoozing in her favourite posture.

Elsa had risen early and gone to her job at the hotel. Ma Draper had not heard her leave in the early hours of the morning. She pushed the rocking chair back and forth with her body, still searching to find a rhythm, her cup, now empty. She allowed the chair to come to a natural halt and placed the cup on the floor. Putting her head back, she drifted into a slumber.

The sun had risen in all its warm splendour, rejuvenating the day when Ma Draper opened her eyes again. Things seem more like the detail she was accustomed to on a Saturday morning. There was a half-smile on her face; she massaged her knee, pounding it with a folded fist saying to herself, "It going to rain today oui."

Without any sense of urgency, she dragged herself out of the chair and proceeded to the kitchen. She prepared a breakfast of coconut bread along with fried salt fish and tomatoes. She sat at the dining table feeling solemn and lonely eating her meal.

After breakfast, Ma Draper readied herself for market and deposited herself on the rocking chair awaiting Sooklal's appearance.

The act of him coming to reap all the mangoes was something she felt compelled to sit back and watch. She had come around to accepting Fitzroy's decision to sell the mangoes. Reluctantly, she too, felt it was the right thing to do. The task of putting out the ripe mangoes at the front gate had started to irritate her. What irritated her most was that people never took the mangoes. For all of the mango season, she performed this daily routine that became ornamental. At one point, she sat on the rocking chair toying with the idea of telling Sooklal that she had changed her mind about the sale of the mangoes. As her thoughts raced, a mango crashed on the roof and hit the ground with its usual thud. Ma Draper sucked her teeth and whispered, "Come on Sooklal, time goin' man."

Sooklal had a thriving business selling Doubles. He had two pitches in Arima and another in Sangre Grande. It was a family business. He and his son sold in Arima and his wife and son-in-law managed the Sangre Grande outlet. He used the green mangoes to make chutney and kuchela condiments to accompany his Doubles. He travelled through the countryside during the mango season buying up as many mangoes as he possible could to make his products. It was far more economical for him to purchase mangoes directly from people, rather than at the market where it was far more costly.

How Fitzroy came to know Sooklal, remained a mystery to Ma Draper and she did not waste time hankering over the notion. She sat on the rocking chair, finally finding her rhythm and a suitable hymn to pass the time as she waited.

Sooklal sauntered into the yard nonchalantly, carrying three large hessian bags under his arm and a long, well-honed cutlass wrapped in newspaper and tied with a piece of string. He greeted Ma Draper politely and handed her some notes rolled up and held together with a rubber band. Ma Draper clutched the wad of notes in her moist hand. Sooklal looked at her without moving and said, "Yuh eh countin' it, lady?"

Ma Draper looked at he notes and at Sooklal, "You count it? She said eventually,

"Yeah! I count it, it all dere."

"Well! Ma Draper said, "No need for me to count it again, eh?"

Sooklal looked up at the mango tree and said softly, "Is up to you lady."

Ma Draper eased herself down the steps with her market basket in hand. She watched the small Indian man as he measured the mango tree with his eyes.

He paid no attention to her as he looked about the tree

with a certain level of curiosity.

"I going to de market now," Ma Draper said to him, "If yuh finish before I come back leave ah few nice ones for me to make some chow."

Sooklal did not say much. He looked at her with scant courtesy and said, "Okay Miss lady." Saluting her, he continued to survey the laden mango tree. Sooklal had never cast his eyes on a mango tree with such an abundance of fruit. Every branch was brimming with mangoes, the ground, littered and stained with the juices of the fallen fruits. He watched Ma Draper as she walked out the gate, her basket swinging on her arm. Sooklal pondered his next move - he could not climb.

"This Mauby missing something today gyul." Ma Draper commented.

"You know you is not de only one to say dat dis morning."

"Den it mus be true den?" Draper laughed.

It was the first time that she had ever left Mauby in her glass. Miss Duncan watched the glass with some scorn, as if insulted by Ma Draper leaving the drink unfinished. She held a rigid stance as Ma Draper kissed her cheeks. Ma Draper sensed the uneasiness and said instinctively, "I going to have another glass on my way home today." Miss Duncan seemed relieved to hear this and a perky expression returned to her face.

A lean lanky East Indian man in a khaki uniform greeted Ma Draper, "Aye Agnes how yuh going gyul, yuh buying out de market or what?"

Ma Draper grinned, replying, "Yes boy, how yuh wife and dem chirren?"

"Well I suppose yuh eh hear! De 'oman leave me about three weeks ago. She shack-up with 'Gouti mouth."

Ma Draper feigned innocence. She had heard the news in

179

market gossip from Radio Trinidad but pretended not to know. "Boy is so life is sometimes yes! Yuh jus' have to carry on with de help and grace ah God."

He shook his head in agreement, "De children still at home. The youngest one just started secondary school and de boy doing engineering down at John D." He gave Ma Draper's hand a little squeeze before disappearing into a small office at the corner of the market. Her eyes followed him into the office until he was out of sight.

She continued her Saturday ritual, stopping to converse with people she only ever saw on market day. There was no urgency in Ma Draper's market routine. She browsed and conversed as she normally would on any given Saturday.

Sooklal searched around the yard and found a ladder that extended just halfway up the tree. He leaned it against the tree and climbed to the top rung, stretching his hand to measure how high he could reach. He un-wrapped the long cutlass from the newspaper and started to chop at the branches. The sharp cutlass and his rapid strokes brought the branches crashing to the ground with most of the mangoes still on their stems.

It wasn't long before the tree stood naked, except for a lone branch that escaped the reach of Sooklal's cutlass. Sooklal began to fill the hessian bags with the green mangoes that were now accessible. He then chopped the bare branches as he went along and piled them up against the trunk of the tree. The verandah was now basking in new light, created by the absence of the thick foliage that usually kept the sun out in the afternoons.

Next door, Sita barked furiously. Sooklal carried on with his task, paying no heed to the bitch on the other side of the fence. He filled the three hessian bags with green mangoes leaving all others scattered about the yard. While doing so, he noticed the abundance of *shadon beni* in the yard and helped himself, ripping a couple handfuls of the plants out of the ground.

The neighbour shouted at the dog, "Sita shut yuh ass and sit down."

The dog fell quiet. Hendry looked over the fence and said to Sooklal, "So de ole girl finally cut down the tree eh?"

Sooklal laughed and said, "Nah man! I jus' buy de mango buh I cyar climb so ah had to cut de branches and dem to get de mango."

Hendry shook his head and looked at the mess Sooklal had made in the yard, destroying some of the floral vegetation as well in the process. Sooklal seemed unconcerned of the damage he had done and, more importantly, the destruction of the mango tree.

He hoisted one of the hessian bags onto his shoulders to take to his small van. He was stopped in his tracks when Dhanraj came over and asked, "Who gave yuh permission to cut down that mango tree?"

Sooklal measured Dhanraj with a cynical stare and proceeded to hoist the bag to his shoulders again. Dhanraj grabbed him, "Mister man you eh going nowhere 'till the ole 'oman come back, yuh hear meh?"

Sooklal laughed in his face saying, "So who going to stop meh, I pay the lady ahreadly for de mango sar."

Dhanraj whipped out the revolver from his pocket, "If you leave this yard before Draper come back, I go shoot yuh in yuh foot." Sooklal's feet started to tremble when he saw the gun. He quickly sat down on the steps mopping sweat from his forehead. His knees trembling as he kept rubbing his hands on his khaki trousers.

Hendry surveyed the damage done to Ma Draper's

plants and the way Sooklal had butchered the mango tree. He shouted across to Dhanraj, "De man chop down de woman mango tree because he cyar climb. Yuh ever hear arseness so in yuh born life?"

The neighbour looked up the lone branch left on the tree, sucked in his lips and shook his head slowly in disgust. He stared at Sooklal in disbelief and asked, "So pardners, why yuh left dat one branch?"

Sooklal in arrogance and fear, eyed Dhanraj with the gun in hand and pointed with the cutlass, "Yuh see any mango on dat branch?"

Dhanraj laughed a slow laugh of sarcasm, "Boy you is ah real joker yes! Shoot him Danny." Sooklal was less nervous now that Dhanraj wasn't pointing the gun at him. He challenged Dhanraj, "Look mister, I paid for dese mangoes an' I going to load meh van, you shoot if yuh want."

Sooklal barely had time to make two steps when Dhanraj lifted his revolver to the sky and fired one shot. "I am telling you now, the next one, won't go into the air." Sooklal scrambled for his cutlass, Dhanraj aimed the gun at Sooklal, "Let's see if yuh cutlass faster than ah bullet?"

Hendry, knowing Dhanraj's temperament, raced from his house over to Ma Draper's yard to placate Dhanraj. He lowered Dhanraj's hand and eased the pistol out of it.

A small crowd had gathered on the road looking on at the commotion taking place. The melee had attracted the attention of a policeman on foot patrol. He walked into the yard enquiring what was happening. Hendry handed Dhanraj his revolver, he holstered the weapon before securing it into his pocket.

"So, gentlemen, what's going on here, everything alright Mr Dhanraj?" The officer enquired with a friendly greeting to both men.

"This scamp here butchered de woman mango tree because he cyar climb and refusing to wait till she come back from the market."

"Officer dis madman threatened to shoot meh," ranted Sooklal.

"I doubt that very much sir, Mr Dhanraj here is a top marksman. If he intended to shoot you, you would not be standing here speaking to me."

The officer suggested that Dhanraj go back to his shop. He nodded at Hendry who walked off casually. The policeman took out a small black notebook and asked, "What's your name mister?"

Sooklal dropped his arms to his side and said, Ramjit Sooklal."

The policeman looked up at him after noting Sooklal's name in his book. "Mr Sooklal, you would have to remain here until Mrs Draper returns from the market, just to get some clarification on what transpired here today. Your address please."

Ma Draper was weary from her market run today. So much so, she failed to keep her promise to return for a second helping of Mauby from Miss Duncan. She had not even bothered to go to the poultry depot to purchase her broilers. Her basket was not as full as it was normally, yet she found it extremely heavier than normal.

There wasn't anyone she could depend on today to assist her with the basket. Elsa was working and it had been weeks since she saw any signs of Watkins. He often came around offering his assistance, knowing that Fitzroy wasn't around. Her feet carried her slowly along. She stopped at a Syrian store, admiring the display in the window. One mannequin was adorned with the new basketball kit. Ma Draper assumed that it was the store that sponsored the basketball team. She admired the kit shaking her head in silent approval. A young Syrian man came out of the store and greeted her, "Morning Miss Draper," He said politely.

"Morning son how yuh fadder?"

"He okay thanks." The young man responded kindly, admiring the window display before returning inside the store.

Ma Draper wearily picked up her basket and waited at the lowered pavement for a break in the traffic to cross the road. A taxi braked and waved Ma Draper to cross the street. She thanked him in a whisper and hurried along as fast as her tired legs would allow her.

She dragged one foot after the other transferring the basket from one hand to the other and rested intermittently. In her mind, she questioned herself as to why she felt so exhausted. She was not overtly tired, for she had retired early and slept soundly that night, waking once, to have a glass of iced water.

The short East Indian roti vendor saw Ma Draper struggling and came to relieve her of the basket. She led Ma Draper to a small wooden bench near her stall and motioned for her to sit down. Ma Draper welcomed the rest, gladly taking the weight off her feet. The roti vendor opened an Apple J soft drink and stuck a straw into the neck of the bottle before handing it to Ma Draper. "Here neighb' sip this slowly. Yuh drink it to fast and de gas does bubble up in yuh nose."

She thanked the roti vendor, stuck her index finger under her head tie and gave her head a vigorous itch whilst sipping on her Apple J.

"Yuh look very weary today neighbour." The roti vendor said rolling a roti as she spoke. She picked up the dough from the board without losing its shape, placing it on the hot tawa for a patient customer.

"Gyul, ah feel tired too bad! I eh know what wrong wid meh today."

The vendor oiled the roti with a home-made apparatus, made with strips of cloth attached to a long wooden stick. She flipped the roti and repeated the oiling process. Ma Draper watched her attentively as she lifted the cooked roti onto a sheet of brown paper. She scooped a spoonful of curried chicken and added a spoonful of potato, then drizzled it with pepper sauce and kuchela. Carefully, she folded the roti into a neat bun, then wrapped it in the paper before placing it into a small brown paper bag for the customer.

"Chile dat sweet drink was nice. Ah think ah needed dat and de rest too."

"Well yuh know what they say? Nothing to quench yuh thirst like ah Apple J."

"And nothing to wash down ah roti like ah red solo," Ma Draper echoed.

The two ladies laughed openly and chatted while serving her customers, keeping a lively banter going.

"So, when Fitzy coming back den?" the vendor pried.

"He not gone away yuh know! He got a job working for one ah dem oil company down South."

"Well I always thought de boy gone abroad, de way he used to talk about ships and ting."

Ma Draper explained to the roti vendor that Fitzroy had abandoned the idea of working on the ships after someone told him that the oil fields were paying good money. She gave the roti vendor details of how much money Fitzroy was working for every month and, how well he's doing.

"Is true yuh know neighb, I have ah cousin wuking off-shore and he wife say he making good, good money; two, three times ah year she going New York oui." Ma Draper had stopped listening to the vendor, she thought only of how nice it would be to have Fitzroy here this morning to help her with her basket. She had always expected one day, Fitzroy would leave home, and she had dreaded the arrival of that day. The thought brought a tinge of sadness to her heart. She sat watching her friend turn out roti after roti with controlled rhythm.

Ma Draper looked across the road at the corner where the nuts vendor would normally park his bike and ply his trade. It was a popular evening spot where Fitzroy and other young men came out in the evening to hang out and discuss politics, sports and global topics and, smoke the occasional joint.

Looking back, this day had similar peculiarities to that day when Fitzroy left. A light breeze gently caressed the trees and the sun did not seem as fierce as it normally was at that time. She remembered also feeling just as tired. High above, cirrocumulus clouds covered the sky. Ma Draper studied the intricate patterns and formations as she remembered Fitzroy's fascination with the sky.

Fitzroy's absence from home made the house a lonely place. She missed the animation that characterised the place when Fitzroy was around. There was always some meeting taking place in Fitzroy's room, or All Fours card games on the verandah into the early hours of the morning or drinking of beers on a Saturday evening after a basketball game, especially if they had been victorious.

Ma Draper knew that she had to come to terms with the fact that Fitzroy was unfulfilled and needed new and exciting challenges to occupy him. When he had nothing to do, it made him miserable. He would often sleep so his day didn't drift by, aimlessly. He was not one who craved applause nor was he fanatic about being first. In fact, he would always let one of the other players collect the prizes when they won at basketball tournaments and tennis ball cricket, even though he was the captain. Ma Draper knew, deep in her heart, the real motive for Fitzroy's moving out. Arima was not big enough to fulfil his insatiable appetite for progress. The town did not provide the motivation or the infrastructure to feed Fitzroy's quest for success.

Ma Draper had disliked it when Fitzroy would go down to the docks every day, hoping to find work on a ship. There was relief each evening when she saw him returned, dejected. She could see the look of frustration on his face, though he never discussed it with her. She felt guilty too, never showing an interest in something he wanted, something that was important to him. Ma Draper felt that not even Mr Draper would have been able to deter Fitzroy from his ambitions. Fitzroy loved adventure, he saw working on the high seas as the ultimate adventure and a way to see the wider world. It was ironic that he found employment on an oil rig.

Ma Draper's eyes followed the movements of the roti maker as she conducted her roti making and continued her conversations with ease, both with the customers and Ma Draper. The place was alive with Saturday morning shoppers and vendors plying their wares on the roadside. People shuffled by, dodging pedestrians and peddlers for pavement space. Drivers were weary of those stepping onto the road to avoid the crowded pavements. A small group of young kids, probably no more than fifteen, stopped to look at the mannequin adorned with the basketball kit. They pointed their fingers at the shop window and made comments before moving on along the busy pavement.

Ma Draper rubbed her knees slowly and rose to her feet. "Ahhh! That feels so much better. Vashti, thanks for the drink gyul yuh save meh life today," she said thankfully to the roti vendor.

The roti vendor who was serving a customer at the time, wiped her forehead with the back of her hand and said to Ma Draper, "Lady yuh doh have to t'ank meh fuh dat. We all on mudder earth to help each other. Jus' remember me in yuh prayers is all I ask."

They both laughed. Ma Draper bid her farewell picking up her basket, she continued her way home.

Across the road, the Chinese take away shop was teeming as usual. Down the street, she could see the commotion with all the vehicles jostling for parking spaces to go into Dhanraj wholesale store. The area looked brighter than it did normally. She looked to the sky to check the sun's position. Bringing her head back down she noticed that she could she her house clearly. Something that was not usually possible, because the mango branches had always obscured the view. She was puzzled but could not figure out what had happened. Her eyes followed the clear view of the house and her tired feet carried her more quickly than it had done all morning.

Nearing her home, she could see the lone mango branch on the butchered tree; she felt her knees wobble. Nonetheless, she reached her gate, where the magnitude of what had taken place dawned on her.

Sooklal sat on the steps without remorse, staring at Ma Draper as she crawled into the yard. The Policemen came towards her and aided her with the basket, carefully placing it on the landing. Ma Draper's lips trembled, unable to utter a word since entering the yard. Dhanraj, seeing her return, could not leave the store to come over to her. He watched her with a tinge of sadness. Ma Draper mopped her forehead with a small handkerchief from her bag. Finally, words formed on her lips, "What in the name of Jezess happened here?"

"Mrs Draper, did you sell the mango from your tree to this gentleman?" the young officer asked, with an official tone.

"No, not exactly, is meh son, he sell the mango a couple weeks now. But why yuh cut down the tree for mister?" she protested, in a soft, gentle voice.

Sooklal stood from his sitting position and defended his actions. "Miss lady, I cyar climb de tree, how else yuh want me to get the mango I paid for? De only way was to cut the branches."

"I could arrest him for malicious damages to your property but that's about it Mrs Draper. You admitted that you sold the mangoes so there's no case there to answer for. However, considerable damage has been done to your property. And that's another matter that can be substantiated."

Ma Draper held her head, she surveyed the damage to the tree and to her roses, lime, anthuriums and her Zebapique vine. The lone branch left on the tree amused her. She lifted her hand in gesture asking Sooklal, "So wha yuh left dat branch...no don't tell meh! dat branch eh have no mango?"

The policeman shook his head and smiled at her remark. He stepped over the strewn branches on the ground. He stood next to Sooklal and looked at Ma Draper, anticipating her decision on Sooklal's fate.

Ma Draper brushed a tear from her eye and said to Sook-lal, "Dis is like ah blessing in disguise yuh know!" Sook-lal and the policeman looked at each other puzzled. "Dis mango tree is as old as this house, Lord Jezess bless us dis day."

Her face was sullen as she recalled Mr Draper's words when he transferred the tree from the centre of the land to its present location in order to facilitate the construction of the house. Mr Draper, in all his stubbornness and ignorance, did not heed advice to get rid of the tree. He protested it was a starch mango tree and kept it.

Mr Draper never lived to see that it wasn't a starch mango tree. No one had any doubt that it would have amused him a great deal to marvel at the abundance of fruit the tree produced. It would have pleased him too, to see the array of wildlife it attracted, providing food and shelter to many creatures, from far and, wide. People commented to Ma Draper that some of the birds came from as far as Venezuela to roost, feed and nest in the shelter of the tree.

The policeman gave Ma Draper a fleeting glance, await-ing her instructions on how to proceed with the mat-ter. She seemed unhindered by the destruction of the mango tree, only occupied by what it represented, the symbolism of its existence. It was not the mangoes that bothered her and entertaining the thought of holding Sooklal in any contempt was far from her mind.

Briefly, she felt as if the pages of her life had been ripped apart and scattered before her. She could see herself and Mr Draper posing for the portrait that hung in her bed-room, the young mango tree behind them. She remem-bered his passing too, not with sadness but with jovial fondness for his life and his visions. The silence his death brought to the house, the loss of laughter, the emptiness it created in her life. Now the fate of the mango tree seemed to bring closure to that chapter. All that had transpired during the day had come to have meaning; the tiredness, the sapping of her strength, the lack of taste in her mouth suddenly made complete sense to her. They were all omens of a disastrous day. She smiled, looked to the heavens, her lips moved in prayer. She lifted her up her hands and whispered, "Jezess, I give it up to you."

"Renwick," Ma Draper addressed the policeman by name, "Once the mister clean up all these branches from the yard let him go about his business. But he needs to clear it all up."

The policeman nodded and looked at Sooklal with a puzzled frown, "Well you heard what the lady said, what are your intentions regarding the request?"
Sooklal nodded in agreement to comply. He even offered to give Ma Draper some money for the destruction of the tree. She shook her head inching her way up the stairs, surveying the disaster. Looking at Sooklal she said, "What is done, is done. Nothing happens without a reason." She retired inside, resting her basket on the table. The officer noted Sooklal's address and allowed him to carry on with his task.

CHAPTER
15TEEN

There was jubilation on the streets as celebrations swept across the Borough. People of all ages were joyous; the news of the newly elected mayor thrilled the entire town. In rum shops, street corners, market stalls, office buildings and even Ma Draper's house, excitement prevailed about Mackie's victory. Ma Draper smiled and stuck her finger under her head tie saying to Elsa, "Ah see you boy clean dem up girl."

The two national newspapers carried the news of the victory on their front pages. The Prime Minister, though reluctant, congratulated Mackie on his victory as an independent candidate who had gained, not just trust, but the respect of the electorate in the Borough. "It should act as a lesson, we in the government can learn from, and seek to redeem the party with the electorate in the general elections." He confided to one of his aides. He treated the victory with caution and vowed to reform his own party in order to regain the confidence of the people.

Mackie smiled at the handwritten note from the Prime Minister, folded it along its original crease and placed it on a stack with other congratulatory notes that had poured in. He made a mental note to send a thank you telegram to Fitzroy.

Moreover, on the night of his win, Mackie hailed it not as a victory for him, but as a victory for the people of Arima. In his speech, he said, "The people of Arima have spoken and they have chosen me to carry out a mandate on their behalf. I shall do so, without fear or favour and without prejudice." He promised there would be no lavish celebrations or the wasting of public funds. He stressed that it was his will to implement thorough investigations into allegations that councillors had been using the services and funds of the Borough to facilitate their private wellbeing and profiteering. If found that they were engaged in such activities, they would undoubtedly face prosecution.

He reminded people that the running of the mayor's office would become transparent, giving the public the opportunity to see how and where public funds were being used and distributed. He stated this in his manifesto and promised under his leadership, that no area of the borough would remain neglected. However, certain areas and issues would take priority over others. A natural form of process, he called it. This promise given by Mackie had helped to persuade the people living in certain districts to vote for him.

Many areas under the previous mayoral leadership had seen total neglect for many years, leaving residents and businesses in those areas reluctant to support the previous administration. Maintenance of roadways and refuse collection along with drainage had been the bane of many complaints to the previous administration. Complaints that were continually falling on deaf ears became the downfall of the former regime.

Mackie was aware of the difficulties ahead of him. He needed to implement new and sweeping changes in an environment that, for as long as he could remember, had been plagued with allegations of corruption and the misuse of public money. The cooperation of current staff and other councillors would be crucial to having a transparent administration. It was the only way forward to successfully implement policies that, in the long term, would eradicate the overt and widespread corruption that allegedly existed in the borough.

Fitzroy's foresight for Arima and ideas by which the Borough would grow through development, truly amazed Mackie. For someone whose ambition had been to work on ships, his intelligence surely, was of better use elsewhere, rather than being wasted floating on the ocean. Some of these ideas frightened Mackie yet, his trust in the intellectual capacity of Fitzroy, knew no bounds. The documents that he produced gave details for every aspect of development. Ways in which to save and more importantly, ways in which to generate funds to meet the shortfall in government allocated funding for local government. Fitzroy had even gone to the lengths to summarise the progress of Mackie's term as mayor, giving recommendations on how a successive term in office could be achieved. It had baffled Mackie, that Fitzroy chose to distance himself from politics. Fitzroy could make a tremendous offering to public service. His genius would have made a major difference should he have extended his services to the country or, as Mackie had always advised, to join a large cooperation where his ideas could make a difference to the wider society.

Mackie looked around the scant office. It surprised him how quickly the offices had been cleared by the outgoing administration. He had expected that any evidence of inappropriate activity within the council would have been disposed of, or cleverly hidden. What really astonished him was the speed at which the transition occurred. He smiled to himself, rubbing his hands together.

With legs crossed, and arms folded, Mackie sat on the edge of the desk and surveyed the office. He reached into his pocket and produced a small black moleskin notebook. The new Mayor made notes of all the work that needed to be done on the office.

Behind him, the corporation flag and the national flag hung from the wall on polished wooden flagpoles. On another wall, a large outdated map of the borough hung with stickers obscuring some areas of the map. He studied the map mentally, picking out areas he knew had undergone development and the construction of new roads were in progress. He examined a huge architectural drawing proposing a new housing scheme for the cooperation. He realised that the drawing was outdated, as the proposed housing area had already been built some years ago. Mackie studied the huge map on the wall tracing it with his eyes. It was the first time he had seen a map of this scale of the borough.

The task of setting in motion, the rebranding of the Borough as an integral Eastern hub, was upon him now. The engines of progress and the challenges of implementing change was the next big step. Despite knowing that there would be elements of opposition to change, he had every confidence in achieving the goal set before him.
The local business sector though apprehensive, had shown confidence in Mackie and pledged to invest on the projects that he outlined.

Mackie was mindful he could be up against rigid opposition with some of the policies that he intended to push through to councillors. They were not unrealistic measures, however, in the process of reaching these milestones; there would need to be a collective agreement, and, in some cases, he would have to rely on the local businesses and importantly the backing of the other party councillors.

Long-term gain for the local business community promised to be fruitful and, he was convinced that along with the new administration he would be able to woo businesses, especially as they would be the ones reaping the benefits of progress.

Elsa cradled her huge tummy, gently caressing it as she strolled slowly towards the gate, taking in the sight that greeted her. She was at a loss as to what had happened to the mango tree. Normally, at this time of day, Ma Draper would be rocking on her chair fanning herself with a copy *Watchtower* magazine. Today she was nowhere to be seen. She was still trying to grasp what had happened to the tree.

Sooklal was so busy chopping the branches into smaller, manageable pieces so they would fit in his van, he did not notice the presence of Elsa. She looked on in disbelief at the destroyed rose bushes, the squashed jump-up-and-kiss-me flowerbeds and the lime tree split in two down the middle, presumably by a falling branch. Her heart sank when she noticed a huge branch on top of the anturium patch. They had only just sent out their vivid red plastic looking textured flowers. As she stared at the void left by Sooklal's savagery, an anger brewed inside her, but she dared not speak or allow it to consume her. A tear formed at the corner of her eye and trickled down her cheek. She moved cautiously over the chopped branches, inching her way to the steps.

She walked past Sooklal without uttering a word; in turn, Sooklal said nothing, he just gazed at her, lifting his eyes as she went by.

Ma Draper emerged at the door holding a glass and a bottle of iced water. She called out to Sooklal who hurried to the step to collect the bottle of water and the glass from Ma Draper.

She looked at Elsa and said, "Don't ask let me sit down and I will give you the full low down." She fanned herself vigorously with the religious publication and groaned as she massaged her knee with the other hand. Elsa settled in another chair beside her and prepared her ears for the details of the saga that unfolded earlier.

Sooklal busied himself in the yard. Before long, he had cleared all the branches and loaded his small van with as much as he could. He promised Ma Draper to return on Monday to clear the remaining rubble and thanked her for her kind gesture. Ma Draper smiled warmly with him and said, "Don't worry, sometimes these things is a blessing in disguise."

Elsa nudged Ma Draper and gave her a furious look. "Why did you let him off so lightly? Look at all the blasted damage he caused. Mash up all the flowers and lime tree and ting."

"Chile, not to worry 'bout dat, is not you self who say I should sell the mango? Well, all this happen for a good I say, look at all this new light it brought into the house."

Ma Draper smiled, "Look! From here, I could see out de road clear as day now. And the leaves and dem won't rot the galvanize. No more mango to clean up and all dat damn chow making finish yuh hear."

Elsa could not tell whether Ma Draper was serious or being cynical. She decided, in the interest of averting an argument she would remain neutral. Ma Draper rocked and hummed to the rhythm of the chair. Elsa watched her in silence, seething inside.

Maybe she is right, Elsa thought to herself. Maybe this is a blessing in disguise as she presumed. She welcomed the new light that flooded the house. For the first time in many, many years, they had the view of the main road from the comfort of the verandah.

Looking at Ma Draper attentively, Elsa noticed a renewed glow in her, something that had been missing since Fitzroy left. A refreshing light emanated from Ma Draper's face. It was a look of content and happiness. The look puzzled Elsa as she watched the old lady rock to and fro on her rocking chair humming in a low tone.

CHAPTER
16TEEN

Elsa groaned and waved her hand at Ma Draper, "Quick, get somebody I think ah going to have the baby."

Ma Draper stood up briskly from her rocking chair and yelled over the fence, "Hendry, Hendry."

"You calling Agnes? Hendry answered from behind the iron fence.

"Yes boy," is Elsie, "she having the baby, go ask Dhanraj to call ah ambulance nah."

"Yuh have to be joking, ambulance go take ten hours to come, I go take she in the car," Hendry said calmly, "get she tings ready."

Ma Draper was about to ask Elsa what she needed. Elsa whispered to her between groans that everything was in a bag on her bed. She hurried along and brought the bag out to Elsa. Hendry skipped through the front gate and supported Elsa down the stairs, Ma Draper following with the bag.

Hendry pointed to the back seat saying, "Ah put a blanket on the seat just in case she waters break and wet up meh car."

"Thank you neigb, you is ah Godsend boy." Ma Draper said politely, putting the bag on the front passenger seat.

Dhanraj observing the commotion, raced to the car to enquire if everything was okay with Elsa. He stroked Elsa's forehead and wished her well as watched the car sped off to merge with traffic on the main road.

Ma Draper in her preoccupation had not given much thought about the living arrangements for Elsa and the baby. It was accepted that Elsa now lived with Ma Draper. However, nothing was ever discussed about what would transpire when the baby was born. Elsa never spoke about the matter and she always gave the impression that she and Marlon were eager to raise their baby together. From this, Ma Draper assumed that they probably had intentions of getting a place together.

The thought of Marlon and Elsa moving in together with the baby brought a smile to her face, as she scratched her head vigorously, shuffling her feet about the house aimlessly. Her mind drifted as she toyed with many ideas, clinging to the thought that Elsa would eventually remain with her.

She felt awkward that such an important matter had slipped her. It was then that she realised too, there was no way of her contacting Marlon to alert him of the current development. Ma Draper comforted herself with the notion that Elsa would ask one of the nurses to contact him. Still, her trepidation lingered as she found odd things to tinker with around the house.

After a while Ma Draper resorted to her rocking chair, from here she mulled over the gender of the baby. A smile came over her face and she was overjoyed with the prospect of becoming a grandmother. She rocked the chair into a familiar rhythm. Everything around her was calm and serene. A moment of happiness had nestled, and she exuded an exuberant glow.

Fitzroy held up the newspaper and showed Petra the headline. "You see that? That is my best friend, the Mayor of Arima"

Petra looked amused by Fitzroy's statement. For all the time they had been together he had never spoken about anything but oil exploration, petroleum products and cricket. On the odd occasion they would discuss a movie they had been to see together or talk about ships they saw sailing on the ocean when they walked together down at the seafront.

Learning, his best friend was now the Mayor of Arima came as a shock to Petra. He had never let it slip, even when there had been negative allegations in the tabloids during the election campaign.

"Is there something you're not telling me here mister man?" She snapped at him.

"What! do you think there is something to tell? He's my friend, my best friend, my brother."

"And there is nothing more to it than that?"

"Well not exactly."

Petra's face was full of exasperation. He had never seen that side of her mood before and, her reaction was least expected, "Did you leave Arima with some bad experiences behind you?"

Fitzroy was able to laugh now, he felt comfortable, "No not at all. As a matter of fact, I haven't got bad experiences anywhere, least of all in Arima."

Without divulging every detail of his involvement with the election manifesto, Fitzroy enlightened Petra of his contribution with Mackie and their friendship. Petra initially, looked a bit apprehensive with Fitzroy's explanation but felt that he had no reason to lie to her.

She listened attentively, folding her clothes and continued with the packing of her suitcase. Looking up at him, she said, "You taking these old shorts with you?"

"But of course, dat is meh favourite shorts. I even wear them to bed."

"Not next to me," she smiled.

Fitzroy laughed loudly, "You wait, when we reach Scotland, you would want me wearing more than dem shorts. It cold no ass up there you know."

"I don't know if I could handle cold weather nah. If it too cold I am leaving yuh ass and come back home yes." There was a jovial exchange of glances.

"Well look at it this way," said Fitzroy. "we are going to have a honeymoon lasting two years, all paid for."

Petra tossed an item of clothing at him playfully and continued packing. She sniggered, "Smart ass."

Fitzroy folded the paper and laid it gently on the floor. Petra sifted through the clothes that she was taking with her and those she was going to give to her cousin. Fitzroy didn't seem at all concerned about packing. In fact, there was not much for him to pack. He owned a minimal amount of clothing and wore mostly coveralls while at work so there was never any need for him to splash out on clothing. Most of his clothes consisted of jeans and T shirts and now he owned a suit. He looked up at her, neatly folding every item of clothing, even the pieces she was giving away. "I will take my suit though." He said to her.

He tried to explain to Petra that she should not take lots of stuff with her given the fact that she would need new clothes to suit the climate when they got there. Petra protested, "You think I leaving all my good clothes behind? You must be crazy."

Petra waved a wad of US notes at Fitzroy. "Here boy *dunseye*."

"You do know is pounds they use over dey?"

"I know that, the Chai's gave me this when they heard that we were going away, $300 US boy, going to change it in the bank tomorrow." She said with a huge grin on her face. She zipped the suitcase shut and shoved it under the bed, scraped back her hair into a ponytail and pinned it with a tortoise-shell ring comb.

Fitzroy sat perusing through the paper, cutting out articles using a razor blade. Petra watched him as he concentrated meticulously on the task before looking up at her when she spoke. "You remember we are going by Merve and Juliette this evening?"

His confused frown told Petra he had forgotten. Fitzroy was laughing to himself as he carefully guided the razor blade around the edges of a picture of Mackie.

"What are you grinning for?" She asked curiously.

"Nah, nothing. Ah just realised that you are packing and ting and I eh ask yuh if yuh have ah passport."

Petra threw the hairbrush at him. "You only farce, I've been to America twice you know, you never even been Tobago."

"True! But I'm more widely travelled than you."

"How you work that out magician?"

"Well I've been to Port of Spain, Grande, Toco, Oropouche, Manzanilla, Maraval, Santa Cruz, Lopinot, Point-a-Peirre, San Fernando, Matelot, Diego Martin, San Rafael...yuh want meh to go on?"

Petra was amused, she laughed until tear came to her eyes. She loved his dry humour and poker face when he was being humorous. He had always been able to make her laugh even when she was at her lowest or seething with anger.

He remembered the first time making her laugh loudly at the restaurant. She wore an opened back top exposing her smooth silky skin and clearly, no bra. When she returned with his order, he calmly asked. "Were you in prison?"

She gasped and gave him a stern look and screamed. "No!

why you ask?"

"Nah I just noticed yuh back outside."

Petra fell into a fit of laughter. She had to rush to the kitchen where she had a drink of water to settle herself before she could go back onto the restaurant floor. As soon as she emerged and saw Fiztroy, her laughing fit erupted once more. The Chinese woman at the counter uttered something in Cantonese and joined in the laughter with Petra.

"Are you going to read every single word in that newspaper then?" Petra shouted at him.

"Oh gosh no ah coming just now, gimme five minutes."

Fitzroy discarded the newspaper, neatly folding the clippings before securing them into his notebook. He flicked through the book briefly, observing that his last entry was on the day before he married Petra. To some extent, he had written, in minute detail what he had done that day. He had left nothing out and nothing was abbreviated. In his mind, he tried to question himself why he would have done that. Seeing the note, he wrote in bold letters, it became apparent. Rubbing his finger along the line, he read to himself what he had written. "Tomorrow will be the start of the rest of my life."

"Aye man yuh coming or what? The papers not going to run away you know." Petra yelled with some level of impatience.

"Okay, okay ah coming," He replied, securing the notebook with the elastic band placing it under the cushion of the chair.

Fitzroy smiled at her as she stood next to the dining table staring at him. "What?" he said looking confused, "Yuh never see nice man yet?"

"No, that is why I was looking to see if ah see one."

He held her hand and kissed her neck tenderly saying, "Come on Mrs Impatient Draper lets go."

Elsa bit her bottom lip as the porter wheeled her into the maternity ward. Every turn of the wheel from the chair, she could feel a new wave of contraction. The porter, unusually polite asked if she wanted him to stop. Elsa not wanting to appear troublesome waved him on with her hand. Her bed was situated to the very end of the ward; next to her was a young Indian girl. She appeared to be no more than sixteen, cradling a newborn baby to her bosom. She had a soft smile that welcomed Elsa. She spoke with the same gentleness as her smile offered. "He doh want to take de breast at all, no matter how ah try."

Elsa eased herself onto the bed with the aid of the porter, gripping the sheets as her contractions became more frequent. In between breaths she asked. "Is dis yuh first child?"

The girl smiled and brushed her long jet-black hair back with her free hand and replied, "No, dis is de second one, de odder one is year and a half. What about you?"

"Ahhhh," Elsa groaned. "Dis is my first, somebody shoulda warned meh."

Between groans and contractions, Elsa and the young Indian girl shared moments of laughter about the antics of some of the patients in the ward, before their babies were born.

Signalling with her head, indicating to another Indian woman at the far end of the ward, she said, "Gyul, dat one, she put dong ah set ah bawling here last night, cussing and carrying orn wid de nurses. Today she quiet like a lamb."

A stout, strong nurse came over to Elsa's bed and attached a band on her wrist with her name and ward. She monitored her pulse and blood pressure then her temperature; the nurse smiled with Elsa then moved on to the next patient.

"Yuh see dat nurse? One ah de best in here, Colette is she name. De rest ah dem like dragon, dey treat yuh as if is ah favour dey doing yuh." The Indian girl lamented.

Elsa cradled her tummy and laughed, they both laughed together as the Indian girl expressed delight, "Oh gosh! look de little bugger taking the breast now yes. Is yuh presence, he like yuh voice." She said smiling with Elsa, encouraging the baby to drink from the reservoir of her breast.

Pausing mid-sentence in conversation, Elsa would grip the crisp sheet as she dealt with each contraction and resuming where she had left off. A trait she must have inevitably picked up from Ma Draper.

A young midwife, probably no older than Elsa came over and chatted with her, explaining the hospital procedures to her. She pointed to a ward on the other side, saying it was the delivery suite where she would be transferred to later. After an examination, the midwife informed her that she would have a short labour. 'You are coping well with the pain though.' The midwife commended.

Elsa chuckled with the midwife saying, "Is only shame that keeping me from bawling down de place oui." She groaned at the end of her sentence, massaging the small of her back with one hand, breathing slowly as the labour pains attacked.

Lying on the bed, she looked around and saw other patients being visited by friends, family and husbands. She yearned to have Marlon at her side, or Ma Draper or Fitzroy. She did not particularly care at this point, just someone to be there with her. For the first time in her memory she felt lonely and abandoned. The sight of the nurses scared her, she wished Colette would attend to her. The smell of medicine made her nauseous and dizzy.

The Indian girl observing her said, "Aye gyul yuh better call de nurse yes." Without waiting for a response from Elsa she yelled, "Nurse! Nurse."

Colette hurried over to the bed to see Elsa looking a bit pale. She monitored her symptoms and gave Elsa a drink of water. Soon her radiance was restored, and she appeared relaxed. After another examination, it was announced that she was almost fully dilated; preparations were afoot to transfer her to the delivery suite.

Elsa snatched a couple breaths as she experienced another wave of contraction. She looked at the midwife and joked. "Dey eh call dis labour for nothing nah, is blasted hard work yes." No sooner had she settled in on the birthing bed there was a gush of water and the amiotic fluid soaked the bedding. The midwife sighed with relief and said, "Well yuh waters break, I think you will have an easy birth."

Silently, Elsa was troubled with the fear of having to undergo a caesarean or the prospect of having an episiotomy if the baby was too big. She felt a wave of relief when assured that she would have a natural birth. The midwife said to her, "Everything will be okay." Elsa clasped the midwife's hand groaning, trying to push at the same time, with encouragement from the birthing team. "Come on, big push, breathe...big push, breathe."

Slowly her eyes opened, Elsa could see Colette standing beside her with a little bundle, her face beaming with a beautiful smile. Colette lowered her hands and placed the baby into Elsa's arms. "Here you go Mrs Nurse, what you going to call her?"

Elsa caressed her gently and kissed her little nose and eyes, she lifted her little hands and kissed her fingers too. Her eyes met with Colette's, she said softly, "Agnes Nubia Nurse- Dudley. Hello Agnes." She said as she caressed her nose with her little finger.

The Indian girl came over and peered into the soft blanket. "Oh my, she's a gorgeous baby eh, ah princess, she's so beautiful."

Colette waltzed over with a huge bouquet and a mischievous smile, "Young lady, you have flowers here from the Mayor of Arima. He's not de fadder, is he?"

Elsa grinned and assured Colette that Mackie was not the father. "Her father is Marlon Dudley."

A worried expression formed on Colette's face, she rushed back to the reception desk. Both Elsa and the Indian girl gave each other a bemused look and continued fussing over Agnes, examining her little toes, fingers and her silky strands of hair. "Like she fadder is Indian? she hair straight, straight."

Elsa laughed, "Is not Indian alone that have straight hair yuh know."

Colette returned a few moments later wit a copy of the *Evening News* in her hand. She gave it to Elsa and said, "I presumed you didn't know."

She looked at the headline and clasped her mouth with one hand, preventing herself from screaming. Tears dropped on the paper, soaking the newsprint. The headline read, ***Newly appointed Supt wounded in gun battle.*** Colette comforted her and assured her that he was okay and resting comfortably in Port of Spain general hospital. She promised Elsa to contact the hospital and convey the good news of Agnes to the Superintendent. Elsa thanked Colette, cradling Agnes close to her chest and allowed herself to cry quietly.

Ma Draper crept slowly along the wooden floor of the hospital ward, stopping at the front desk to ask for Elsa's ward. Colette smiled with her amicably saying. "You daughter and little granddaughter are both doing well, last bed down on the right." Colette signalled with the wave of her hand.

She carried with her a bag packed with essentials she knew Elsa would need and a bowl of chicken pelau that was still warm. In another bowl she had cucumber and watercress salad with slices of tomatoes.

Elsa did not wait for Ma Draper to get o her bed, as soon as their eyes met each other she dragged her weary legs to meet her, Agnes in arms.

"My, my, she so cute; look at dem beautiful brown eyes eh. Just like yuh mudder." Ma Draper cried with delight.

Elsa handed her the baby and took the bag from Ma Draper. The bag was hefty, Elsa rummaged through to find that Ma Draper's intuition was almost spot on. She yearned for some pelau and coleslaw. She was equally delighted with the cucumber and watercress salad, picking up strands of watercress with her finger putting it into her mouth and chewing slowly.

Ma Draper and the Indian girl conversed, exchanging childbirth stories as Elsa tucked into to the bowl of pelau.

"Dat is ah beautiful bunch ah flowers, Marlon send yuh dat?"

Swallowing a mouthful of rice, she replied, "No Ma, dat is from Mackie. Marlon was wounded in a police shootout this morning, he in town hospital the nurse over there trying to contact him now to give him the news."

"Oh gosh child I really hear about the shooting on de 12 'O' clock news but dey didn't give details." Ma Draper rocked the baby in her arms as she looked at Elsa with a worried gaze, giving the baby her little finger to suck on.

"Mum dat is the nicest pelau I've had in a long, long time. Thanks ah million."

Elsa ate heartily, savouring every mouthful of the soft rice, pigeon peas and tender chicken, cooked just the way she liked.

Ma Draper waited until Elsa was finished then tenderly handed baby Agnes over to her. The baby was fast asleep, Elsa settled her into a tiny cot next to the bed. "She weighed 7lbs 7ozs and twenty inches long you know." Elsa said without looking up at Ma Draper, tucking a small blanket over baby Agnes.

The ward was busy with families and friends visiting new and expectant mothers. Most visitors had brought home cooked food for the patients they were visiting. The aroma of the various foods somehow overpowered the medicinal reek in the ward.

Colette stood up and shouted at the top of her voice, "Listen people! Could you keep your voices down dis is not ah fish market."

A deafening silence gripped the room for a few seconds before the cackle of human voices began to filter through the ward again in a more subdued tone.

Ma Draper gathered Elsa's soiled clothing, folded them neatly, before stuffing them into the bag. Elsa wanted to stop her she knew there was no point of getting into an argument with Ma Draper now. Also, there was no one available to come and look after her, she allowed Ma Draper to proceed with her motherly manoeuvres and to fuss as much as she felt necessary.

The ward was quieter now. Visiting time was over, most of the visitors had vacated, leaving exhausted mothers to rest and look after their babies. Most of the babies were now fast asleep except for the Indian girl next to Elsa. Her baby was still up, latched on to her breast and was happily feeding cradled in his mother's arms.

Elsa saw the *Evening News* at the foot of the bed and reached for it with long slender arms. There was an obscured head shot photograph of Superintendent Dudley in his police uniform alongside the bold typed headline. She started to read the article and suddenly went pale. She attempted to get out of the bed and collapsed onto the floor, unconscious.

"NURSE!" The Indian girl screamed, waking, almost everyone on the ward.

Colette and a colleague rushed to the bedside and hoisted Elsa back on the bed quickly administering a whiff of salts of ammonia near her nostrils. Elsa twitched and groaned, slowly opening her eyes. Colette fanned her with the newspaper as she regained consciousness.

"She was reading the papers good, good den next ting ah know she jus' collapsed." The Indian girl related to Colette. "Her husband wounded in a shootout with bandits this morning," Colette whispered as she continued to fan Elsa. "I don't want to see him again," Elsa mumbled. "I never ever want to see him again."

Colette cradled her and comforted her, "Yuh upset child, he will be okay you know, is just the shock now hitting yuh."

Elsa looked at Colette shaking her head from side to side. "You don't understand, he killed my best friend. The father of my child killed my best friend thinking he's ah bank robber." She grabbed Colette and screamed into her shoulder, sobbing and shouting No, No, no why Watkins?

Fitzroy stared at the newspaper held together with clothes pegs on a piece of string tied to a disused gateway. He dipped his hand into his pocket, fiddled for some coins and exchanged them for a copy of the newspaper from the vendor.

His hands trembled as he held the newspaper and looked at the picture on the front page. Fitzroy could not bring himself to believe the picture he was looking at on the front page of the newspaper, with a headline that read: **Trinidad's Most Wanted Man Shot Dead by Police**. "There must be some mistake, this can't be true..." He whispered to himself. "Watkins? There must be some mistake." Reading through the article, the reality of what he was reading became tremendously difficult to digest. He needed to sit down. Walking a short distance, he found a low wall along the narrow street and sat on. His legs numb, his chest ached, and a bitter taste rushed to his mouth. Tears welled up inside him and trickled down his face. Fitzroy felt he was bleeding inside as the numbness gripped and paralysed him for moment.

All his life he had known Watkins and even before he left Arima, he thought he had come to know him even better. If the latest events are true, then Watkins had concealed his criminality with great success. He never splashed about any excessive cash at any given time and, he showed no outer signs that he was involved in any illegal activities.

There were times, Fitzroy remembered, when he had to lend Watkins money to pay his team membership. Comprehending the scale of the situation was beyond Fitzroy. How can Watkins be a part of this fiasco he thought, it can't be true. He crumpled the paper into a ball and smashed it on the pavement. The ball of paper rolled a couple feet in front of him. He stared at it and waited, like a master patiently waiting for his dog.

Flashbacks occurred in his mind as he stood glued to the spot, his eyes never leaving the crumpled paper. He questioned his memory, searching for answers. He looked back at the times when Watkins was absent from a game or failed to turn up for practice. His memory was acute, and he recalled that no robberies ever took place during the late evenings when a game was on or even during practice sessions. He knew that Watkins was involved with several socialite girls, one of them a prominent politician's daughter. Who she was Fitzroy had no idea. Watkins was careful never to divulge details of any of his girlfriends with his basketball team. He was a closed person and hardly ever talked about his experiences in the army either. He was an excellent sportsman and a good team player. No one knew much about him apart from that.

Watkins had joined the army straight out of secondary school. Army life had changed him, but not his love for basketball and neither did he forget his friends. But no one knew about his personal life; he remained an enigma.

Fitzroy took out his diary and leafed through the pages until he came to the page of his last entry. He read the entry to himself and closed the book. Lifting his foot, he kicked the ball of paper. Fitzroy watched it roll away down the sloping street, he could still visualise the headline in his mind.

Turning to walk away, he then hurried to the spot where the ball of paper had settled. Quickly, he unfurled the paper from its crumpled state and scanned the headlined article with his finger along the text as he read. He read aloud as he got to the sentence that grabbed his attention. Dean Watkins was shot dead in a police shootout by newly appointed Superintendent Marlon Dudley of the Flying Squad.

The words that he read troubled him. He knew the name; it was Elsa's boyfriend. Fitzroy had no idea that Marlon was such a high-profile officer. He knew Marlon worked in the Flying Squad, but his position was not candid. Fitzroy tried to synchronize his thoughts with his emotions. Did Elsa really know Marlon? If she had, she never discussed it in any conversation they had in the past. Again, Fitzroy crumpled the paper into a ball, this time kicking it into the air. He walked away, not waiting to see or caring where the ball of newsprint fell.

There was a sudden emptiness. He felt hollow with only visions of Watkins filling his thoughts. His feet carried him aimlessly until he found himself near the waterfront. The smell of the sea and the stale stench of fish met his nostrils. Pulling his shirt over his face to block out the rancid smell he eased his way nearer the water's edge.

In the distance he heard a voice call out. 'Hemmingway', the small group that regularly gathered to haul in the fishing nets had given him the name after observing Fitzroy writing in his diary whenever he visited the shoreline.

Fitzroy lifted his hand and acknowledged the greeting. His eyes wandering across the ocean. The sun sparkled on the open blanket of water; the rays of the sun seem to dance on its surface. Tears streamed from Fitzroy's eyes. He stood motionless with his hands deep into his pockets watching the vessels chop through the calm waters effortlessly.

The pain he felt inside was inconsistent with anything he had felt before. There was no pain when Mr Draper died, only a void. The emptiness in the house took some years to adjust to and eventually it healed, but there was never pain. He had known his father was nearing death after lengthy illness. Somewhere in his subconscious he had accepted the inevitable, the day when Mr Draper would be no more. In his memory, he could hear Ma Draper saying. "Mister man, yuh better cut down on dat rum drinking yuh hear, it go kill yuh one ah dese days." She said it to Mr Draper every weekend when he would spend hours in the rum shop near the market. "Look woman," He would say to her. "you trying to take away my one recreation or what? Anyway, we all have to dead one day."

Fitzroy remembered his own first drink in the very rum shop with Watkins. They had both finished school and started working at a local hardware store. The Portuguese rum shop owner had questioned their age but served them all the same. They celebrated their first wages with cold beers and salted peanuts. They felt there was nothing greater in the world than sitting in a rum shop, like grown men, swigging beer and eating salted nuts.

The memory made Fitzroy smile. He wiped away the tears from his face with his hands. His smile turned to laughter as the memory of that day became vivid. Watkins, he thought had lived his life exactly as he had wanted. He had charted his own destiny, the path he wanted to follow as far as Fitzroy's memory could recall. Maybe this path that Watkins had taken was an unspoken phase of his existence. He struggled to understand it, nevertheless.

Fitzroy tried to piece together why Watkins would have deviated from a normal life to descend into a den of criminality. There were no signs to read. Whatever he got up to, it was well concealed.

This new revelation did not fit in with what Watkins represented. During his time in the army, he had set up many youth clubs for young people to get into sports and, persuaded many of the youngsters to join the army. At one point, Watkins was the face of the army's recruitment drive. He was good at reaching out to young people. He travelled around the country visiting schools and local communities to encourage young men to find a career in the army.

Through a maze of unanswered questions and theories to the why's, how's and when about Watkins, Fitzroy concluded that he could not allow the unfortunate demise of Watkins to be burden on his future. He reached into his pocket, fetched his diary and read the last line of his entry, "Today is the start of the rest of my life." He closed the notebook and secured it into his pocket.

"Superintendent Dudley?" The nurse asked politely. She had a pleasant oval shaped face with welcoming eyes and a warm smile to accompany her posture. Her presence alone was medicine to any sick man. Marlon looked up from behind the newspaper and answered with his eyes. She extended her smile and Marlon returned a it. "So, what can I do for you nurse?" sensing some officialdom.

"There has been a call earlier from Arima District Hospital to inform you that you are now the proud father of a beautiful baby girl."

Marlon doubled the paper and placed it beside him

on the bed. He paused in his thought of action and attempted to swing his legs off the bed. Clenching his fist, he grimaced as pain took hold of him. He discovered painfully that he did not have full control of his body. The nurse shook her head, giving him a cautionary stare, "And where do you think you're going young man?"

He looked down at his bandaged legs and smiled amidst the pain. "Well your majesty, if its not too much trouble, do you think it is humanly possible for me to go down to the reception to place a call to ADH to find out how mother and daughter are doing.?"

There was a smile at the corner of her lips, Marlon could sense that she wanted to smile freely, but she also wanted to assert herself on her ward, "You can't pull rank in here Mr Superintendent. This is not police headquarters you know."

Marlon clasped his hands as if to offer a prayer and whispered. "Please!"

A smile beamed from her lips, she said in a soft tone, "I will send a porter down to get you." He mouthed a thank you to her as she continued her duties.

No sooner had she turned her back, Marlon disregarded her caution and tried to ease off the bed. The paroxysm he experienced through his legs caused him to cry out in agony, deterring him from making any further attempts to leave the bed. He bit hard on his lips while he waited for the porter.

The hospital ward was unusually quiet. Most of the patients seemed to be asleep. The two that were awake had visitors around their beds. At the far end of the ward the patient had one visitor, a female who sat on a low chair holding his hands. He could see a ring on her finger and assumed it was the patient's wife.

From his bed, Marlon could tell that they were sharing a tender moment. He watched the way she held his hands and caressed his fingers. The moment was tender, romantic and pleasing to witness. He thought of Elsa, alone with the baby in hospital and yearned to be at her side with his baby girl in his arms. Marlon wondered if the couple had children of their own.

A young man, barely about thirty pushed a wheelchair along the aisle in Marlon's direction. Marlon psyched himself for the arrival of the chair, readying himself for the onslaught of pain he would experience transferring from bed to the chair.

The porter dragged his feet along the aisle taking forever to get anywhere near Marlon's bed. Marlon looked on in disbelief, the porter went straight past his bed without a glance in his direction. The agony of the pain gripped him as he struggled to get the porter's attention. A plump nurse at the other end of the ward shouted, "Aye Bertrand, is bed number 49."

Without urgency, Bertrand manoeuvred a turn in the aisle and continued with the same pace to Marlon's bed. He positioned the wheelchair in a manner that would minimise the efforts of Marlon getting into the chair. Once settled the porter proceeded to wheel him to the reception desk. Marlon looked up at the porter and asked. "Who is that couple over there?"

"He is ah policeman just like you. Some bandits shoot 'im up, but he alright?"

"Take me over there Bertrand."

"Yes sar," Bertrand proceeded without question.

On seeing the Superintendent, the officer shuffled in his bed, sat up and saluted with his left hand.

"No need Cpl Clyde. Did not know you were in here as

well. How's your wound?"

"Not bad Sir, no nerve damage or anything like that, was very lucky."

Marlon nodded and extended his hand to Cpl Clyde. "Good work Corporal. Who is the lovely lady?"

Cpl Clyde smiled broadly and said, "This is my wife Linda, married two weeks next Tuesday."

Marlon offered his congratulations and informed Cpl Clyde that he was now a proud father of baby girl. The delight showed on Marlon's face as Clyde congratulated him. For a moment Cpl Clyde looked on and thought that his superior was about to cry. Marlon composed himself and said to Clyde, "Luckily I am alive to see her and, know her."

Linda offered her slender hand to Marlon, "Congratulations Sir on the birth of your daughter. What's her name?"

"Agnes. That is as much as I know right now."

Marlon again congratulated Clyde and Linda on their marriage and signalled to Bertrand that he was ready. He lifted his hand to stop the porter. With a pained voice he said to Corporal Clyde. 'I am sorry that you got wounded on this operation. I had intended to not have any married men with children in the squad in the event of situations like this."

"Sir none of this is your fault. We have a job to do, its part and parcel of who we are and what we do. Putting ourselves on the line in the course of our duty, is a normal day's work."

Marlon smiled and saluted Clyde before signalling the porter to take him to the front desk.

The nurse at reception gave a broad smile on seeing Marlon and she offered a friendly joke. "I see you have arrived by slow coach." Marlon laughed, the porter sucked his teeth loudly and parked Marlon at the desk.

"Why yyyyou eh come and ppppush it... faster nahhh?" Marlon looked up at Bertrand and then at the nurse. She paid no mind to the porter, addressing Marlon. "So, Mr Superintendent I hear you is ah daddy and, ah big hero too? I just trying now to call Arima, hold on eh."

Through the window behind the nurse, Marlon could see the towering hills in the background dotted with yellow blossoming poui and, immortelle trees in vivid orange blooms. He remembered fondly the poui tree just outside their house that bathed their yard in a carpet of yellow flowers. His father, every morning would look out their back door and cuss the tree for littering the yard with leaves and flowers.

The memory made Marlon smile, thinking how his father; despite his profanities would still bring out his Polaroid camera and take several shots at different angles of the magnificent tree in bloom and of the beautiful carpet on the ground. Many of the Polaroid shots hung proudly on the walls of their home and, even relatives were given framed prints when they visited from abroad.

The nurse disturbed his vision when she said, "Supt Dudley...," Marlon looked up, retracting himself, thinking her address to him had turned very formal. "... I was just informed by the nurse at Arima that Miss Nurse doesn't want to have any contact with you at this present time."

Marlon forgot himself and tried to stand. The excruciating pain reminded him that he couldn't. Through the pain he squeezed the words out of his mouth. "That is absurd, why would she not want to speak to me?"

Shaking her head from side to side offering commiseration in her gaze, she crouched down next to Marlon and said softly. "Sir, it turns out that the man you killed was her best friend. I will get Bertrand to take you back to your bed."

He looked up at the nurse. She could see his eyes welled up with tears, but they did not flow. "In my line of duty...," he said to her. "....I do, what is necessary within the limits of the law and, I have no regrets for any of my actions for protecting the wellbeing of the people of this country and I will always put duty before emotion." He looked away from the nurse, blinked and a stream of tears rolled down his cheeks. Without waiting for Bertrand, the nurse wheeled Marlon back and assisted him onto the bed.

"You are a very kind nurse. Thank you."
Her smile was a comforting smile. "Thank you, sir, it's not often we get complimented."
Marlon's eyes followed her as she daintily made her way back to her desk.

CHAPTER
17TEEN

The taxi eased its way along the congested main road before joining the busy highway, at moderate speed. Fitzroy sat with his hands clasped on one knee, leaning forward slightly, gazing out of the window. He watched as the car left the expanse of sprawling sugarcane plantations fields. Their pinkish, lilac arrowhead flowers, dancing in the wind like masqueraders, on carnival day. It mesmerised him to watch the gentle breeze providing the rhythm for their dance. The cane fields waved at him, the car gathered momentum on the highway, the radio low in the background but he did not pay attention to it.

Miles and miles of lush green crops hugged both sides of the highway punctuated with small villages along its path. Most of the houses in the low-lying areas were constructed on pillars, some wooden while others in the permanent stability of concrete. Their walls washed in vivid colours of pink, blues, yellows and reds, giving a colourful backdrop to the undulating lush landscape. Rice paddies, cabbage, tomatoes, corn, ochro, watermelons, cucumbers, peas and sugarcane created a food basket landscape for the eyes.

Fitzroy's eyes followed an aged Indian man on a bullock cart. The huge black animal pulled the cart without effort. The elderly man sat on the edge of the cart with a long whip in one hand. His body looked drained of what little moisture there might have been in his once lean, strong frame. His thick grey wiry hair unkempt, his trousers tattered, and mud stained, and he was bare foot.

Soon, the bullock cart had disappeared as fast as it had appeared in his vision. Along the green verges of the highway, small wooden structures basked in the sun, stacked with freshly harvested crops. From the rough wooden rafters hung blue crabs, their legs and pinchers bound with mangrove grass. A woman, her features weathered and dressed in bright orange Indian wear, sprinkled the creatures with a splash of water from an iron bucket.

Looking across to his right, Petra sat next to him, unconcerned with the vanishing view, her eyes buried in a Mills and Boon novel.

"You seem pretty relaxed," Fitzroy said fixing his gaze out the window again.

"Shouldn't I be? I am only meeting my mother-in-law you know," she said without lifting he eye, flipping the page as she continued reading.

"Suddenly, I feel a bit apprehensive about the visit."

"What you mean?" Petra probed, without interruption to her reading.

"I don't know really. Mackie is now Mayor, Watkins dead, you and I making a fleeting visit. Maybe it's the anticipation, I don't know?"

There was a prolonged silence. Fitzroy did not even hear the radio. He adjusted himself on the seat and clasped his hands on his other knee as the car zoomed past villages and more expanses of green vegetation.

"Stop fretting and relax." Petra said eventually, resting the open book on her leg. She rubbed his shoulder gently and squeezed his ear lobe between her fingers. Something she often did when Fitzroy appeared tense.

He held her hand, kissed her fingers saying thank you. She smiled and kept his hand, picked up her book with the other, and continued to read.

Petra had convinced Fitzroy that they should visit his mum before they left the country. She reflected to him how morally wrong it would be to leave the country without telling or, even seeing his mum. She pointed out too, the proximity of the airport and where his mum lived.

She lifted her head from the book, placed her hand on his and said softly, "How are you feeling about seeing your mother with a wife on your arm Mr Draper?"

"She going to cuss like hell, but I prepared," he laughed.

"Well that's your own fault not mine, you should have invited her."

He avoided a response to Petra's words, "I must go and see Watkins' parents as well, whatever we do."

Meeting Watkin's parents was more daunting than visiting his own mother and introducing a daughter-in-law to her. The death of Watkins served as a catalyst for Fitzroy's return to Arima. He felt the need to visit the place where Watkins presence could be felt; a place where there was a connection. He could envisage the basketball court, huge moths darting about the bright floodlights, illuminating the court. He could feel the atmosphere of the game and hear the profanities from the spectators when they made an error on the court.

The sugarcane fields had long disappeared, and the landscape was now saturated with dwellings of all description and colours. Further ahead, tall patches of bamboo grooves were visible. In the distance, a huge river divided the landscape, its murky, orange looking waters flowing silently under the bridge that reconnected with land. Above, in the clear skies, aircrafts descended on their approach to the airport. They both looked through the windows as they watched the aircrafts landing gears engaged for touchdown at Piarco Airport. Fitzroy held Petra's hand, "We will be on one of those soon."

The sight of houses gave way to agricultural plains, as the taxi negotiated onto another highway. Huge industrial buildings flanked both sides of the dual carriageway, followed by rows of luxurious houses with exotic plants adorning the gardens. Petra lifted her head from her book and marvelled at the expanse of industrial estates that lined the highway. She had never seen a sugar factory before. Thick grey smoke billowed from the chimney stacks high above the roof, towering into the sky. The sweet smell of crushed sugarcane filled the air. "That aroma is so intoxicating, it invigorates your senses," she said, clearing her throat.

Fitzroy laughed, "You make sugar sound romantic."

"Yes! It's the sweetness of a bitter labour," she said with a curt tone.

"Oh! you know of its bitter history then?"

"Mr Draper yuh eh bet yuh farce with yourself. I have three lots of history, the African and the Indian and Portuguese."

Fitzroy laughed. "Creolification, that equals dougluese."

Elsa slapped him playfully on his leg and mouthed, "shut yuh ass."

The landscape around them started to become familiar, nothing seemed to have changed in Fitzroy's eyes. He narrated to Petra as the taxi followed the winding road into Arima. "Up there is where they killed and buried that English woman." The taxi driver appeared to make a mental note of it, slowing the taxi as they went past, looking up the incline. Soon they were crawling in slow moving traffic. Fitzroy could recognise a few familiar faces on the streets.

Ma Draper sat in her rocking chair, humming as usual, as she had been accustomed to doing. She sat, taking in the panoramic view that was now visible since the mango tree was gone. She stood up, seeing Fitzroy. He stood aghast at the emptiness before him, his lips trembling. He hurried to meet Ma Draper at the stairs embracing her. "Oh God Fitzroy, is really you?" she screamed. Her eyes streaming with tears, her face beaming with a joyous smile. She squeezed Fitzroy close to her and allowed her tears to flow.

"What happened to the mango tree?" he blurted out.

"Long story boy," Ma Draper responded. "we will talk later."

He cleared his throat and looked at Petra, "Ma this here, is your daughter-in-law Petra."

Ma Draper hugged Petra warmly and kissed her cheek, both sides. She scrutinised Petra thoroughly clutching her hands lovingly. "Welcome to our humble little home my daughter."

Petra reciprocated a warm smile, she squeezed Ma Draper's hand gently, saying thank you.

Ma Draper turned and gave Fitzroy a long stare then landed a solid slap his arm. Her hand stung him and, he yelled, "What was dat for?"

"I wasn't good enough to come to your wedding?"

He looked at Petra and she turned away leaving him to explain himself. "It wasn't like that Ma it was a spur of the moment decision."

Ma Draper buried her finger under her head tie and scratched vigorously. She beckoned them both inside with a wave of her hand. "Come, it have ah surprise in here for you."

She led them both into Fitzroy's room, in the corner stood a small pinewood crib. There was a whiff if talcum powder in the air. Agnes lay in the crib, fast asleep. She stirred with the commotion in the room. Petra whispered, "Oh my gosh, she's just so adorable."

Fitzroy touched the baby's nose with his finger, and she stirred again. Petra slapped his hand, prompting him to stop before he disturbed her sleep and woke her up.

"That there is Agnes," Ma Draper said, "She's such a cutie, sleeps all day, once fed and all through the night."

"What happened to de mango tree?" Fitzroy asked impatiently.

Ma Draper laughed and shook her head, "Boy, dat is your fault. Dat Sooklal come one Saturday to pick de mango, while I gone to the market. He cut down all the blasted branches, say he cyar climb."

Fitzroy stood stunned in disbelief. He walked onto the veranda inspecting the truck of the tree that was left. Pink sap stained the bark of the tree where the limbs were severed.

"So, what you do?" he asked Ma Draper, half expecting some form of sarcasm from her. "Did you ask him to compensate you?"

"Nah! Sometimes things are a blessing in disguise. Dhanraj wanted to shoot de man. In the end, I just asked him to clear up the mess and get rid of the branches."

Fitzroy surveyed the mango tree, devoid of its thick foliage that once partially shrouded the house from view. He was relieved to learn that Ma Draper had taken the demise of the mango tree with such optimism. He had quietly hated the mango tree and welcomed the new light filtering into the house. He could now see the house fully when he approached.

Inside the house, he could hear Ma Draper and Petra engaged in conversation. They were jovial in their dialogue. It made Fitzroy happy that Ma Draper had, without any fuss, accepted Petra. He had no doubt that she would. He had half expected her to be angry with him. While she did present a sign of anger, it was short lived. Her welcoming nature made Petra feel at ease and at home. The warmth Ma Draper extended made her feel very much a part of the family.

Ma Draper came out to the veranda where Fitzroy stood, looking at the mango tree. She patted him on the back and said, "Son don't fret about de mango tree. Everything has its reasons and purpose. De day Sooklal chop down de mango tree, a new life came into this house. Jezess entered, with a joyous breeze to bless this place, praise Jezess name for it. Praise Jezess, praise de Lord, hallejujah." Ma Draper wept.

"Ma, I have something to tell you."

Ma Draper wiped her eyes with her dress sleeve and stopped him, "Shut yuh mouth, yuh wife tell meh everything ahready. I am proud, very, very proud of you son. Who would ever think you would go to university to study oil?"

"Yuh not mad?"

"Of course, ah blasted vex, yuh eh invite yuh own mother to your wedding, but I understand. And yuh have yuh own life to live now, so go and live it damn well, enjoy every minute of life, you and your lovely wife. She nice too bad."

Fitzroy could not believe the new Ma Draper he was seeing and hearing. This paradigm had stunned him, yet, pleased him. His mother had a renewed happiness, something he had longed to see in her. Ma Draper had even allowed Elsa to freely rearrange the house so that it was practical for the baby. Several new framed pictures adorn the newly painted walls, and, colourful curtains brought extra light and ambience to the rooms. Ma Draper's happiness could be felt as well as seen. She had a new lease of life and a new rhythm in her step.

"Where is Elsa then?" Fitzroy asked.

"She gorn to de grocery, she should be back any minute." Ma Draper's face grew sullen and she started to hum a psalm. She held Fitzroy's and Petra's hand as she prayed.

"You hear what happen with Watkins?"

Fitzroy nodded.

"Elsa don't want anything to do with Marlon anymore. She eh even want him to see de the child. I glad yuh come, talk to her and make her see some sense. The child must know she father." She gripped Fitzroy's hands tightly and prayed as she kept her a hold of both their hands.

Fitzroy sympathised with Elsa's rationale, realising how hurt she must feel. The man she had envisaged spending the rest of her life with and, more importantly, the father of her child had killed their friend. He knew it was not healthy for Elsa to carry around this bitterness, he had to find a way of convincing her to forgive and move forward. Nothing at this moment was lucid in his head but he prayed that before he departed, he would think of some resolution.

Petra stood in the doorway, cradling baby Agnes in her arms, she mouthed to Fitzroy. I want one. They both smiled and Ma Draper chimed, "Girl yuh looking good with dat child yuh know, next ting we know yuh come back here with ah little Scotsman or Scotsgirl."

Laughter erupted as Agnes stirred in Petra's arms. She

rocked her gently in her cradled arms. Agnes settled again in the comfort of Petra's warmth, making little noises.

In the distance at the top of the street, Ma Draper caught a glimpse of Elsa creeping along at snails' pace. She hurried Petra and Fitzroy to stay out of sight as her eyes followed Elsa dragging her weary feet along, looking lost and wounded. she inched her way to the house, her head buried to the ground as her feet carried her. Ma Draper rocked and hummed on her chair. There was no rhythm as she watched Elsa, her heart saddened by Elsa's state.

Elsa climbed the stairs with a lingering sigh.

"You take a long time today gyul, everything okay?" Ma Draper pried with a worried tone.

Elsa perched her head and listened. "A, A, like dat child smell meh? I could hear her making funny noises in there."

"Better go and see she must be hungry now."

"Is about two 'O' clock now, almost her feeding time." Her voice drained and, her eyes weary. "she didn't wake up since I gone?"

"No gyul she slept right through, even when Duncan came ringing dat kiss-me-ass bell."

"Ah cyar stand dat man nah," Elsa said with lurid scorn.

Entering the doorway, Elsa saw Fitzroy standing inside the room, his arms outstretched, welcoming her. She dropped the bags and threw herself onto Fitzroy, almost toppling him to the floor. Tears of joy trickled down her face as she embraced Fitzroy with every bit of emotion she could conjure, she kissed his lips and apologised. From the corner of her eyes, she could see a young woman standing, smiling broadly, holding baby Agnes in her arms.

Elsa dried her cheeks quickly and smiled. She looked at Fitzroy and asked. "So, who is this then?"

"That is your sister-in-law, Petra," he replied with a smile.

She made a fist and buried it into his arm. Fitzroy groaned, "But wait nah, allyuh go kill meh just now?"

"How you could get marrid and not tell us? You is ah dog boy!" she said playfully.

Fitzroy offered her no explanation. Elsa embraced Petra, not expecting an explanation either. She looked at Agnes, quite content in the cradle of Petra's arms. "She could stay there all day if you give her a chance, she like hand too bad."

"Fitz yuh come back for good? I see suitcase and ting."

Before Fitzroy could digest Elsa's question, Ma Draper shouted from the veranda. "Gyul, he going Scotland, some place called Edinborough to study about oil, could you believe dat?"

"Edinburgh Ma, Edinburgh," He corrected with a wink.

"Is true?" asked Elsa animated with excitement.

"Yes, it's true. The company sending me on an all expense trip to complete a course in Petroleum Science and Engineering. And, we are getting a free honeymoon out of it too."

"So how you two meet?" Elsa probed, as she changed baby Agnes, securing a fresh white cotton diaper on her and dusting her with talcum powder.

"He used to come to the restaurant where I worked, pestering me, until I finally said yes to go out with him."

Elsa laughed aloud and lifted Agnes above her head. "Here you take her, she likes you."

Petra offered her hands in a cradling position. Elsa settled Agnes in Petra's arms. The smell of talcum powder perfumed the air, Petra caressed Agnes' little nose with hers.

"Ma was right you know," Elsa commented quietly. "A lot of positive things came in the wake of dat mango tree being chopped down."

Caressing baby Agnes, Petra asked. "What do you mean?"

"Well since Sooklal butcher de tree, Mackie won the election, Agnes was born, Fitzy get married and a university scholarship. You can't get better blessing than that now, can you?"

A tear trickled down her cheek and she brushed it away gently with her finger and another followed then she burst into fitful sobbing.

"Are you okay?" Petra asked softly, taking care not to alarm Ma Draper or Fitzroy who were sitting on the verandah.

"Agnes' father is a policeman. A Superintendent, he shot and killed one of our closest and dearest friends. I am sure Fitzroy told you already. I can't bear to live with him, see or touch him after that. I don't even want him seeing or touching Agnes...ever."

Petra sat holding Agnes, lost for words to comfort Elsa. She felt awkward, refraining from saying anything. There was a tinge of sadness, knowing that she could not find the right words to ease Elsa's pain.

"Should I put her in the crib?" Petra asked awkwardly, getting up from the edge of the bed. Gently, she settled Agnes into the crib. Agnes little limbs fell gently on the soft cotton blanket without a stir. Petra kissed her finger and placed the kiss on Agnes' forehead. She returned to the edge of the bed and sat next to Elsa, comforting her.

Clutching Petra's fingers, she mouthed, thank you. Silently, tears began to trickle down her cheeks.

Petra sat in silence, allowing Elsa to drain the grief away through her tears. She could feel Elsa's body relax, allowing herself to be comforted. Petra seized the moment. "You should talk to Fitzroy, he too was devastated with the news, it almost killed him. He didn't eat for days."

Her hand still clutching Petra's fingers, Elsa said with a warm voice. "Thank you! Fitzroy is very lucky to have found you."

Petra smiled. "We are both lucky, and so are you."

"Dat is not luck nah girl. How can I have a meaningful relationship with the man who killed our best friend?"

There was a long pause before she responded to Elsa. "It is extremely difficult given the job that Marlon does..." Petra waited, hoping that Elsa would respond instead, she sat quietly clutching Petra's hand looking at baby Agnes in her crib, fast asleep. Finally, she let go of Petra's fingers, dried her tears and said. "Told you she would sleep all day once she's fed and cleaned."

"Right now," Petra said, "you're feeling raw and it's only to be expected, but I am sure that you will work through this situation and come to some understanding. Perhaps in time it will heal, some wounds take longer, but they do heal and, we do get better."

It was vivid in Elsa's eyes that she was wrangling with her emotions, pondering on how best to bring some resolve to the situation that confronted her. She knew too, Agnes should have her father. She wanted nothing more than for Agnes to have her dad. In her tormented heart, she knew it would take forever before she allowed Marlon to touch her. She knew too, it wasn't fair to him, neither to Agnes. At present, she did not have the answers to all the questions she asked herself daily.

"Do you believe I am being unreasonable?"

Petra contemplated on the question, twisting strands of hair around her finger.

"No! It's not unreasonable, but you must take the other person's situation into consideration as well. You are both hurting, in different ways, but hurt is hurt."

Elsa paced the floor, stopping to monitor Agnes intermittently, touching her soft skin as she did so. She looked out of the window. Birds pecked away happily at the ripe bananas on the tree. She smiled and looked at Petra. "This place full of love and life, you can't deny that for sure."

Petra tried not to absorb too much of the emotions that flowed. In the few hours she had known Elsa, she had absorbed a great deal of Elsa's pain. In a few days, she would be far removed from any emotions that Elsa, or anyone in Trinidad was faced with. People would get on with their lives, wounds would appear and open emotional scars. While scars remain as a reminder of the hurt, they are also a testimony of healing. She wanted so much to assure Elsa that all would be well in her life and that she should allow forgiveness to overcome bitterness and anger, but she didn't know how.

For once, Petra grasped some understanding of how Fitzroy might be feeling. It all made sense to her now, why Fitzroy was so badly affected by the death of Watkins. The close-knit relationship that they all shared. It was far beyond anything she had experienced with her friends or family. Coming to Arima had also opened an entire new dimension for her in understanding Fitzroy and what made him the man he was. She saw his environment, the happiness, the closeness of all those around him. The jovial aura that existed in the house itself, filled her.

Petra felt that if anyone possessed the faculty to coax Elsa back from the abyss into which she was descending, it was Fitzroy. He was gentle, patient and dutiful. His understanding of human nature was exceptional. He approached everything with optimism and never envisaged problems and, when they did occur, he had what almost seemed like prepared solutions. She knew Fitzroy had a solution. She knew too, he had no idea yet that he could make things better. Petra thought of the pain and the trauma that Elsa must be going through. She prayed that Fitzroy would somehow dig deep into his treasure trove of wisdom to ease the pain for both sides.

Fitzroy took two envelopes from his pocket. "This is for you."

Ma Draper opened the envelope and stared at the cash inside. "What dis for boy?"

"Ma it is for anything you want it to be."

He handed her another and whispered, "That one is for Elsa, give it to her when we leave, otherwise she would not accept it from me, she too proud."

She laughed heartily with Fitzroy. "Boy you know she too well."

Ma Draper looked at Fitzroy with emotional pride and a tear trickled down her cheek. Fitzroy tried to speak, Ma Draper lifted her hand and stopped him. She maintained the momentum of her rocking and said, "I am proud of you! I know this small place is not big enough for you, it never was. As a boy yuh was always going to Port of Spain, to shop, for carnival, big city was made for you. But now, even dey small too."

He knew that Ma Draper was going to miss him. He was no longer just in San Fernando and could visit her at any given time. The reality of his impending departure was only just beginning to register with him, and it frightened him a great deal.

Ma Draper, as if she could read his mind said, "Don't you go fretting yuh little head about me yuh know. I have Elsa here and I will be busy wid meh little grandchild." She clasped her hands together and shook them in the air. "Praise Jezess for all our blessings, praise de lord. Hallelujah!"

Elsa walked over to the crib and caressed Agnes as she slept. Looking across at Petra, she said calmly, "What about your parents, what do they do?"

Petra lifted her head, smoothed her dress over her legs with her palms. "My parents are no longer with us. My dad died when I was quite young and my mum, she passed away a couple years ago."

"I am so sorry," Elsa responded in shock.

"It felt a bit sad when I got married that they weren't there but that is life. We evolve through its cycle."

Elsa beamed a lively smile and said to her, "Well, a whole new life is ahead of you in Scotland, a gateway to the entire world. You and Fitzroy will be very happy. Just remember to send me some snow."

They both laughed watching Agnes sleep in her crib. "She is quite sweet," Petra said softly.

Ma Draper sat in her rocking chair, watching an aircraft high in the sky until it disappeared into the clouds. In her hands, she held the airmail envelope that contained three photographs and a short letter from Petra. She had read the short letter many times over and, admired the photographs. She especially adored the one of Fitzroy and Petra standing next to Big Ben in London. The other two were taken outside Buckingham Palace and Piccadilly Circus. After studying the pictures, she would find her rhythm and continue her cycle of rocking and humming her favourite hymns.

She looked at the spot where the mango tree once stood in all its splendour and magnificence, adorned with its rosy fruits seemingly like Christmas lights dangling from its branches.

Ma Draper had decided to have the tree completely removed after Sooklal had butchered it in his attempt to harvest the mangoes. Never once, did she hanker over its loss. Dhanraj and Hendry had tried to persuade her to make Sooklal pay for the damage done to the property. She assured them that there couldn't be a price on blessings. The man was honest she thought, he cannot climb. Should we punish a man for a disability she would say, time, and time again.

Ma Draper always maintained that what transpired was an act of faith and she was never once angry about the outcome. Sooklal was sent to do a deed, she protested to her neighbours, especially Dhanraj who could not understand why Ma Draper would allow this travesty to go unpunished. She had grown accustomed to the absence of the mangoes crashing onto the iron roof. She did not miss having to clear the bruised fruits from the ground every morning and selecting the unblemished ones to offer to those who never took them. Now, she was happy caring for baby Agnes, who brought untold joy to the home and that was much more rewarding than picking up mangoes and making chow.

From her rocking chair, she surveyed the clear view she had, now that the mango tree was gone. Next door, Hendry too was relieved. He no longer had to rake up dried leaves and clear away fallen mangoes from his yard. Though he never complained, he had found it a nuisance.

The roar of aircraft could be heard, high above the house as they disappeared into the clouds. Across the road Dhanraj's business thrived with its usual influx of customers. The aroma of orange and lime blossoms in the yard continued to perfume the air. The flowerbeds blossomed once again as bees, butterflies and humming-birds frolicking happily from flower to flower, in the warm sunlight.

Ma Draper reached on the floor for her Bible. She paused, the rhythm of the chair stopped, having found the desired page in the book she resumed her rhythm, perusing silently through the book of Psalms.

Ma Draper prayed and thanked God that Fitzroy had managed to encourage Elsa to have some dialogue with Marlon. She was thankful too, that Petra had twisted Fitzroy's arm and insisted that they visit her before leaving for Scotland. From the look on Elsa's face Ma Draper could sense that she was more at peace with herself and that the trauma that was tearing her apart was now beginning to ease. Mackie had gotten her a job at the Council. She headed a department set up to deal with residents and business complaints. The job kept her busy, it also allowed her time for her emotional scars to heal. She was happier, her radiant smile was returning. Ma Draper noticed she no longer dragged along but moved with a rhythmic gait. So much so that Dhanraj began to tease her lovingly again.

Marlon was free to visit Agnes whenever he chose, without appointment or prior notice. He would spend time trying to convince Elsa they should get married and be a family. This idea was dismissed but Elsa still held some reservation about their relationship. She accepted and understood Marlon's predicament in his line of duty. She resolved that this duty of Law bound him, and nothing should compromise the office he held and his duty for country.

Marlon had made a visible difference in reducing crime, achieving what his predecessors had failed to accomplish for many years. His promotion to Assistant Commissioner meant Elsa and Agnes saw less and less of him. His visits to Agnes never coincided with when Elsa was present, and they soon became less frequent when he was promoted to post of Police Commissioner. He came by one afternoon and left a letter for Elsa. Ma Draper looked at him and squeezed his hand, "Son, you have tried and done your best. I know it is difficult for both of you. I know you will never abandon your child. Elsa loves you. And I know you love her bad. Maybe one day she will come round."

Marlon embraced Ma Draper, he said very little and bid her goodbye. She watched him walk out the gate, metal scraping the concrete as he shut the gate behind him, get into his car and drive off.

Petra sent regular letters accompanied with photographs of spectacular landscapes in Scotland. In one letter, she suggested to Ma Draper that she should visit Scotland. Ma Draper smiled at the thought, she stuck her index finger under her head tie and massaged the itchy spot on her head. She reflected on a framed photograph of Petra and Fitzroy together, both clad winter coats and tartan scarves standing with Edinburgh Castle in the background. Ma draper loved the sight of the beautifully kept gardens, it amazed her how vivid the gardens were with flowers in the freezing winter.

Many years ago, she had seen a documentary on television where lakes and streams froze over in the winter.

In the news, she saw that in Scotland, snow was knee deep, and people went about their lives unhindered. She smiled in anticipation of when Petra would send photos of them in the snow. She laughed, recollecting how Petra described her first experience with scotch eggs and haggis. Moreover, she marvelled at the news of Fitzroy's obsession to visit every whiskey distillery in Scotland. Ma Draper was always thrilled to see the airmail envelopes in the hands of the post woman as she made her way towards the house. It pleased her too, that she got letters written by both Petra and Fitzroy. Whenever Petra wrote letters, she always included photographs.

Next door, Sita was yelping and tugging at her chain in excitement, the commotion Ma Draper knew so well. Sita only made those noises when Hendry came home from work. Today he was exceptionally earlier than normal, and it made Ma Draper curious. She lifted her head slightly and called out to Hendry, "Aye man, yuh home early today boy."

Hendry yelled at Sita to be quiet and replied, "Power cut neighb, nobody cyar work. I bring something for you macumere." In his hands, he was clutching three huge pineapples. Ma Draper went to the fence and collected the fruits. The aroma from the pineapples was so pungent, she could smell them even before she got to the fence. They were huge pineapples and she struggled to keep them from falling from her grip as she wrestled with them.

Once inside, Ma Draper allowed the pineapples to roll onto the kitchen counter. Putting her nostrils to one of them, she inhaled the honey-like aroma. Without hesitation, she took a sharp knife and pared away the tough skin to expose the firm juicy golden flesh of the pineapple. The sticky juice from the fruit settled on the table. Carefully, she cut the pineapple into small triangular shaped chunks. Outside the Blue Jays were merrily pecking away at the peppers on the tree. She listened to them, smiling as she went into the back yard. The birds did not attempt to fly off. Ma Draper selected the broadest *shadon beni* leaves she could find in the undergrowth.

She looked at the tall banana tree. The weight of the huge bunch of bananas caused the tree to lean precariously. Some of the ripe bananas were already attracting a flurry of small, black and yellow birds. Clutching her *shadon beni* leaves, she shook her head in awe at how tall the grass had grown. The lime and orange trees were abundant with blossoms and young fruit. The passion fruit vine had wrapped itself around the sugarcane stalk, producing a single flower - a promise of fruit.

In her head, Ma Draper made a mental note reminding herself to get Rookmin's son to come and clear the tall grass and persistent weeds that overran the yard. She laboured up the back steps, returning to her chopped pineapple. She washed the *shadon beni* leaves and crushed them between her fingers, rubbing it over the pineapple, with the same methodical diligence undertaken when making her mango chow. Ma Draper proceeded to prepare her mixture for the pineapple. Stopping, she savoured the piquant aroma of the *shadon beni* that filled the house. The smell pleased her, a warm smile formed on her face and she stopped, listening as Agnes stirred.

The crushed, vibrant emerald green leaves of the *shadon beni*, the red peppers, cracked peppercorns and crushed garlic pearls against the golden hue of the pineapple presented a colourful contrast in the bowl. Ma Draper studied the mixture, tossing it in the bowl, coating the chunks of fruit with seasoning. She tasted a wedge of pineapple. Her expression revealed, she was pleased with the result. Daintily, she selected another piece of pineapple with her fingers and chewed it slowly. "Hmmm! Pineapple *chow*, now that is something that might catch on."

Printed in Poland
by Amazon Fulfillment
Poland Sp. z o.o., Wrocław

60856419R00143